Praise for P.D. Cacek

'P.D. Cacek is the most lyrical – and the scariest – writer to emerge in the horror field.'
S.P. Somtow, author of *Valentine*

'Cacek is certainly one of horror's most important up and comers.'
Matt Schwartz, Horror.net

'Fascinating [...] Readers will find this a rewarding exploration of the emotions felt both by those confronting their own deaths and those left behind to mourn.'
Publishers Weekly on *Second Lives*

'*Second Lives* is a wonderfully stunning novel, and a definite candidate to reread.'
The Haunted Reading Room

'P.D. Cacek's *Second Lives* is every bit heartbreakingly beautiful as it is compelling.'
Cedar Hollow Horror Reviews

'A spellbinding and original exploration of reincarnation... [a] wondrous concept brought to life.'
Well Worth a Read on *Second Lives*

'Fantastic, original, character-driven and exciting. Looking forward to more from Cacek!'
Library Thing on *Second Lives*

P.D. CACEK

SEBASTIAN

This is a FLAME TREE PRESS book

FLAME TREE PRESS
6 Melbray Mews, London, SW6 3NS, UK
flametreepress.com

US sales, distribution and warehouse:
Simon & Schuster
simonandschuster.biz

UK distribution and warehouse:
Marston Book Services Ltd
marston.co.uk

Thanks to the Flame Tree Press team.

The cover is created by Flame Tree Studio with thanks to Nik Keevil and Shutterstock.com. The font families used are Avenir and Bembo.

Flame Tree Press is an imprint of Flame Tree Publishing Ltd

flametreepublishing.com

A copy of the CIP data for this book is available from the British Library and the Library of Congress.

HB ISBN: 978-1-78758-688-8
PB ISBN: 978-1-78758-686-4
ebook ISBN: 978-1-78758-689-5

Printed and bound in Great Britain by Clays Ltd, Elcograf S.p.A

P.D. CACEK

SEBASTIAN

FLAME TREE PRESS
London & New York

To Mike and Elizabeth
Ari and Peter
and Joe

and with special thanks to
Dallas Mayr

The honor of your presence is requested
at a private reception to celebrate the life and memory of
Christine Morgan Riley
immediately following the service at
The Ruth and Raymond G. Perelman Building
at the Philadelphia Art Museum
2525 Pennsylvania Avenue, Philadelphia, Pennsylvania

Light refreshments will be served.

She showed us the world as only she could see it…
What wonders will she see now?

-0-

Morgan didn't want to talk about it.
He didn't want to think about.
But he took a deep breath and began.

CHAPTER ONE

My mother wasn't crazy.

At least not certifiable.

She was an artist, and artists think differently than the rest of us. They're more focused and obsessive and, yeah, self-centered, but that doesn't make them crazy.

Well, maybe a little. You have to be a little crazy to look through a camera lens and take photographs that aren't like anyone else's. I could get a camera and set up a shot that was identical to one of hers…I mean, a perfect imitation, and take a picture and that's all it would be…a picture.

My mother took photographs, artistic photographic representations of whatever it was she saw.

She was an artist with film.

I can take a picture.

Do you understand the difference?

So, my mother wasn't crazy; she was driven, devoted to her work, and more receptive to things. Yeah, that sounds better…not crazy, just more open to seeing things that the rest of us missed.

That's what made her a success.

She saw things through the lens of her camera that the rest of us poor simple mortals don't…or can't…and she was able to capture it on black-and-white film that was processed in a darkroom with chemicals and time…and not uploaded to a computer screen.

Not that she couldn't have gone digital. My mother wasn't a Luddite; she knew her way around computers, but in her mind there was no art in manipulating software to create an image.

She even sued one critic who voiced the opinion that one of her photographs had been digitized…because it was just too good to have been done in the darkroom.

I think the man's writing online supermarket ads now.

Not crazy…focused…especially when she had the idea for a new series. She'd get an idea and you could see it in her eyes…the wheels turning, as my dad used to say. 'Careful, Morgan, your mom's wheels are turning, best stay out of the way or she'll run you over.'

Yeah, funny, but still true.

The wheels would turn and it consumed her…it consumed all of us. I was her favorite model, once. The world watched me grow up and it used to bother me, a little, when I was younger. I mean, sometimes.

What? Yeah, I once got into a fight. I was about twelve…no, thirteen, and in middle school and we'd just gotten back from winter break when one of my classmates in Homeroom pulls out my mother's calendar for that year and opens it to December.

It was a good photograph – she'd taken it during a snowstorm and you could barely see my face through the swirling flakes…my feet were freezing by the time she finished and I couldn't feel my nose – but there was just something about the way my classmate said, "Oh, look, we have a celebrity" that set me off.

I jumped him when school let out and gave him a bloody nose.

He gave me a black eye and swollen lip.

The Boys' VP took us both to the principal's office and called our mothers.

Mine brought her camera and took what was to become the first photograph in her Friends Forged in Fire *series.*

It worked. Chet and I are still best friends.

It could be grueling sometimes, posing and all that went with it, but that was just part of life with an artist and I didn't mind, I really didn't. I was used to it.

★ ★ ★

Morgan leaned back against the front door and imagined he could still feel the heat through the wood and the two shirts – one polo, one button-down, both from his mother – he'd slung over his shoulder. Compared to the hot, humid September evening he'd just left, the house's constant 72°F temperature/40% humidity almost felt cold.

It felt wonderful.

Morgan closed his eyes and took a deep breath.

Then opened his eyes and walked into the gentle breeze from one of the foyer's mini ductless splits before taking another breath. All he could smell was Freon, chemicals wafting up from his mother's darkroom in the basement, and the various other scents and odors an old house gathers into itself over the years...but what he didn't smell was Chinese takeout.

And he should have.

It was the second Monday of the month and from the time Morgan had discovered the culinary pleasures of fried wontons, boneless spare ribs and sweet-and-sour chicken, the second Monday of every month meant sitting down at the formal dining room table and waiting in anticipation while his father opened up the many mysterious cartons that filled the air with exotic aromas and his mother talked about the next series of photographs she wanted to take.

His father had his law practice and his mother had her gallery openings and exhibitions and juried competitions and business trips, but the second Monday of every month was their time together as a family.

After his father died, he and his mother ate in the kitchen. When he got married his new wife knew not to expect him home the second Monday of every month...and still didn't, eleven years later.

So, where the hell was the Chinese takeout?

Morgan knew it was the right day...his mother had called him the night before and asked that he bring a couple of shirts, casual ones, something he'd wear on a hike, which meant, he knew from experience, it wouldn't just be dinner and discussion...she had an idea for a photograph.

"Mom?"

His cellphone pinged to alert him of a text.

Morgan took his cellphone from his pocket and thumbed the screen open. "You've got to be kidding."

SAW YOU PULL UP IN ATTIC BE RIGHT DOWN

Morgan walked to the foot of the staircase that divided the house left to right, now gathering shadows, and draped the shirts over the newel post that had been the site of his first and last attempt at Boy Scout wood carving. The effort did not earn him a merit badge but the photograph his mother took of the attempt did win the Grand Master's Award at a national photography competition.

And also made the front cover of the next issue of *Boys' Life* magazine.

Morgan took a deep breath and lifted a cupped hand to his mouth. "OKAY, MOM!"

Ping.

THAT WAS NOT FUNNY MORGAN

"I thought it was."

NO IT WASN'T. THAT'S WHAT PHONES ARE FOR

Morgan slowly lowered his hands but kept his eyes on the dark second-floor landing as he backed away from the stairs. Sometimes she really scared him.

Leaving the shirts on the newel post, Morgan turned and walked into the library/gallery across the entrance hall from the living room. When he was still living in the house, the living room was just that, a room for living where he'd sneak downstairs early to watch Saturday morning cartoons while eating handfuls of sugary cereal right out of the box or sit on the sofa next to his father, watching westerns and eating popcorn, or build elaborate cities out of Legos while his mother developed film.

Now it was a living room in name only, a place for entertaining and interviews filled with a pristine arrangement of furniture that his mother covered for holidays and when his daughter stayed over for the weekend... just in case. The walls were covered with just enough of his mother's photographs and pictures – family and school – on the mantelpiece over the working fireplace, to promote the illusion that they weren't just background scenery.

Morgan much preferred the library/gallery...it didn't pretend to be anything other than what it was: a showplace of his mother's talent. The soft gray walls were hung with framed originals of her best-known photographs and plaques that were too large to fit into the low glass-front curio/award cabinets that lined two walls.

It also didn't hurt that a good many of the award-winning photographs were of him and his daughter.

Chairs had been set up around the room in optimal spots. Morgan chose one of the two upholstered wingbacks in front of the room's multipane window and turned on the small lamp on the table between them. The room opened onto the massive covered porch his grandfather had built regardless of the fact that it didn't architecturally work with the original Tudor Revival design. His mother always kept the sheers drawn, much the same way his father had.

The room had originally been his father's office, inherited from his father along with the Philadelphia law firm the old man had started back in the forties. Morgan was supposed to follow the tradition, become a lawyer and take over the practice as well as the office.

His father had died long before Morgan even realized he didn't want to be a lawyer. He never saw his son graduate, with honors, with a master's in Finance and Investments, or become a senior financial advisor, and then senior VP of investments for a nationwide banking firm.

Not that it would have softened the blow.

Morgan had helped his mother pack away the office and found a wrapped desk plate with *Morgan Riley, Esq.* engraved on it. The gift tag had read: *I am so proud that you are my son. Love, Dad.*

He never told his mother about it and still had the desk plate in one of his father's old shoe boxes in the back of his closet.

Morgan leaned back and listened to the occasional thump or thud until the sounds coalesced into definite footsteps.

"Morgan?"

Morgan stood and walked to meet her at the bottom step. Once, years ago, in an interview, a reporter had written that she was very much like one of her photographs, tending to wear only monochromic tones with *"...hair so blond it appears white and eyes of startling ash-gray-green rimmed in charcoal...."*

Obviously the writer was a failed artist, but minus the purple prose, his mother's taste had always been to clothes that were black and white and gray – they were easier to separate and wash – and had blond hair that, now at 72, was more platinum than gold...but her eyes were hazel, had always been hazel and would continue to be hazel.

But they did look pale gray rimmed in charcoal in photographs.

Today she wore light gray linen slacks and a loose white top... her shoulder-length hair held off her neck with a black plastic claw clip.

Black and white and gray except for the clothes she was carrying. They looked familiar.

Morgan kept looking at them – small clothes, toddler-sized shirts and shorts – as he leaned in to kiss her cheek. She smelled faintly of dust and cedar.

"No Chinese food?"

His mother sighed. "Well, hello to you, too, dear son."

"Sorry. Hi, Mom. So, what's this?" Morgan picked up one of the shirts. "Hey, this is my old *He-Man, Masters of the Universe* tee, isn't it? I didn't know you kept it."

"I saved some for Hannah."

Not that his daughter would ever need a size-two boy's t-shirt with a faded logo from a TV show that ended twenty-nine years before she was born.

And he wasn't even going to think about the movie with Dolph Lundgren.

Morgan held the shirt up by the sleeves. It still had a stain running down the back from where he'd crawled under a newly painted fence. He didn't remember doing that, but his mother had taken a photograph.

"Mom, Hannah's a little big for this. Are you trying to tell me something? Am I finally going to get the baby brother I always wanted?"

"Did you see him?"

"See who?"

"He's in the living room. Come on, let me show you." His mother reached for the newel post as she started down the stairs, knocking off the shirts he'd brought. "Why did you bring shirts?"

"You wanted me to," Morgan said, picking them up.

"Oh, that's right. Well, why don't you put them upstairs and I'll just throw these in the wash." She was already hurrying down the hall toward the laundry/mud room off the kitchen. "But don't come into the living room until I tell you to."

Jesus, she got a dog. After all these years she got a dog. I wanted a dog… didn't get a dog…still can't…place is too small…no yard…but she got a dog. Morgan tossed the shirts back over one shoulder as he climbed the stairs and wondered what kind it was and why it hadn't barked its fool head off when he walked in.

Maybe it's a cat.

Turning left off the stairs, Morgan passed the upstairs bath and double-wide linen closet, then reached for the cut-glass handle to his old room. His mother's room, the master suite and bath, was at the opposite end of the hall. The attic stairs directly opposite had made sneaking up there all the more difficult when he was a child...unless his mother was in the darkroom his father had built for her in the basement.

The pink teddy bear-shaped name tile – *Hannah's Room* – rattled against the dark wood as he opened the door. When this was Morgan's room, it had been pale blue and gone from teddy bears (blue) and Tonka trucks through He-Man and Ninja Turtles to wall posters of swimsuit models and athletic pennants. Go Eagles.

Now it was all white lace curtains, pink walls and pretty, pretty ponies. His old twin bed, still serviceable even after all the wear and tear he'd put it through, had been repainted white and piled high with a menagerie of stuffed animals, mostly of the equine variety, and pillows.

Morgan walked over to the room's closet and opened the door. Hannah didn't need any of his old clothes – his wife always packed a few extra outfits and changes of underwear to leave at Grammy's when their daughter visited and his mother was always buying her outfits – and he still had enough slacks, polos and dress shirts that he really didn't have to bring anything from home.

Except that it did clean out his closet at home of all the things that only *really* look good in a black-and-white photograph when everything would be in various shades of gray.

Including him.

Morgan hung the fuchsia polo and melon rind-green and purple pinstriped shirt between a salmon windbreaker and gray Penn State sweatshirt he wore when he came over to do yard work and closed the door.

His mother was waiting for him beneath the living room's peaked archway.

"His name's Sebastian," she said, taking his hand. "Well, what do you think?"

It wasn't a dog.

CHAPTER TWO

I don't know why I thought it was a dog, but it doesn't matter, that's not the point. It could have been anything, because whatever it was didn't matter… not then…not at the beginning. See, it was never about the subject, it was the inspiration it created.

In her.

I know, it's difficult to explain, but my mother would see something…something ordinary, something that most of us would not even give a second glance…and be inspired by it.

Yeah, yeah, I was in a lot of her photographs, but it wasn't me…do you understand? It wasn't me, Morgan, her son. I was just a part of whatever it was she was really photographing. I could have been anyone or anything; it didn't matter.

Even a dog.

I don't think it always came to her, but once she was inspired by something, God, it consumed her. The inspired obsession…yeah, that has a nice ring to it. The inspired obsession…but it didn't last long, a few weeks, maybe a month or two if she was particularly enamored by the subject, but eventually it would end and she'd disappear into her darkroom and come out with enough photographs for a new series.

And that was the way it was supposed to be. If you focus too hard on one thing, you'll go….

She wasn't crazy, just obsessed.

★ ★ ★

"Sebastian, huh?"

Morgan looked at the manikin standing on its white metal plate in the middle of his mother's living room and nodded. It was naked – probably the reason his mother had been going through his old clothes – about the size of a two- or three-year-old, sexless – thank God – faceless, hairless and molded or cast – or however they made them – from white plastic with an eggshell finish.

And the only reason he knew that was because he'd repainted the kitchen cream with an eggshell finish.

"Isn't he adorable?" His mother latched on to Morgan's arm and pulled him closer. "Did you see the toes? And look at the fingers? Each finger and toe has a nail, isn't that amazing? Look at the detail!"

Morgan nodded, but had to admit the detail on the toes and fingers was amazing. Each finger and toe was separated from its neighbor, which had to be a whole other manufacturing step. Arms at its side, hands open, the fingers were bent slightly toward the palm. The feet were arched and the toes flat against the stand except for one little piggy that had none; it was crooked over the top of the little piggy that had roast beef.

Aw.

It was one of the more elaborate…and creepy props his mother had found. But at least it went with the color scheme.

"Yeah, cool. So, where'd you rent it?"

His mother stopped being amazed by the details and looked up at him. "I didn't."

"You mean you bought it? Why?"

"Of course I bought him." She seemed surprised by the question. "They don't let you just walk out of the store without paying, you know. You remember that children's boutique on Germantown Pike, the one on the corner? Well, it's going out of business and…." Her eyes narrowed. "And don't you even think about asking how much he cost."

Morgan was already raising his hands in surrender. He should never have asked. Besides it being none of his business, he didn't care what she spent or on what. It was just the fact that he was and always would be 'a banker', and bankers were only concerned about the price of things.

"You know I would never do that."

"Well…." Morgan lowered his hands when her face softened into a smile. "He was only $39. I can't tell you why, Morgan, I just saw these little manikins in a corner, huddled together under a sheet of plastic, except for him." She cupped her hand against the smooth head. "It was like he was peeking out and I got this idea. You know how much I love Halloween."

Morgan nodded. Everyone in the tri-state area and beyond knew how much she loved Halloween. Every October 31st members of the news media – print, digital, and televised – would crowd into the five-house cul-de-sac to capture the spectacle and send it on to their affiliate stations and the Internet.

As a kid, he'd been the envy of all his friends whose own Halloween decorations consisted of parent-carved jack-o'-lanterns, plastic skeletons, half-buried zombies, tissue-paper ghosts hanging from tree limbs or various inflatables. Not that they were bad, but no one could outdo his mother.

"I'm thinking haunted house. Can't you imagine Sebastian draped in sheer gauze under a black light? He'll make a wonderful ghost."

Morgan nodded. "Yeah, that should terrify the kids."

"Oh, no, he's a good little ghost. The kids will love him…especially Hannah. Do you think you can get her to dress up like a ghost, too?"

Now it was getting creepy. "I think she wants to be a witch, but I'll ask. Why Sebastian?"

"What?"

"Why the name Sebastian?"

"Why not…oh and don't you dare look at me like that. You named your car."

"Don't speak ill of Ralph."

It was his first car, a 1970 Ford Falcon, bought with very little of the money his father had left him. A 'project car' was how it was listed in the Classifieds section of the community throwaway paper, but more a clunker in reality, its once lemon-yellow paint reduced to faded, rusty cream. Morgan had christened it Ralph after he drove it to school and all his friends simultaneously pretended to vomit in unison.

"I guess Sebastian's a good name for a dummy."

"Manikin. A dummy is just a form molded out of plastic, but a *manikin* is a life-sized, articulated and anatomical representation of the human body. The name comes from the Flemish word *manneken*, meaning 'little man, figurine'." She smiled. "I Googled it."

"Ah. So, I guess a manikin doesn't need to have a face?" She stopped smiling. "And it's articulated?"

"The arms move. Okay, be right back." His mother patted the dummy...the *manikin's* head and Morgan's arm before walking out of the living room and through the dining room into the kitchen. Her voice echoed slightly when she spoke again. "I called Chet earlier and he's expecting us, but we should hurry. It's getting dark and I don't want to keep him too late."

Morgan looked down at the manikin and nodded. Now it made sense.

"My coat and tie are in the car," he said when she came back in carrying a plastic Wawa bag, her camera case over one shoulder, "but don't you think I should change my shirt? There are plenty of others upstairs."

His mother gave the plain blue wrinkled short-sleeve a look and shook her head. "No, you look perfect for what I have in mind. Oh, here."

Morgan opened the bag and peeked inside. "Mom...."

"I know," she said, "it's not Chinese food, but a BLT with hot peppers and vinegar is still your favorite, isn't it?"

Morgan took the classic hoagie out of the bag and pressed the paper wrapper to his nose, inhaling the mingled scents of bacon, vinegar and pepperoncini peppers deep into his lungs. His stomach growled as the flood gates opened. He had to swallow before answering.

"It is. And Chili Cheese Fritos, too."

"Am I forgiven?"

"Totally," Morgan said, using his daughter's current and most annoying expression. "Thank you."

"You're welcome. Do you need a bottle of water?"

"Have one in the car."

"Great, let's get going."

Securing the camera bag by slipping the strap over her head, his mother walked over to the manikin and started to pick it up.

"Hang on!" Morgan put the sandwich back into the bag and handed it to her. "Let me do that, okay?"

"Morgan, I carried Sebastian out of the store and into the house. I'm perfectly capable of taking him out to the car."

"I'm sure you are." Morgan grabbed the manikin around the waist – it was cold – and lifted. "You want it in the backseat or—"

"Not like that!"

For some reason, he thought the manikin would be much lighter than it was. It was only made of out plastic…*solid* plastic as he found out and damned near weighed as much as a child that size. He hadn't expected that.

Or for the arms that were held on by magnets to suddenly pop off or for the rod holding the quarter-inch-thick metal stand to slip from the hole in the back of the manikin's left leg and land squarely on his foot.

"*Jesus Christ!*"

"*Don't drop him!*"

And somehow he didn't.

Somehow, foot throbbing and eyes watering, he'd managed to hold on to the armless, faceless torso and neither drop it nor pitch it through the window.

Morgan took a deep breath. "Ow."

"Oh, Morgan, I'm so sorry. No, just hold him one more minute…" He felt the weight lift off his throbbing instep. "…until I get the rod back. Okay, you can put him down now. Carefully. Good. Are you okay?"

"Fine. You didn't tell me the arms came off."

"I told you they moved. How do you think they dressed him?" His mother handed him the Wawa bag then picked up the arms and reattached them. Morgan flinched at the sound of metal meeting magnet. "Why don't you head on over and we'll follow?"

It was tempting. "No, it's okay. I know you can handle it, but I'll take it out to the car."

"Fine, let me get the hand truck."

"You have a hand truck?"

"Of course, in the laundry room. It's the one I use to move potting soil. Sebastian's a little awkward to carry, but thank you for trying." She patted his cheek the same way she used to when he'd done something exceptional, like picking up empty film canisters without putting an eye out. "You can help me put on his bungee cords."

Morgan listened to her footsteps echo down the hall and looked down at the manikin.

"Boy, you'd better be worth it."

★ ★ ★

Graybryer Memorial Gardens and Mortuary was all that remained of the Lewison-Graybryer Estate, the onetime summer retreat for a Main Line millionaire and his family. On a par with Orson Welles's imaginary Xanadu in *Citizen Kane* and any of the du Pont properties, this American castle had its own spring-fed lake, tennis court, miniature golf course, rose garden, riding stable, Presbyterian chapel and cemetery.

It was the cemetery that saved the family after the Depression had wiped out their bank accounts and stock portfolios clean. The chapel began non-denominational services, the groundskeeper's cottage was turned into a full-service funeral home, and the gates of the wrought-iron fence that enclosed the thirty acres of rolling grass and woods were opened to the public.

The Graybryer Memorial Gardens and Mortuary was the place to await the Final Judgment Day and had a waiting list that far exceeded its remaining seven thousand available plots.

Unless your dearly departed was famous.

Or in the armed forces.

Or a first responder.

Or a friend of the family.

Like Morgan's father.

"Wakey, wakey, buttercakey."

Morgan opened his eyes to the softly lit room where he and his friend had once played their own version of cops and robbers called, because of the caskets that had been on display, Dracula and Van Helsing. Morgan always had to play Van Helsing and always had to lose to the bedsheet-caped and plastic-fanged vampire because Chet's father owned the place.

Back then the nave still had rows of pews and a marble altar beneath the stained-glass window of a lone lighthouse standing vigil on a cliff as the sun, flaring bands of red and orange and yellow, set into a sea of purples and blues. A single clear beveled jewel had been set into the window sometime after the chapel became part of the memorial gardens. It was supposed to represent the evening star, but Morgan always thought it looked like a flying saucer.

Now, aside from the refrigerated floral display case between the men's and women's bathrooms and the leather-bound reference books on Graybryer's full line of caskets and other funeral items – including prices and payment options – discreetly placed, it looked like any other nondescript waiting room…cream-colored walls, gray carpeting, soft indirect lighting, a sound system, comfortable chairs and sofas and black-and-white photographs on the walls. His mother's photographs… headstones and the younger version of himself at his father's grave.

A Boy's First Grief was still one of her best sellers.

When they first arrived, Morgan had gone to see his father while his mother pushed the manikin down the road in the opposite direction.

Morgan sat up and took the red plastic cup his friend held out to him. He might not have followed in his father's footsteps and become a lawyer, but Chet had and took over the business, lock, stock and Internet-ordained ministry when his dad retired three years earlier.

"Thanks." Morgan took a tentative sip – it was sweet iced tea – then downed half before coming up for air. "I needed that."

"I saw that. Makes me think you don't trust me." His friend took a normal swallow. "Although I did think about adding a shot of Everclear."

"Everclear?"

Chet took another sip and nodded. He'd exchanged the white shirt, black suitcoat and tie he'd had on when they arrived for a black Def Leppard t-shirt that made him look more like the skinny, iron-knuckled, dark-haired, big-mouthed kid he once was than the successful, distinguished, salt-and-pepper haired, paunch-gut businessman and licensed embalmer that he now was.

"Yeah, thought you could use it after all that." He swept his cup toward the modern 'antique glass' windows fronting the office. His mother was still out there, taking more pictures of the manikin among the tombstones. "But I figured you might not want to spend the night… although I do have some really comfy coffins in the back. I've tried a few and they're not bad."

"Thank you for your— You're sick, you know that?"

"I try." A big, toothy grin almost split the man's face in two. It was the same smile; the only difference was that the wrinkles were a little deeper around the eyes and mouth.

Morgan nonchalantly ran a thumb across the crow's feet in the corner of his right eye.

"Just between us," his friend pulled up a chair next to Morgan's and leaned forward, lowering his voice, "those pictures she was taking…."

"Photographs."

"Sorry?"

"Pictures are…." Morgan waved the rest away. His mother took photographs. He and most everyone else in the world who wasn't a photographer took pictures. Explaining the difference had almost become an unconscious reflex. "Sorry. Go on."

"It's not that I don't love your mother's work; I do and so did my dad. Obviously. I mean they're wonderful. I'm just saying that watching her take pictures of you and that little thing was a bit creepy."

Morgan nodded. "Yeah, I don't know what she's planning for the series, but I know she's going to turn it into a ghost for Halloween."

"Well, cool, my kids love coming to your mom's house. So do I. She always gives out full-sized candy bars. So, okay, now I get it. It's supposed to look like a ghost so naturally she brought it out here to take pictures." Chet grinned and nodded and took another sip. "Still creepy, though."

"Oh, yeah."

"There you are."

They both stood up as his mother wheeled the hand truck with its bungee-tied 'ghost' toward them. She'd draped the camera bag off the back of the truck; the camera, lens cap in place, was still around her neck.

Morgan finished the tea and handed his friend the cup. She probably wasn't finished, but he could hope. "Are you ready to go?"

"Almost," she said. "There are a few more shots I'd like to take in here, if I can. Chet?"

"Sure, but I'm not sure what the regulations are concerning putting a manikin inside one of my caskets."

His mother looked horrified. "Oh my God, no! I would never put Sebastian in a casket. That's a horrible thought."

Chet looked at Morgan and mouthed "Sebastian?" Morgan nodded as his mother wheeled the manikin to the stained-glass window that had once backed the chapel's altar.

"It's gotten so dark.... Chet, can you turn on some lights?"

"Sure." Chet finished off his tea as he walked back to the reception desk and turned on the recessed lighting. "You want them on full or half? I have two independent dimmer packs so can do pretty much whatever effect you want."

"Wonderful. Morgan, come sit in this chair and face right. Good, now cross your legs and rest your head on your hand. Like that, good. Chet, can you lower these lights? Too much. There. Perfect. Now, take down the ones behind it...slowly.... Stop!"

Morgan stayed in position while his mother unstrapped the manikin and dragged it across the carpet until it was next to the chair. She took off the lens cap, dropping it to the floor as she raised the camera.

—click—flash—

Without moving, Morgan watched his mother walk back to the manikin and turn it toward him, repositioning the right arm so that it seemed to be reaching for him.

His mother stepped back and lifted the camera.

"Okay, Morgan, close your eyes like you're asleep."

—click—flash— —click—flash— —click—flash—

"Perfect."

CHAPTER THREE

Do you know why she only took black-and-white photographs?

Because blue isn't always blue.

Get it? No, I'm not being funny. I know, the first time she told me that I didn't understand it either, but listen, I'll explain it the way she did. Let's see.... I need a color. Oh, my sweatshirt, how's that. What color is it?

Green, right. It's called Eagle's Green, but let's just call it green for right now.

Now, is the green you're seeing the same green I'm seeing? Think about it. I know what I see and you know what you see, the color green, but I don't know if my green is the same shade and tone as the green you're seeing.

Get it?

I know, it's confusing, but that's why my mother only took black-and-white photographs. Black-and-white photographs allow the viewer to add colors as they choose. You show people a color photograph of a yellow rose and they all see a yellow rose, but if you show those same people a black-and-white photograph of that rose...that gray rose...they'll put a color to it inside their head. That rose could be yellow or pink or cream or even lavender...it could be whatever color that person thinks it is.

Now do you understand how blue isn't always blue?

Plus, black-and-white film was cheaper when she started out. There also seemed to be less competition in the black-and-white categories of the photography contests she competed in. And history, as they say, was made. First came blue ribbons, then grand championships, and let's not forget the hefty prize money that accompanied them, then gallery shows and merchandise – calendars, note cards, gift store prints from photos she called her 'bread-and-butter' shots...good, but not what she'd consider a prize winner.

And sometimes good is enough for some things.

There aren't any bad Christine Morgan Riley photographs – no mediocre negatives hidden away and no less-than-stellar prints stuck into file cabinets. None.

I know, because I helped her burn them.

I don't know when she started or if my father knew – when he was still alive, we'd do it when I got home from school or on Saturdays when he golfed with his friends, but every few weeks or so she'd drag our old Weber barbeque grill out to the middle of the backyard and ask me to help her carry up some boxes from the darkroom.

The boxes were full of photographs she'd taken and their negatives. I know I sort of joke about her becoming famous because there was less competition, but it was her talent that did it and some of the photographs in those boxes were good. At least I thought they were.

But she didn't.

Sometimes she'd tell me what was wrong with it – too ordinary, anyone could have taken this, a blur…no blur – before tossing it into the barbeque. When it was almost full, she'd squirt on some lighter fluid and toss in a match. Then… WHOOSH!

I don't know when she started doing that, probably way before I was born, but she only asked me to help when I was in fourth or fifth grade…old enough to help and man the garden hose, just in case one of the burning photographs escaped. And I only asked her once why we were doing it and she told me something about how you couldn't keep everything in your life so you had to decide what things were worth keeping and which weren't.

And if something wasn't worth keeping, you got rid of it.

Made sense to me and it was fun. Hey, I'm a guy and fires are cool.

So, we'd stand around burning the prints my mother didn't think were worth keeping and when we'd finished, we'd throw some charcoal briquettes on top of the ashes and cook hamburgers.

My mother wasn't crazy, just a perfectionist.

★ ★ ★

Morgan shifted his weight and burped, tasting an odd combination of sesame chicken, hot-and-sour soup and crab rangoon. His mother had made up for the previous month by ordering all of his favorite dishes and insisting they sit down and eat as soon as he walked in. They ate in the kitchen, at the breakfast nook, because the dining room table was covered with prints that she wanted him to look at after dinner.

He often reviewed her new work before she showed it to her agent, because he knew how much she valued his opinion – as an average, non-artistic plebian and potential buyer.

It was a role she believed he excelled in.

"For a banker," Morgan said, saying out loud what he was sure she thought, as he turned on the Italian cut crystal chandelier and looked at the photographs that covered the 42" x 96" table. The manikin was in all the photos, a small faceless ghost wandering the graveyard; Morgan was in five.

A triptych—

Mid-shot of him standing at the grave of a child named Jackie Graybryer Ketchum, born and died the same day, January 24, 1919, the manikin in the far background, barely visible among the headstones.

Same, same with the manikin standing on the child's grave facing him.

Same mid-range with Morgan reaching toward the manikin.

And two others—

Seated in the chapel with his head on his hand and his eyes closed with the manikin standing next to the chair and reaching for him.

And an extreme long shot of him at his father's grave. He had no idea she'd taken that.

He had no idea why she'd taken any of them.

Jesus, what was he going to say? He couldn't tell her the truth – *could he?* – that he thought the photographs were – *repulsive* – offensive and macabre and no one in their right mind, not even the most ardent Christine Morgan Riley collector, would buy a photograph of what looked like the ghost of a naked child wandering a deserted cemetery. *"Look dear, it's the ghost of a dead child…shall we hang it in the nursery?"*

What the *hell* was she thinking?

It was one thing to buy a kid-sized…no…a *toddler*-sized manikin to dress up for Halloween, but this….

Morgan took a deep breath and was glad she'd insisted on eating before she asked him to look at the photographs. If it'd been the other way around, he might have missed another month of Chinese food. He wouldn't have been able to eat, and not because she'd have thrown him out; she would have simply looked at him in that *special* way she had when she wondered if something was worth her camera's attention, then thanked him for his opinion.

Even if he was just a banker.

Morgan walked out of the dining room and down the hall to the door to the darkroom, automatically checking the light sconce mounted next to it before keying the intercom. When his father had the basement remodeled, he'd paid extra to have both a warning light and intercom installed so no one – meaning him – would accidently walk in while his mother was developing film. His mother had added the DO NOT ENTER IF LIGHT IS ON sign even before Morgan could read.

Not that he needed to. He'd been taught the rules long before that. If the red light is on, you do not open the door. If the red light is on and you need your mother – see appendix A for what constitutes a viable need – you press the intercom button and wait for her to answer. But above all, if the red light is on you DO NOT OPEN THE DOOR.

And he never did. All the way through his childhood and early teens he never opened the door except on the day his father's paralegal assistant called. He'd answered the old landline phone in the kitchen where he'd been doing homework, expecting it to be Chet with ideas for an upcoming bike trip. At first he couldn't understand what the woman was saying. She spoke very fast and her voice was low, but she kept saying "your father, it's your father" and then she suddenly stopped and began to sob.

Morgan had dropped the phone and ran to the door, screaming for his mother when he yanked it open and heard her scream back, *"Morgan! What have you done?"* but all he could do was paraphrase the voice on the phone.

"It's Dad. It's Dad."

When his mother ran into the kitchen, he stayed in front of the open basement door, afraid to move even after he heard her hang up. It was only after the flash went off that he was finally able to turn around and look at her.

"It was a heart attack, Morgan. Your father's dead. It was very quick, he didn't feel any pain. Don't move."

Click. Flash.

The series *A Boy's First Grief* won the Grand Champion ribbon and a cash award of $20,000.00 in an International Photography contest.

Morgan pressed the call icon. "You can come up now, Mom."

"Will do."

He heard her footsteps on the stairs – she must have been standing next to the intercom waiting for him – and stepped back when the door opened. Oh, God.

"Mom…."

"Hold that thought." She pulled the door closed behind her and headed for the kitchen. She came back a moment later with the unfinished carton of kung pao shrimp and a fork. "It's true what they say…a half hour later and you're hungry again."

"It's been fifteen minutes."

"Is that all?" She stabbed a shrimp as she walked past Morgan and into the dining room. "Ummm…."

He had no choice but to follow her. "Mom."

"Son." She ate another shrimp. "Well, what do you think?"

Damn.

Morgan walked back to the table and picked up the photograph directly in front of him. It was the one image he almost liked. She had placed the manikin on a slight rise at the end of a long double row of elaborately carved headstones and taken a low-angle shot to increase the forced perspective illusion.

To the viewer the manikin just looked like another grave marker, which in Morgan's opinion, made it the best photograph of the lot. His mother put her fork into the carton and took the print carefully by the corner.

"I like this one, too," she said. "It was the last one I took…you don't think it's too dark, do you? I wasn't sure there was enough daylight left, but I think it works."

"It's perfect."

"I think so, too." His mother put the photograph back on the table and speared another shrimp. "I'm thinking of calling the series *Little Boy Found*. What do you think?"

"No."

The fork stopped an inch from her mouth. "What do you mean no?"

Tell her, you wuss. "Mom, about the photographs...."

"You don't like them?" She dropped the shrimp and fork back into the carton and stared at his face. "Oh my God, you don't like them."

"I didn't say that."

"Then what are you saying?" But she didn't give him a chance to answer. "You have to tell me, Morgan, because I haven't been this excited about a project in a long time. This little.... Sebastian has inspired so many ideas. Morgan, tell me what you think."

His mother never doubted herself or her work. She knew what worked and what didn't, and if it didn't she'd burn it. No muss, no fuss, no second thoughts. His opinion and those of critics were just that, opinions, and up until that moment, Morgan would have sworn she secretly didn't care what the public thought about her work as long as it sold.

She waited for him to answer, clutching the takeout carton so tightly that it had started to crush between her fingers. Morgan took it from her.

"When are you going to show them to William?"

"Tomorrow or the next day, but you haven't answered my question, Morgan. What do you think about my new series?"

Morgan took a deep breath and did what any son who loved his mother would do – he lied and hoped her agent would tell her the truth. William Ahern had one of the most successful photography agencies in the business – with offices in Philadelphia, London and San Francisco – and had been his mother's agent for almost as long as Morgan had been alive. Obviously with that much time under his belt, he must have had to deal with the harsh realities once in a while.

"Does William know anything about it?"

"Some. I told him about Sebastian, but do you mean the photographs? No."

"It's wrong…the name. You should call it something like…um… *Peek-a-Boo* or *Hide and Seek*…or…."

"*Hide and Seek*! That's perfect, Morgan, *thank* you!" She started to take back the carton and stopped. "You finish. You deserve it."

Morgan jabbed the last shrimp with the fork, popped it into his mouth and handed her back the empty carton.

"Nom, nom, nom, nom."

"Take something else, there's plenty of leftover."

"No, thanks, you keep it. You know what they say, you'll probably get the munchies in another half hour."

"Hah, hah. Well, at least take the fortune cookies home to Hannah."

"That I'll do."

While his mother walked back to the kitchen, Morgan turned in the opposite direction and took the slightly more direct route through the living room to the hall coat rack.

Daylight Saving Time might have ended five weeks ago, but night had pretty much started to invade the house. There was just enough light from the dining room's chandelier and coming in through the living room sheers from the 'historically accurate' reproduction streetlamp at the entrance of the cul-de-sac for Morgan to navigate a path without risk of barked shins or bruised egos.

Which wouldn't have been a problem if he hadn't suddenly noticed it standing in the shadows next to his mother's chair.

And sidestepped. Quickly. In a sort of hop-jump.

"*Jesus!*"

"Morgan?" His mother came in from the hallway carrying an ACME shopping bag. "What happened?"

"I tripped." Lying was becoming so much easier.

"Well, no wonder, it's dark in here." His mother walked over to the small table next to her chair and turned on the lamp. The manikin wasn't naked anymore. It wore a pair of pull-up dark brown corduroy pants and a gray *ALF* hoodie. Morgan remembered the hoodie from family pictures his father had taken.

"Here." She handed him the bag. It was heavier than it should have been for just cookies. "Don't get mad but I know how much Holly loves boneless spare ribs and you like mu shu pork more than I do, and they always give me so much rice.... What are you looking at?"

Morgan let the bag dangle on his fingers. The manikin was still barefoot. "You put clothes on it."

She turned and nodded. "Oh, course I did. I couldn't just leave him naked."

"No, you couldn't. What would the neighbors say? Why is it in the living room?"

"Where else would he be?"

Morgan thought a moment. "I don't know...the closet?"

"Why would I put him in the closet? It's nice having him around and the kids love it when I put him in the window. They wave to him when they get off the school bus. I could photograph it from behind him...but the front hedge just cuts the image.... Maybe I can.... Oh, I'll wait until the leaves fall and spread them on the yard and have the kids play in them and then photograph him looking out. Perfect. I hope we get an early snow. Can you imagine Sebastian in the snow?"

"Appropriately dressed, of course."

His mother looked up at him and blinked. "I am so sorry, Sebastian, I do get carried away sometimes, don't I?"

"Morgan."

"What? Morgan, of course, Morgan. Maybe you're right," she said, push/pulling him into the hall. "All those darkroom chemicals have finally eaten holes in my brain. Now, drive safely and give Hannah and Holly my love. And tell them to enjoy. Now good night. I love you."

"Yes, Mom. Good night, Mom. I love you, Mom."

"And thank you again for the title change, Morgan, I take back everything I ever said about you not having an artistic soul. You do. Drive safe."

"Will do."

The motion-sensor path lights came on as Morgan stepped off the porch steps and turned toward the driveway. He heard her tap on the glass as he walked past the living room and was already raising his hand to wave.

He didn't exactly jump; it was more of a side-shuffle stumble that just missed taking out a light.

She'd put the damn manikin in the window, his little egg-shaped, blank face peeking out over the bottom sill, its right arm up as if it was waving. Morgan couldn't see her, but he knew she was watching and probably had both hands pressed over her mouth to muffle the sound of laughter.

Morgan waved back and started whistling as he fished the keys out of his pocket and aimed the fob at the car. He could still feel her eyes on his back as he walked away.

"Cute, Mom, real cute."

CHAPTER FOUR

God, I used to love Halloween.

What?

No, that's not what I mean. I still do, but it's different when you get older and become a parent.

Sometimes.

★ ★ ★

By the time they'd reached Chestnut Hill and had been directed through the convoluted detours surrounding his mother's house, Morgan could feel his makeup and patience wearing thin.

The police routinely closed the side street leading to the cul-de-sac to vehicular traffic on Halloween, positioning themselves and community support volunteers discreetly around the neighborhood to insure the constant and continuous flow of pedestrian traffic. Morgan knew he could use his 'I'm Christine Riley's son' card at any of the roadblocks and be granted access to wander the residential streets in search of parking, but he'd done that only once, when Hannah was still a baby – dressed as a pumpkin – and could still remember the nasty looks he got as he drove by.

Full dark had fallen just after they got off 422 and swung onto Ridge Pike. His daughter had wanted to take the route Morgan usually drove when they visited his mother to see the decorations, but relented after he reminded her of how long that way took and how quickly trick-or-treat candy disappeared.

His wife had given him a hard side-eye, but it wasn't as if their daughter hadn't already plundered their covenant-controlled community and the neighborhoods where her best friends lived. Two large mixing bowls filled with candy sat on the kitchen counter, waiting inspection when they got home. Morgan felt no shame.

Irritation, low-grade road rage, frustration and growing fatigue, yes...but not shame.

"Everybody's a zombie, Daddy," Hannah yelled from the backseat, "just like you! Look, there's a witch, like me, except she has an orange wig...and there's a werewolf and a cheerleader and..." She sighed. "... more zombies. Why is everybody a zombie?"

Because, Morgan thought, it's an easy costume. You find some old clothes, rub some dirt on them, put in a few more holes, a little makeup, a little blood and *voila*: zombie.

When the brake lights flashed on the SUV in front of them, Morgan used the moment to glance at his daughter in the rearview mirror. The red light had turned her green witch makeup to brown and ignited her long brown hair to the color of flame.

"We're coming to get you, Bar-ba-rah," Morgan said.

Her face disappeared into shadows as the SUV crept forward. Morgan took his foot off the brake and eased the Escort into a crawl.

"Who's Bar-ba-rah?"

"It's from an old movie," his wife said as red light filled the car again. "About zombies."

"Can I see it?"

They both said "No" at the same time.

When they passed the last side-street roadblock, Morgan turned in to a nondescript neighborhood of modest split-level *Brady Bunch/Leave It to Beaver* homes and began the search for a parking spot along the car-lined streets.

"There!"

Morgan looked where his wife was pointing and watched the Action News 6 van pull away from the curb. "Good eye."

"Which one?" she asked and nodded the twin bloodshot eyes of her deely-bopper at him, her silver tinsel flapper wig sparkling. Her costume was equally zombie-easy and most of it she'd gotten on a trip to the Dollar General: wig, deely-bopper, silver lamé-like leggings with matching cape, and gray makeup. She'd already had the Roswell, New Mexico 'Alien Abduction' sweatshirt from the last vacation trip they took before Hannah was born. She'd added the fuzzy black legwarmers and knee-high UGGs when the temperature dipped into the mid-forties as the sun went down.

Morgan never got a chance to quip "How about the one in the middle?" Hannah's shriek of delight as he pulled into the empty parking space ruined the moment. His ears were still ringing but some part of his daddy-brain recognized the sounds of a released and discarded seat belt and door handle being yanked.

His daughter tested the child-safety lock three more times before giving up.

"Daaaadd!"

"Just hold your broomstick for a second, Miss Witch." Morgan turned off the car and turned so he could face both his wife and daughter. "Do you have everything?"

His daughter held up the black and orange witches' cauldron goodie bag with her left hand, her right still wrapped around the door handle.

"Button your cloak."

His daughter sighed. "Witches don't wear cloaks."

"They most certainly do," his wife said. She'd removed the sleeves and cut down an old coat she was going to donate. "Especially if they want to go trick-or-treating."

While their daughter buttoned her makeshift coat-cloak, his wife unbuckled her seat belt and turned toward him. She looked particularly smug. "Ready?"

Morgan unlatched and turned toward her. "Feeling confident, are we?"

"Always."

"Okay. One. Two. Three."

Her scissors cut his paper.

"Yay, Mom won!"

Morgan glanced back at his daughter. "You don't like me going with you?"

"I do," she said, "but you eat all the Laffy Taffys."

She knew him too well.

"Only the banana ones," Morgan said and unlocked the back door. The car's interior immediately flooded with light – from both the back and front passenger side doors. His wife's victory in their annual Rock-Paper-Scissors contest won her the right to accompany their daughter up to any house that looked particularly scary while he watched from the sidewalk.

Without the possibility of filching even one banana Laffy Taffy.

Morgan reached into the back footwell for the Dollar General foam rubber arm he'd picked up that afternoon and got out of the car. Neither his wife nor daughter, already halfway up the street and skipping hand-in-hand, turned or slowed down when the door locks beeped.

Morgan stuck the foam rubber arm in his mouth and quickly shambled after them.

"Ban-nan-nan Laffy Taffy," he moaned in his best zombie voice. "Ban-nan-nan Laffy Taffy."

★ ★ ★

Morgan picked up his daughter when they reached the ROAD CLOSED barriers at the mouth of the cul-de-sac so she could see over the throng of reporters and parents gathered on the blacktop and the herds of trick-or-treaters that started at his mother's house before moving counter-clockwise around the circular sidewalk.

"Wow."

Morgan looked at his wife and nodded. There was little more he could add to that.

It was obvious his mother had not only decided the theme for her own yard decorations, by far and above the most elaborate and labor intensive, but for her four neighbors as well.

Waves of fog rolled across the manicured lawns from dry ice machines concealed among realistic tombstones or crypts to fill the street ankle deep and turn the sidewalks, outlined with blue rope lights, into glowing pathways. Flickering torches and grinning jack-o'-lantern faces peered through the mist while hidden speakers filled the night with the sound of rushing wind and disembodied moans.

The cul-de-sac, Buttonwood Court, had become a haunted graveyard, but while his wife and daughter oohed and ahhed, their heads swiveling from one display to the next, Morgan couldn't stop looking at his mother's house.

It was filled with ghosts.

Most of them hovered above the glowing fog that covered the front lawn where he and his friends once played football. Their diaphanous bodies fluttered as they swayed in the wind and tugged at some invisible cord that tethered them to the ground. Others swung suspended in the shimmering blue light that filled the porch and spilled out into the night.

His mother, dressed in a hooded white cloak, sat in a chair at the top of the porch steps surrounded by children…surrounded by ghosts.

"They're helium balloons."

"What are?"

"The ghosts."

His wife hip-checked him. "Well, I didn't think they were real."

And his daughter squirmed her way out of his arms. "I want one!"

"Hannah!"

Fortunately, the crowd slowed her progress just long enough for Morgan to grab her shoulder and pull her to a stop, the parental reprimand dying on his lips when he felt his wife grab the back of his moth-eaten sweater/costume.

"Go on."

With his wife hanging on, Morgan hoped he sounded sincere as he steered his daughter through the multitude.

"Sorry." "Excuse me." "Witch comin' through." "Sorry." "Pardon."

"Hey! Wait your turn."

"I got kids, too, you know."

"Entitled son-of-a—"

"The line starts back there, sir." The police officer who'd stepped in front of them wore a reflective Community Service vest and a smile.

His wife bumped into Morgan when he stopped. Smiling back at the officer, he pulled his daughter in close.

"I know, but this is my mother's house and she's expecting us."

The officer kept smiling but cocked his head to the very long line of costumed trick-or-treaters that lined the sidewalk behind him and stretched out beyond the cul-de-sac.

"Well, we're keeping things moving pretty quickly, so if you'll just take your family to the end of the line, sir."

"I know how it sounds. I really am her—"

"*Grammy!*"

His mother stood up into the blue light as the last group of trick-or-treaters ran down the stairs and headed for the driveway. Because she wore a black sweater and slacks under the cloak, she seemed to be nothing more than a head and a pair of hands.

It was a very cool effect.

Morgan slipped the foam rubber arm up his sleeve then pulled his cellphone out of his back pocket. He took a picture just as his mother raised one hand.

"It's okay, Hank, that's my family. You can let them in."

His daughter took off before the officer could step aside. The fog swirled in her wake and set the ghosts along the walk dancing.

"Sorry, Mr. Riley," the officer said. "It's been crazy."

Morgan looked at his mother sitting among her ghosts and nodded.

"I can imagine." Morgan slipped his phone back into his pocket. "Thanks. You're doing a great job."

"I'll give you a minute, but we really need to keep the line moving."

Morgan understood and took his wife's hand. "Of course, thanks."

Hannah was already on the porch hugging his mother as a kid in an old-fashioned-not-inspired-by-Stephen King clown costume watched, but even though the front walk was outlined with white lights, the constant shift and movement of the fog and balloon-ghosts gave Morgan the sensation that he was walking through a carnival funhouse.

"Where do you think it is?" his wife asked as they neared the house, and Morgan didn't need to ask her what *it* she was referring to. He'd told her about the manikin and his mother's Halloween plans for it when he got home after the photo session at Graybryer. She hadn't been surprised. "I don't see it."

"It's kind of small so I don't think she'd have it out here. It's probably up on the porch, tucked in a corner and under a spotlight."

His wife squeezed his hand. "You don't think it'll bother Hannah, do you? I don't want her having nightmares about it. She is only eight."

"Naw, she'll be fine."

"I don't know."

"Mom, Dad, come on! Sebastian wants to meet you!"

"Who's Sebastian?" his wife asked. Morgan turned and hoped the ghost lights were bright enough for her to see his smirk. "You're kidding. She named it?"

"Yup, and I don't think we have to worry about Hannah."

"No, but now I'm worried about your mother."

"Join the club, we have jackets."

Morgan had stopped watching his feet slink through the fog when they reached the porch steps and looked up. His mother was sitting in her chair, a bowl of candy bars on her lap, watching Hannah and the little clown. The voices of the awe-struck crowd floated on the air behind him.

"It's not a ghost."

"What's n— Oh. Wow."

Morgan pulled the foam rubber arm out of his sleeve and stuck it between his teeth as he climbed the stairs. "Grrrr."

"Lovely." His mother put the bowl down next to the chair and stood up to accept a hug. "You make a truly wonderful corpse."

"T'anks. Grr."

"And Holly, you are a very fetching alien. So, what do you think of all this? We had a little neighborhood meeting and everyone really got into the spirit of the thing." She laughed. "I can't believe I just said that. And I know, I went a little crazy."

"Uh iddle?" *A little?*

"Morgan, will you please get that out of your mouth?" his mother said, but looked vaguely disgusted when he did. "Now, what were you trying to say?"

His wife answered instead. Which was probably for the best.

"Your decorations are amazing, Christine. I mean, all the houses are unbelievable, but this…." Her deely-bopper eyes gyrated above her head as she nodded. "It's…fantastic!"

"Thank you." His mother turned toward Morgan, expecting more of the same. "What do *you* think?"

Morgan looked down at the manikin in its black-and-white clown costume, with belled jester's cap, opposite color ruffles at the wrists and ankles – white on the black side, black on the white – and the two large patch pockets on the legs to fill with candy. Once upon a time, when he'd worn the costume, the white pocket had a monogrammed *M* done in silver thread, the black pocket a gold *R*.

The *R* was still there but the *M* had been replaced by a silver *S*.

For Sebastian.

Morgan didn't remember the clown-faced shoes, curly wig or foam nose taped to the center of the manikin's face.

He knew the shoes and wig and nose were red, even though they looked gray under the black light. He'd seen enough of her photographs to recognize the shade.

Black and white and gray…the perfect Christine Morgan Riley color palette.

"I thought you bought it as a Halloween decoration."

Morgan heard his wife sigh.

"Among other things," his mother said and picked up the candy bowl. "Holly, would you mind taking over for a minute? I need to get my camera."

"Of course you do," Morgan said, low enough, he thought, so she wouldn't hear.

He should have known better.

"Only if you want Halloween pictures," she said. "I don't have to get my camera."

Morgan could feel the weight of his wife and daughter's stares without needing to look, and what was even stranger was that he thought he could feel the manikin staring as well.

He rolled his shoulders against the sensation. "Sorry, Mom. Yes, please, get your camera."

"If you insist." Fortunately, she was smiling when she said it and still smiling when she waved at the officer manning the walk. "Okay, Hank, send up another group."

Suddenly the recorded sounds of wind and ghostly moans were replaced by a very real and semi-harmonized chorus of "trick-or-treat" as two zombies, one Iron Man, a miniature Wonder Woman holding the hand of an even smaller yellow-masked Minion and a kid in a long lab coat with a rubber chicken stuffed in the pocket charged the porch. The tethered ghosts momentarily disappeared behind a wall of swirling fog.

"Daddy! Help!"

Hannah was dragging the manikin backwards toward the glider swing at the far end of the porch, the metal stand leaving scratches in the painted wood floor. Morgan reached her in two strides and set the manikin upright.

"What are you doing, baby?"

His daughter looked back at the trick-or-treaters and then up at him. "He's too little, Daddy. They'll knock him over."

Possibly, Morgan thought. "Okay, but let me, it's too heavy for you."

"He," his daughter corrected at the same moment an errant breeze must have slipped down the collar of Morgan's sweater and run the course down his spine.

Remembering the incident with the stand and his foot, Morgan laid the manikin across one arm and carried it horizontally past the floating ghosts tied to the railing. It was darker at that end of the porch, so when the flash went off it momentarily blinded him.

Morgan heard the stand clunk against the floor and his daughter's quick intake of breath when the second flash went off.

"Sebastian's okay, Grammy," his daughter said from beyond the yellow/purple after-image haze. "Daddy, you have to be more careful."

"Sorry. Mom, a little warning next time, okay?"

"You're right, but it was a perfect shot. Holly…can you handle another group while I take a few more photographs?"

"Sure." His vision cleared enough to watch his wife settle back in the chair and wave. "Okay, Hank…release the krakens!"

His mother still hadn't apologized when she turned and walked toward them. Hood thrown back, shoulders hunched forward, head low, camera hiding her face, she seemed to float toward them through the blue light… just one more ghost.

"Hang on, Mom." Morgan pulled out his cellphone and swiped open the camera app. His *picture* might not contain all the nuances of a Christine Morgan Riley photograph, but it was Halloween and his Father-Given Right to take pictures of his child – even if she was standing next to a manikin wearing his old costume.

But that really was the beauty of digital photography. All he had to do was edit, crop and delete whatever he didn't want.

Bye, bye, Sebastian.

Morgan lifted the phone out in front of him and took aim. "Okay, Hannah-Banana…say Cheddar."

"Cheddar!"

"Perfect." Morgan put the phone back in his pocket as he turned. "All yours, Mom."

She nodded and got back into her photographer's crouch. "Thank you. Okay, Hannah, now…I want you to bend down like you're telling Sebastian a secret. Good." *—click—flash—* "Now, open your bag and show him the candy. That's per—" She cleared her throat. "That's good, Hannah."

—click—flash—

Morgan walked back to his wife as the lightning storm of clicks and flashes continued behind him and another group of zombies thundered down the stairs and took a sharp right at the THIS WAY OUT sign pointing to the driveway.

"Having fun yet?"

"Tons." His wife stood up and handed him the candy bowl. "Here, you take over. I need to use the little alien's room before we head out."

She leaned forward and lowered her voice. "We *are* heading out soon, aren't we?"

"Just let me get a few more of Hannah," his mother answered, "and then I want one with all of you."

Morgan pointed to his ears and mouthed "Like a bat" as he sat down. His wife nodded and headed for the hosue.

"Oh, and Holly would you mind bringing out that bag of extra candy when you come back? Thank you. Okay, Hannah…just like that…."

—click—flash—

He sat back in the chair and took a deep breath. "Okay, Hank."

"TRICK OR TREEEEEEEAT!"

* * *

Morgan called it after the third wave of zombies and others came and left.

"Mom, I really hate to break up the party, but it's getting late and people are going to be turning off their porch lights soon."

It might have been hitting a little under the belt, but it worked. Hannah got up from the floor where she'd been kneeling to put candy into one of the manikin's pockets and headed for the exit. Morgan managed to stop her at the top of the stairs.

His mother followed more slowly. "You're right, but I need one photograph of all of you."

"Aw, Grammy…it's getting late." There was a faint, but definite whine in his daughter's voice. She was getting tired.

"Just one," Morgan said. "Then we're off."

His mother nodded. "Just one. Hank, hold up, please? Okay, everyone gather around Sebastian."

"Mom…."

"Morgan, just do it and stop wasting time."

His wife handed him a full-sized Oh Henry! bar and showed him the Mounds bar she'd palmed for herself. "Compensation for time served. Where do you want us, Christine?"

"Here is fine. Okay, Morgan and Holly in back, Hannah in front and

Sebastian…" She moved the manikin in front of Hannah. "…right here. Hannah, put your hands on his shoulders. Lovely."

—click—flash— *—click—flash—*

"You said *one*, Mom."

"Math was never my strong suit." She stood and let the camera hang from its strap as she held out her hand. "Do you want me to take a picture with your phone?"

Morgan handed her the phone and the case flashed blue as she raised it. "On the count of three. One. Two. Three. Cheddar!"

"Cheddar."

—click—flash—

Done.

"Thank all of you for putting up with me. I'll be right back." His mother handed him back the phone and walked into the house.

"Where's she going?"

"To get Sebastian's trolley," Hannah said with a yawn.

Morgan was about to ask what she was talking about when his mother came out pushing the hand truck.

"You can't be serious."

"We *have* to, Daddy! It's Sebastian's first Halloween ever!"

His mother shrugged. "A child's imagination is a wonderful thing… and it is his first Halloween. Come on, Morgan, it'll be fun."

"Yeah," he said, "fun."

"Yay!"

His wife gave him a thumb's up. "Yay?"

Morgan decided to save his comments until they were home and alone, and bent to the task of strapping the manikin onto the hand truck. He'd had a lot of practice during the photoshoot at Graybryer.

"I put the bag with the extra candy under the chair, Christine," his wife said as she helped their daughter down the stairs. "I think Hannah wants to hit a few more neighborhoods after this, but we'll try to stop back before we leave."

"That would be wonderful. Happy hunting, Hannah!"

"Okay, Grammy. Come *on*, Mommy."

"You two go ahead," Morgan said as he carried the hand truck and manikin down the stairs instead of rolling it down one step at a time because it was faster and he was quickly losing the holiday spirit. "I'll catch up."

Another *—click—flash—* went off as he set the truck/manikin down on the sidewalk next to the exit sign.

"Sorry." His mother said as she sat down and put the camera in her lap, covering it with the cloak as she picked up the bowl of candy. "I was taking it off and accidentally hit the flash. Sorry."

Morgan nodded and grabbed the truck handles. The rubber-coated metal felt slick against his palms. If he was lucky everyone would think the full-grown zombie pushing a manikin in a clown costume on a hand truck was just part of the spectacle.

"That's okay." He rolled his shoulders and leaned the truck back toward him. The bells on the jester's hat tinkled. Jesus, he'd forgotten about the bells. "Okay, we shouldn't be too long, Hannah's getting tired."

"Of course. Morgan, can I ask you to do one other thing for me? If it's possible, could you try to keep people from taking Sebastian's picture? I really would appreciate it."

"I'll try, but—"

His mother shook her head. "Oh, never mind, I'm being silly."

Morgan nodded.

"He's wearing a costume, it's not like anyone will recognize him. Forget I mentioned it. Go have fun. Okay, Hank, I'm ready for another group."

Only the ghosts watched them leave.

* * *

While the news coverage might have made it look like something out of the zombie apocalypse in which all of Chestnut Hill and Germantown Pike was inundated by trick-or-treaters, it was really an optical illusion.

There were no crowds beyond his mother's cul-de-sac, only the standard number of costumed kids and teens wandering the less notable streets and, by the time they'd made it halfway around the adjacent neighborhood, there were more dark houses than ones with lighted porches and glowing jack-o'-lanterns and Hannah had faded into a slumped form on Morgan's shoulder.

He blamed the damned manikin because if he didn't, he'd have to blame his daughter for wanting to bring the thing along and he couldn't do that. She was just a kid and the manikin wasn't much more than a big doll to her...a big and really creepy faceless doll, but a doll nonetheless.

She'd been all sparkle and hype all the way around the cul-de-sac, the manikin's self-proclaimed protectress who'd placed herself between it and the groups of sugar-crazed trick-or-treaters and, with polite determination, cleared a path for the hand truck up to each and every house.

"*Excuse us, please. Excuse us. This is Sebastian's first Halloween and he's really excited. Excuse us.*"

"*Aw...how cute.*" "*Isn't that adorable.*"

Morgan was glad some people thought so.

They did get some raised eyebrows and a few parents had pulled their kids away. No one asked to take a picture, although one news team – he hoped from a public access station and not prime time – had filmed Hannah, after getting her own candy, pointing back to the manikin and asking for a second piece that she carried back to the manikin and put into the pocket of his old costume. Who could refuse?

Happy Halloween.

When they left the cul-de-sac, Morgan had graciously offered the hand truck to his wife, reminding her and their daughter that he'd lost Rock-Paper-Scissors to be that year's trick-or-treat parent.

His wife had graciously declined the honor until Hannah handed him a banana Laffy Taffy and asked to be carried.

"Okay, Hannah-Banana, wake up. We're back."

She moved sluggishly against his shoulder. "Home?"

"Nope, just at the car." Morgan set her down on the sidewalk and opened the back door. "Okay, climb in and buckle up."

She climbed in and settled back into the booster seat she'd almost outgrown and closed her eyes. Morgan set the candy-filled bag in the footwell beneath her feet and began strapping her in.

"Have a good time?" he asked.

"Uh-huh. Sebastian did too."

"Well, that's nice."

"Uh-huh."

"Is that why you wanted him to come with us?"

"Nuh-uh."

Morgan brushed back the hair sticking to her makeup and wiped his fingers across the front of his sweater. What's another stain to a zombie?

"Hannah?"

"Hmm?"

"Why did you want to bring Sebastian?"

"Grammy said to."

"She did?"

His daughter nodded without opening her eyes. "She said I could have a ghost. Don't forget my ghost, okay?"

"Okay, you go to sleep and when you wake up, we'll be home."

She nodded again as he closed the door.

His wife pushed the manikin up to the car. "You want to put this in the cargo space or try to get it in the backseat next to Hannah?"

Morgan didn't look at either option. The manikin might have fit by itself but the hand truck probably wouldn't without lowering the back side seat…and it was just too late for that.

"I'll push it back and you drive over and pick me up. I think it might be easier if you follow this out and come back up Germantown Pike." He pulled out his phone and checked the time. It was just 8:35. "Things should be winding down by now."

In fact, things had wound down completely. The barriers had been moved to the sidewalk adjacent to the entrance awaiting removal and all the porch lights and fog machines were off. Most of the neighbors had already dismantled some of their portion of that year's spectacle, but not one of his mother's ghosts remained.

Morgan pushed the manikin up the dark front walk and past the pile of deflated balloons and night-damp material.

"So where is everyone?"

Morgan watched her materialize from the shadows beneath the dark porch. She'd taken off the white cloak and pulled the thick black sweater tighter around herself as she walked down the steps. The night had gotten colder but she'd sat in the dark and waited for them.

"Hannah got tired so we stopped at the car first. Holly should be here in a few minutes."

"Did Hannah have a good time?"

"She sure did."

"And what about Sebastian?" Bending forward, she carefully peeled off the foam nose then brushed her thumb across the hard plastic where it had been. "Did he have a good time?"

It might have been less creepy if she'd looked at him instead of the manikin. Or not.

"I don't know," Morgan said, "why don't you ask him?"

She looked up and there was just enough light from the streetlamp for him to see her face. For a moment it seemed as if she was considering doing that, then threw the nose at him. Morgan made a grab for it but ended up swatting it onto the lawn. It was too dark to search for it and he was too tired to even try. She'd find it in the morning.

"Funny man." His mother stepped back and pointed to the costume's bulging patch pockets. "What are in his pockets?"

"Candy, what else? Hannah's idea."

"She made sure Sebastian had candy…my God, Morgan, that is so sweet."

"Well, it was his first Halloween."

"It was, wasn't it? Thank her but that's a lot of candy. Maybe you should take some…and you can tell her that it's because Sebastian is so small, we don't want him to get a tummy ache."

She laughed and Morgan hoped the sound he'd made passed for something similar.

"Okay. Is that why you told Hannah to make sure we took it with us?"

She stopped laughing. "What?"

"So she'd get more candy. She said you told her to bring it."

"I did? Oh, yes, maybe that was it. I think I said it was too bad Sebastian couldn't go trick-or-treating or something like that. I forget, but you know how...inventive children's imaginations are. But it really was a very sweet thing for her to do. Now admit it, you had fun, too, didn't you?"

"A blast."

"You really are becoming more of an old woman than I am, Morgan. Lighten up."

Lighten up. Okay. "Whee."

She reached into the manikin's pocket and took out a piece of candy, offering it to Morgan. It was a Banana Laffy Taffy.

"No thanks."

His mother unwrapped the candy and popped it in her mouth. He'd had no idea she liked those. "What about pictures?" she asked. "Did people take a lot of pictures of him?"

"No."

"They didn't?"

"A few did, I guess, but it's Halloween, Mom, there were a lot of strange things wandering around. No one really paid much attention to it."

"They didn't. Well, now it's up to us to change that, isn't it?" Morgan again got the feeling that the question hadn't been directed at him. "Oh, there they are. Here, let me."

His mother took Morgan's place behind the hand truck as his wife pulled the Escape into the driveway and groaned when the headlights swept across the empty yard and discarded ghosts.

"Oh, my God, I promised to give Hannah a ghost!"

"That's okay," Morgan said, maybe a little too quickly, "she'll be fine without it."

"But I promised."

"It's really okay. I'll tell her...um...something, don't worry. It'll be fine."

His mother nodded but didn't look convinced. "Is Hannah asleep?"

"Probably."

"Well, then, I won't wake her. Tell her I'll give her two kisses goodbye the next time I see her."

"I will," he said and kissed her cheek. "You shouldn't have been sitting on the porch, your skin's like ice."

"I'll make some hot cocoa when I go in. Now scoot."

"Okay, but let me just help you get it on the porch."

His mother tapped his hands out of the way. "No need, I'll just roll him around to the back and go in through the patio doors. No stairs and the kitchen's right there. We'll be fine. Now, go on, it's late and you're right, it is cold."

"Okay, good night, Mom." He gave her another kiss and quick hug. She kissed him back but didn't let go of the hand truck. "We can stop by Saturday if you like."

"Give me a call on Friday. I need to talk to William about something and might be busy." She lifted a hand and waved to his wife through the windshield. "Give Hannah a hug for me and don't forget to tell her that Sebastian thanks her for the candy. Oh, do you want more candy?"

Morgan held up his hands and walked backward to the car. "No, really, thanks. Hannah has more than enough and we haven't even sorted it yet."

"Okay. Happy Halloween, Morgan."

"Same to you, Mom."

Morgan opened the passenger side door and leaned down. "Want me to drive?"

"Nope, just get in."

He didn't need to be asked twice and sighed happily as the heated air washed over his feet and face. As his wife backed up, Morgan watched his mother walk up the driveway, her shadow stretching ahead of her until the back motion sensor lamp went on and split her shadow and the manikin's in two.

The light went off as they pulled away.

Halloween was over for another year.

CHAPTER FIVE

Life goes on, right?

Day by day, minute by minute, and we don't even think about it. I mean, unless we're going through something like a major illness or…death…we don't really sit down and consciously think 'I am alive and this is my life.' It'd be nuts to do that, right? I mean, we'd never get anything done. So we don't think about that.

John Lennon said it best. He said, 'Life is what happens to you while you're busy making other plans.'

My mother called them series and they were her life.

Our *lives, hers and mine.*

Of course, sometimes I wasn't the main focus, but I was always there. Like when Hannah was born. You can guess who took over my spot, but, hey, first grandchild and all? What? No, I wasn't jealous. I was proud like any new father and my mother was over the moon.

But she was also and always Christine Morgan Riley…so she wasn't your typical grandmother. She hadn't brought her camera to the hospital, which kind of surprised me a little, but it was probably the right thing to do. I don't think my wife would have been very cooperative at the time.

My mother didn't take one photograph of Hannah until she was two months old. That's the age babies start smiling.

For six weeks my mother only took pictures of Hannah. I don't know how many rolls of film she used, but she'd only printed out fifteen photographs. Fourteen beautiful, award-winning, as it turned out, black-and-white photographs of my baby girl. Plus the last one she took for the series.

It's a close-up of Hannah in the portable bassinet we'd set up next to Holly's side of the bed. Hannah was asleep and I'd come in just to check on her. I didn't know my mother had followed me. It was at night and I'd left the bedroom door open so when I reached for her the shadow of my hand fell across her chest. The next thing I know my mother is telling me not to move and the flash goes off.

Hannah didn't wake up.

That was the first photograph in the Protector *series. It was just my daughter and my shadow, but I'm still in the photograph. I'm still there.*

Okay, I know what you're thinking and it's not true. I'm not in every *photograph she ever took...look at them, I'm not. Yeah, I'm in a lot of them but, hey, I was always there and I worked cheap.*

Sorry, but I was always there.

Life happens when you're busy making other plans, but I was always part of those plans. I was her son and I loved her and she knew I'd always be part of her plans...part of her life...even if it was only to set up her shows or bring Chinese takeout.

⋆ ⋆ ⋆

They took turns doing Thanksgiving and this year his mother was in charge of the feast – which meant far less physical work cleaning, shopping and cooking, but significantly more emotional stress for his wife.

Although Morgan could remember the days when he woke up to the house smelling of roasting turkey and pumpkin pie – while the Macy's Thanksgiving Day Parade, followed by football, played on TV – after his father died his mother made reservations at five-star restaurants, politely declining invitations from her agent and friends because Thanksgiving was a family holiday.

She never said it out loud, but it was obvious to Morgan that even though he and his mother were a team, the two of them didn't qualify as 'family' anymore.

That changed after Hannah was born. Bringing an infant to five-star eateries could be problematic at the best of times, so a new *family* tradition began.

Holly loved to cook and bake and the years they hosted Thanksgiving the condo was filled with the smells Morgan remembered.

His mother had Thanksgiving brought in by whatever caterer she was using that year for her local gallery openings.

It was a perfect compromise…with one exception that always began with the same seemingly innocent question: "What can we bring?"

To which his mother would answer, "Nothing. It's all taken care of."

And thus his wife's emotional turmoil would begin.

"We *have* to bring something, Morg."

"No, we don't."

"We can't just show up empty-handed."

"Hon, yes we can."

"Wine?"

"N— Perfect."

He brought two bottles of wine – a white Burgundy and a Sauvignon blanc – and Holly brought a bouquet of autumn-tone mums and a large covered dish of corn pudding that she made from the recipe Hannah's teacher had given the class before Thanksgiving break.

Hannah carried the flowers, the burgundy mums a near-perfect match to the velvet and lace party dress she wore.

Regardless of the locale – their house or his mother's – appropriate dress was required.

His mother wore a long chiffon vest in swirling autumn colors over a soft gray turtleneck and herringbone slacks, appropriate and yet unobtrusive, and had been thrilled by the flowers and wine and smiled at the covered dish.

"Oh, Holly, you really shouldn't have."

"Hannah helped me make it." Which was not a lie, their daughter had held the recipe card and cracked the eggs…and gotten out most of the shell that dropped into the bowl. He hoped.

"Well, then, I can't wait to try it. Come on, you two, let's get these in water and find a place for Hannah's pudding."

"What do you want me to do?"

Taking the bottles from him, his mother nodded toward the living room. "Why don't you go sit down. We'll call you boys when we're ready."

"Fine, fine…if we're not wanted…."

Morgan made a sad face as he trudged from the hall to the living room and heard his daughter laugh, expecting to find his mother's agent as the other 'boy' she mentioned.

He should have known better.

The manikin stood in front of the fireplace, just left of center, facing the hallway, the banked flames highlighting the hard white plastic head in rose gold. It wore another dapper 1980s hand-me-down outfit: dark gray corduroy pull-up pants, black clip-on bow tie and a black V-neck argyle vest with white and gray diamonds over a bright yellow button-down shirt.

The shirt was new.

And the only reason Morgan knew that was because he'd never worn a yellow shirt in any of the color pictures his father had taken. The original shirt had been white, but that wouldn't have been enough contrast in a black-and-white photograph – white shirt, white plastic head? No, the bow tie would have looked like it was floating in midair.

The yellow shirt would read medium gray in black-and-white photographs and that's all that mattered.

Morgan glanced toward the dining room's sliding doors, which would remain closed until the big reveal, and watched a shadow move from left to right along the narrow crack beneath them.

He was still looking at the doors when Holly walked in from the hallway. If they were celebrating at home, she would have had an apron over a nice pair of slacks and semi-fancy top, but since his mother was hosting, his wife wore a plum-colored midi dress with three-quarter-length kimono sleeves and a gold lavalier necklace that matched the earrings peeking out from beneath her dark blond pixie-bob.

Morgan had decided on brown business casual with a cream-colored shirt and pumpkin-orange tie that his daughter picked out…under a rust-colored argyle vest with black and white diamonds.

"I think we're going to like this caterer," Holly said, coming into the room. "I haven't been able to stop eating these. Her—" The kalamata olive stopped short of her mouth when she saw the manikin.

Morgan took the olive and popped it into his mouth. "Thanks."

"You know, if you'd worn a bow tie you two could be twins. Well, at least now we know why you have an obsession with vests."

He took his time swallowing.

"Yeah, yeah, I know…I'm ugly and my mom dressed me funny."

He expected her to laugh.

She didn't.

"You're not ugly." She was still looking at the manikin. "How many of your baby clothes did she keep?"

"Beats me. Maybe it's her subtle way of pushing for another grandchild."

Holly finally looked up. "Subtle? Your mother? When was the last time she *subtly* reminded you that Hannah's her only grandchild?"

Morgan licked the brine off his lips. His mother had never been subtle about any subject, unless it was in a photograph.

He and Holly had talked about having more children but never with the sound of anyone's biological clock ticking away in the background. If they had another child, great, if not, they had Hannah and she was enough.

For them.

It didn't matter if he was alone on the second Monday of the month or had his wife and daughter with him, his mother would always manage to find the perfect moment to ask: "And how is my only grandchild today?"

Subtle, while being both effective and intrusive.

Except….

"Did she mention it to you?"

Holly shook her head. "Not yet. You?"

"No." He couldn't remember the last time she had. Morgan looked at the manikin.

"Well, don't worry about it," she said, "I'm sure she will before the night's over. Is she going to keep it?"

"What? That…I guess. She keeps a lot of her props."

"In the living room?" Morgan watched Holly cross the room and straighten the manikin's collar. "Shouldn't it be in a closet or something?"

"I asked her the same thing."

"And?"

Morgan walked over to his mother's chair and sat. Turning, he reached over the arm and pulled back the sheer drape.

"She puts it in the window so the kids on the street can wave to it."

"That's.... Morgan, that's creepy."

He let the curtain fall back into place. "That's my mom. Have you two met?"

She finally smiled. "I'm serious."

"And I'm getting hungry. The caterers probably set everything up, so what's taking so long?"

Holly pointed toward the manikin's feet. "It's wearing shoes."

"Appropriate dress, remember?"

She looked up. "What? Oh, hah-hah. I guess everything's ready, but your mom went looking for a crystal serving dish from the buffet for the corn pudding."

"Did you get a look at the table?"

"No, she shooed me out of the kitchen so I would stop eating the extra olives. You should see all the containers. There's enough food still for *three* Thanksgivings. I think it's safe to say there'll be plenty left over to bring home. I hope she doesn't expect us to do this big a production number at Christmas."

"You mean she doesn't want to do Christmas *here*?"

Holly cocked her head to one side and just looked at him...and Morgan imagined he felt the temperature in the room, despite the computer-regulated thermostat and decorative gas fire, drop. *That* was not a subject to joke about.

When they were first married and for the first few years of Hannah's babyhood, Christmas Day had been based on the song 'Over the River and Through the Woods'. And God, did they go to Grandmother's house. After their own rushed early morning celebration at the condo, they'd drive to Holly's folks in Doylestown, where they'd have breakfast/brunch, depending on the time they arrived, usually around 10:00-10:30, and spend their time, usually around three hours, exchanging gifts and taking pictures. Any other time of the year driving from Doylestown to Chestnut Hill would take a half hour…but Christmas Day was never normal. Weather and traffic could keep them on the road close to an hour. There was never a road less traveled that they could take to Grammy's house for more oh-how-lovely's – and posing for photographs – and you-really-shouldn't-haves – and posing for photographs – an early dinner (catered) and, of course, posing for photographs.

He'd never tried to impose a time limit with his mother. It wouldn't have done any good. Art could not be rushed.

It got easier when Holly's parents moved to Florida, sent their gifts via UPS and were happy to watch Hannah open her gifts on Skype; easier still when Hannah was older and wanted to stay home and play with the toys Santa brought her. Morgan had originally been nervous about asking his mother about coming to the condo to celebrate, but was beyond overjoyed when she not only accepted the change but agreed it was best for Hannah.

For the time being.

Holly shifted her weight, still looking at him.

"Sorry." He pressed his hands together in front of his lips. "Sorry."

"Yeah, well…."

Whatever else she might have said was cut short by the dining room doors opening just enough for their daughter to squeeze through and bang shut immediately behind her.

A dark ringlet escaped the French braid her mother had worked so hard on that morning and bounced against her cheek.

Morgan took his cellphone out of his pocket. "Okay, my little cranberry, say Happy Thanksgiving."

His daughter lifted her chin and pointed her nose at the phone. "Happy Thanksgiving!"

He put the phone away. "So, is it time to eat?"

"Mama, Papa…um." Her smile dropped. "Wait a minute."

She turned and opened the sliding doors just wide enough to stick her head through. Morgan could hear her ask something and his mother answer but couldn't make out what either had said. His wife walked over to him.

"What do you think that's all about?"

He shrugged when Hannah closed the doors and turned around.

"Mama, Papa...lou dinner S survy."

"Excuse me?"

"*Lou dinner S survy*. That's French, Daddy."

"Oh."

"It means 'dinner is served'."

"Ah." *Le diner est servi*. Three years of high school French was not wasted after all. "*Très bien, ma fille!*"

"Huh?"

"It means 'very good, my daughter'." Morgan took Holly's arm and headed for the dining room. "Okay, let's eat! That American for let's eat."

"*No!*" They both stopped in mid-step. "Not yet! You have to close your eyes and wait until I tell you to open them."

"Okay." Holly nudged him with her hip. "Presentation is everything. Ready, Daddy, let's close our eyes."

Morgan took a deep breath, his mouth filling with anticipation, and closed his eyes to the rumble of the dining room doors opening.

"Okay, Mommy and Daddy! Open your eyes."

Morgan didn't know about Holly, but he had to blink twice before his eyes adjusted to the dazzling display before him. The Irish linen-draped table (with matching napkins in silver leaf-shaped rings), laid out with the *good* bone china, which was rarely taken out of its cushioned storage containers, Waterford stemware, and heirloom silverware that seemed to shimmer and gleam in the light from the chandelier, looked like something out of *Martha Stewart Living Magazine*...and he was relatively sure it would be once his mother's agent sent a photograph.

A turkey the size of a small pterodactyl sat at the center of a universe of food-laden bowls and casseroles and platters. A minor system of condiments – including the kalamata olives – bread baskets, fruit and cheese plates and two pies: pumpkin and pecan – orbited from the buffet.

There was enough food spread across the table to feed the entire cast and crew of *Downton Abbey* and it wouldn't have surprised Morgan at all if he looked up and saw Mr. Carson sneering at them from a corner.

"Well, don't just stand there." His mother came in from the kitchen with another cut-glass bowl. The camera dangled from the strap around her neck as she made room for the new dish. "The corn pudding… looks delicious. Now, Holly, Hannah, sit down. Morgan, could you pour the wine and juice, please? I'll be right back."

Morgan almost asked how much more food there was before his mother walked away from the kitchen and into the living room. He looked at his wife, who shook her head and sat down.

"Hannah, your napkin." Removing her napkin from its ring, Holly spread it over her lap and held up her wineglass. "I'll take some of the burgundy."

His daughter raised her Waterford water glass. A second water glass and place setting sat to her left.

"And I'll have the cranberry-apple, please."

"Oh, you will, will you?" Morgan said.

It wasn't much, but it made Morgan smile and gave him just enough to do while his mother wheeled the manikin in. The hand truck had been replaced by a square aluminum dolly with large casters that raised the manikin high enough so his mother could maneuver with one hand on its shoulder without stooping…and allowed it to have a place at the table.

Morgan filled his wife's glass as his mother pulled back the chair next to Hannah and wheeled the manikin in front of the empty place setting. The chair, which had been part of the dining set, had been modified. The seat had been removed and extra bracing added to the back and sides to keep the gutted chair vertical and from folding in on itself.

When his mother pushed the chair back in around the manikin, it looked like it was sitting.

Holly took a healthy sip and put her glass down.

"Mom, white Burgundy or Sauvignon?"

"Sauvignon, please."

Morgan put down the Burgundy and picked up the sparkling juice, reaching over the turkey toward his daughter.

"Hannah, glass on the table, please," he said and waited until she had before filling it three-quarters full.

"And don't forget Sebastian." His mother pushed the empty water glass next to Hannah's. "Just a little."

Morgan poured in just a little and put the bottle back on the bar before walking around the table to fill his mother's glass.

"Think there's enough food, Mom?"

Holly snorted into her glass. His mother didn't seem to notice. She'd walked to the head of the table, Morgan's place now, and was taking a photograph.

"I'm sure there is, dear. I know I may have overdone it a bit."

"A bit?" Morgan waited until his mother looked up before picking up his wineglass and taking more than a healthy swallow. "How big is that bird? Twenty, twenty-five pounds? You don't like to waste food. Mom—"

"I don't think that will be a problem," Holly said loudly, wisely interrupting him. "Everything looks so good. And I love having leftovers."

"For the next month?" Everyone, except the manikin, looked at him. "I love leftovers and this will make me the envy of my coworkers."

He smiled at his wife. *Too much*, her eyes said over the rim of her glass, but she nodded.

"I'm glad, but I do have a confession to make," his mother said.

Holly gave him another look: *Whatever it is you're thinking, don't say it.*

He didn't.

"I'm thinking of having a holiday party and this is a new caterer. William recommended them, I think his niece or grandniece owns it, but I thought this would be a good way of sampling some of their dishes."

"Well, William's niece or grandniece has wonderful taste in olives," Holly said.

"And you can write this off as a business expense," Morgan said and wished to God he hadn't. "Good wine."

His mother picked up her glass and took a sip. "Hmm, it is. A toast…."

All of them lifted their glasses. Except the manikin.

"Thank you for being with me today. You are my reason for waking up in the morning. I love you. To family!"

Morgan raised his glass and echoed "to family" before downing the rest of the wine. "That was beautiful, Mom. And we love you, too."

"Raise your glass again, Morgan. Now don't move."

And the moment was gone.

—click—flash—

"Okay. Now, Hannah, could you stand up, please and pretend like you're pushing Sebastian's chair in? That's right. Perfect."

—click—flash— —click—flash—

"Mom."

"Just one more." *—click—flash—* "Now, take Sebastian's napkin and tuck it into the front of his vest…no, vest, honey, I want to see the bow tie. That's right."

—click—flash—

"Mom!"

She looked up. "You can start carving and Holly, would you mind serving the children, please? Just a little for Sebastian."

"Mom, you can't be serious. You just said you don't like wasting food and you want to pretend to feed a dummy."

"Sebastian isn't a dummy, Morgan."

"Right, manikin, whatever."

"It won't go to waste, Morgan, and I need it for the series and calendar. Now, this is Thanksgiving. Let's enjoy ourselves and don't pay any attention to me…just pretend I'm not here."

If only.

Morgan refilled his and his wife's glasses before walking to the head of the table to pick up his father's carving set *—click—flash— —click—flash—* and pierce the breast skin, clear juice seeping down the golden-brown skin like fresh blood, *—click—flash— —click—flash—* before drawing the knife down across the meat.

—click—flash—

The toast had thrown him; she'd never been one for sentiment, but now that it was back to being background props for her photographs, he could relax and enjoy himself.

In the moments between camera flashes.

"No one move."

Morgan held the slice of breast meat caught between the carving knife and fork and waited for the flash while his wife froze holding a bowl of mashed sweet potatoes behind their daughter's chair. It was a standard pose and at the moment thousands of families might be taking the same picture.

More or less.

"Holly, give Hannah a scoop and then walk around to Sebastian's left side. That's right. Now, put some on his plate. Stop. Morgan, you can keep carving. I'm using a tight focus, you're not in the shot."

—click—flash—

"Okay, before you dismantle the bird completely, let's get a photo for the album. Okay, everyone say Happy Turkey Day!"

"Happy Turkey Day."

—click—flash—

Morgan ignored the after-image as best he could and continued with the job he'd been given. A copy of the photograph, an 8x10, would arrive a few days later in a stiff photo-mailer along with whatever other 'family shots' his mother would take that day. They would be beautiful, some breathtaking and all of them precious, but not one would be shown at a gallery or end up on mugs or in calendars.

And that was perfectly fine with him.

"Done. Morgan, cut off a drumstick and put it on Sebastian's plate. Hannah, fix his napkin, it slipped. Holly, I need you to add some sides… let's see…what would he like? Peas and …stuffing, of course. And a biscuit cut and buttered like you did for Hannah."

"What about my corn pudding?"

"Of course." His mother picked up the cut-glass bowl and set it down next to the manikin's plate. "But be sure to save some for me, Holly."

His daughter laughed. His wife didn't. *—click—flash—*

"And cranberry sauce."

—click—flash—

"What about gravy?"

"Sebastian doesn't like gravy," his mother said. "Hannah, sit back a little and just look over at Sebastian and smile. That's my girl."

—click—flash—

"Now…can you look at the turkey leg and look surprised at how big it is?" *—click—flash—* "You are so good at this. Holly, we should get her modeling lessons, she's a natural."

Holly returned to her chair and picked up her wineglass.

"Morgan, give Hannah the other drumstick."

"But I don't like drumsticks."

"I just want you to hold it up for the shot."

"But I don't like—"

"You don't have to eat it," Morgan said as he put the second drumstick on her plate. "Just hold it up for Grammy."

—click—flash— —click—flash—

"That was perfect, thank you, Hannah. Why are you all just sitting there? Don't wait for me. Your food's getting cold. I'm fine. I'll just get a few more shots."

—click—flash— —click—flash— —click—flash— —click—flash—

While his mother was getting a few more shots, Morgan removed the offending drumstick from Hannah's plate and deposited it back on the serving platter.

"Would mademoiselle care for white or dark meat?"

Brow furrowed, his daughter considered. "One of each."

"A lady after my own heart," Morgan said and gave her small enough pieces of breast and thigh meat that she'd be able to cut them by herself. "And remember there's more when you finish. A *lot* more."

He rolled his eyes to make her giggle even though he hadn't been exaggerating. Even legless and reduced by half it still looked bigger than any of the turkeys he'd ever bought.

"Thank you, Daddy. Can I have some gravy, please? I *like* gravy."

His wife laughed in her napkin while Morgan poured. "Yes, you do and yes, you may. Just be careful."

—click—flash— —click—flash— —click—flash—

Enough.

Balancing the meat platter in one hand, Morgan took his mother's arm and walked her back to her chair.

"Morgan."

"You said it yourself, the food's getting cold. Now sit down and eat."

In the momentary silence that followed Morgan could hear the fire crackling in the living room. His wife and daughter had stopped eating and stared at him. The manikin contemplated its meal. And his mother burst out laughing.

"Oh my God, your father used to say the same thing to me."

"For good reason. Camera."

His mother took off the camera but didn't hand it to him.

"The lens cap is in the living room. Let me just put it away and I'll come right back."

"Okay. White or dark."

"Breast, please."

"Would you like me to make you a plate, Christine?"

His mother smiled. "That would be lovely, thank you, Holly."

"That was impressive," his wife said.

"What was?" Hannah asked.

They both looked at their child. "Eat."

Morgan looked at the manikin. "You, too."

His daughter laughed.

His wife didn't.

Morgan refilled his wineglass.

* * *

"How are you doing?"

Morgan burped the disposable container's lid closed and handed it to his wife, who packed it into the smaller of the two reusable Trader Joe's totes he'd brought in from the car. He'd expected his mother to try and send them home with *all* the leftovers, like she did every year, and was slightly more surprised than glad when the subject never came up.

His mother did give Holly all the remaining kalamata olives, however.

And she was still eating them.

"How can you?" Morgan asked as he watched her take another from the quickly diminishing quart container.

"I know." She popped the olive in her mouth. "Stop me." He went to close the container and she slapped his hand away and took another. "Okay, *now* stop me."

Morgan moved the container out of her reach before putting on and burping the lid.

"Thank you," she said, and added the sealed container to the bag. "That last one did it. I'm ready to explode." Then groaned. "I may never eat again."

Morgan pulled her into a one-armed hug. "Why don't you go into the living room and sit down while I take these out to the car."

She leaned into him and sighed. "Don't tempt me. I'm afraid if I sit down now, you'll have to carry me to the car."

Morgan tightened his grip and pretended to lift her. "Whoa.... Okay, maybe you shouldn't have had that last olive."

Even with heels, Holly was a few inches shorter than his own six-foot-three and delicate of frame, but could punch like a deranged mule.

Morgan rubbed his arm. "You could have taken off your ring."

"You know weight is never discussed during the holidays." She patted Morgan's extended belly above the belt he'd already loosened. "Or are we going to change that rule?"

He grabbed the totes and backed away slowly. "No, ma'am. I'll just put these in the hall."

"Good. I'll just finish rinsing these." She picked up one of the cut-glass bowls. "I am glad your mother liked the corn pudding."

"Seemed to. You want some help?"

Holly shook her head. It hadn't taken much to convince his mother to let them dismantle the turkey, box up the leftovers and wash the serving bowls and cutlery. They left the stemware and china, scraped clean of food and neatly stacked next to the sink, for his mother.

Or whoever she got in the next day to help with the cleaning.

"This shouldn't take long," Holly said, putting the bowl on the top rack of the dishwasher. "Ask your mom if she wants me to start it before we leave. Oh, and make sure Hannah uses the bathroom before we go."

"I will."

Morgan left the kitchen in the slow trudge of a man whose overindulgence had condemned him to Dante's third level of Hell, where he would be forced to consume leftovers for all of eternity… but even so was unable to stop inhaling the scents that still lingered in the air.

Swallowing the belch back where it belonged, Morgan walked into the living room and stopped.

The fire had gone out and his mother had only turned on the lamp next to her chair, leaving the rest of the room dark. She read from the large hardcover book in her hands, her voice just on the edge of being too soft for Morgan to make out the words.

Hannah sat cross-legged on the floor in front of his mother, her back straight, hands folded in her lap, the skirt of her dress spread around her like the petals of a flower. The manikin stood next to the chair's left armrest, facing his mother, the slight forward tilt of its body making it appear as if it was listening.

When Morgan cleared his throat, his mother stopped reading and lowered the book.

"Ready to head out?" she asked and his daughter turned to give him a double dose of puppy-dog eyes.

"Not yet, Daddy. One more chapter, please?"

"Must be a good book," he said, flexing the stiffness from his fingers after he put the leftover-laden totes down on the coffee table.

After straightening the attached ribbon bookmark over the page, his mother closed the book and turned the illustrated cover toward him. *The Wind in the Willows.*

"Oh yeah, that is a good book," Morgan said. "It was one of my favorites."

"And mine." She set the book down on the table. "I found it when I was going through your old things and began reading it a couple of months ago. But tonight we started back at the beginning for Hannah, right?"

"I like Mole, he doesn't like to clean his room either."

Morgan laughed so hard it actually hurt. His mother had a bit more control, not much, but a bit. The hall lights came on while they were both still trying to catch their breath. His wife appeared in the doorway a moment later.

"What did I miss?"

"Just your daughter being brilliant." His mother stood up. "Do you have everything?"

Morgan retrieved the totes and held them up for verification. "And then some. Okay, Hannah-Banana, hit the restroom and we can head out."

"But we can't go home yet," his brilliant daughter said without making any effort to stand up, "Mole just met Toad."

"That's the first chapter, isn't it?" His daughter nodded enthusiastically. "Bathroom. Now."

"*Awww.*"

Morgan handed his wife the totes then walked over and lifted his daughter bodily off the floor. She immediately went limp and he found himself holding the human equivalent of Silly Putty. It had been her signature move since she was three.

"Hannah, Daddy's too full for this right now." He started to set her down but the moment her legs touched the floor they folded under her. "Come on, Hannah. Stand up."

She looked at him and gave him a smile that was much too old and knowing. "One more chapter."

"Stand! Up!"

Her legs instantly straightened and held firm but the victory was not without its cost. He'd yelled at her…raised his voice, but loud enough for the sound to echo, which was exactly the right volume to induce tears.

God help him when she became a teenager if this was just the embryotic stage of her manipulative skills.

"But...just...one...more...chapter?"

Morgan took a deep breath and felt himself begin to melt.

"Not tonight, Hannah." His mother yawned...dramatically. At least now he knew where his daughter got it from. "I'm a little tired."

"I'll just put these out in the car," Holly said, ending the debate. "Hannah, bathroom. Now."

His daughter headed for the downstairs powder room as his wife turned in the opposite direction and headed for the door. Morgan still stood where he had been standing...directly in the middle. His mother patted him on the back.

"Sorry about that."

"Oh, it's fine and I really am a little tired."

"Yeah, we all are. Hey, can I borrow the book and bring it back when we finish it?"

"No. I'd rather read it to her. Here. It's a grandmother thing."

There was no way Morgan could, or would, argue with that. "Holly rinsed the serving bowls and things and loaded them into the dishwasher. Do you want me to turn it on before we go?"

"No, I can do that." She yawned again and this time it looked real enough to trigger a response from Morgan. "Sorry. Actually, I might just leave everything...well, after I put the food away. You did take enough, didn't you?"

"Plenty." There was the sound of water rushing through pipes and a moment later his daughter appeared. "Here, get your coat on and give Grammy a hug."

Holly came back to double-check that everyone was ready.

"Thank you again, Christine, everything was wonderful. And thank William for recommending the caterer."

"I will." His mother followed them as far as the porch steps. "Oh, it got cold, didn't it? Okay, kisses all around and then get in the car."

"Good night, Grammy."

"Good night, Christine. And thanks again."

Standing on the second step, Morgan only needed to lean in to kiss her cheek. "Good night, Mom."

"Good night, dear." She shivered, rubbing her arms as she turned toward the house. "I need a sweater. Go on, I'll be right back."

Whenever he brought Hannah over, his mother would always stand on the porch and wave as they drove away.

She was back on the porch, wrapped in a bulky dark sweater, by the time Morgan reversed out of the driveway.

And she wasn't alone.

She was kneeling next to the manikin, waving its right arm up and down. Hannah had lowered her window so Morgan could hear everything his mother was saying.

"Good night, Grammy! Good night, Sebastian!"

"Good night, Hannah! Say night-night, Sebastian. Night-night, Hannah!"

There was a flicker of movement in the rearview mirror and Morgan knew what he'd see if he looked, his mother on the porch waving the manikin's arm, so he stared only at the road he could see in the headlights as he made the turn out of the cul-de-sac and sped away.

CHAPTER SIX

The last time we had takeout was in December…
…and I didn't even get to bring it.

★ ★ ★

When Morgan pulled in there were already three cars parked in the private lot behind the gallery: his mother's dark green Land Rover, Old Faithful; her agent's gleaming white Audi A8; and a road salt-splattered black Toyota Camry Hybrid he guessed belonged to the gallery owner.

He parked the equally road-wearied Escape next to the Camry.

When his mother called and told him to meet her at the gallery, he hadn't needed to ask which gallery. Ground Floor Loft Studio Gallery was at the 'other' end of Germantown Pike, separated from the glitterati boutiques and gourmet shops by small businesses and ethnic eateries. It had started out life as a grocery store and, his mother told him, still had a cold case in one corner for the milk, cheese, eggs and soft drinks it sold to subsidize its less-than-lucrative retail art supplies/ framing business.

The photographs lining the walls were mostly the owner's with the occasional 'show' of new talent.

His mother had noticed that one day when she'd gone in to buy mat board. The next day, she drove the five blocks with her portfolio and drank four 7-Ups while the owner, a retired photojournalist, looked through her unmatted prints.

Her first show opened a month later.

One of Morgan's favorite pictures – *picture*, not a photograph, taken by his grandfather, George Riley – was of his mother, a hippy chick in basic black, standing in front of the studio's front window holding a check in the amount of $12.00 for the sale of her first photograph.

His mother's work later appeared in other galleries that were larger and more prestigious, with price tags which reflected that, and routinely vied for the opportunity to debut her latest series. Not that any of them ever got the chance. Every one of his mother's series and shows debuted at the small – but lavishly remodeled – visual arts gallery at the 'other' end of Chestnut Hill.

Morgan got out of the car and hit the automatic lock as he walked to the EMPLOYEES ONLY door. The new show – *The Sebastian Series*…Jesus – would open to the general public on the First Friday Art Walk in January, with a private show for critics, the media and selected clients the last week in December, but this close to the holidays they needed to finalize the layout and decide on how many and which of her photographs to show.

He would do the actual physical setup a few days before the show while she watched and made minor adjustments to the modular wall displays and photo sequences. He'd been setting up her shows since high school and had learned the correct mathematical equation for hanging photographs – four inches apart, the size of a man's hand, fingers closed, and fifty-seven inches from the center of the photograph to the floor, the eye level of an average adult – long before that.

Her agent was waiting for him in the gallery's back room.

"Morgan, good to see you."

"You too, William. Mom didn't tell me you were coming. I mean, you're more than welcome to join us, but we're only going to do a walk-through and then grab dinner. Of course if you want to come back and schlep display panels when I set things up…great...maybe in something less formal."

The old man looked down at his tailored three-piece suit, the room's overhead shop light adding a sheen to the dark blue mohair fabric, and tugged a sleeve.

"I'll have you know I once schlepped a fourteen-by-ten-foot bright pink art installation piece in the shape of a monkey wrench down 5th

Avenue in a cutaway tuxedo and top hat." He lifted his hand. "Don't ask, but neither of us has to worry. Everything's set up."

"You're kidding." The old man crossed his heart. "That's weird. I wonder why she didn't tell me…or why she wanted me to show up."

"I have no idea."

Morgan looked up. "Yes, you do. What's going on?"

The old man lifted his hand to his lips and turned an imaginary key. "I've been sworn to secrecy. Ask me anything else but that."

"Fine. Have you seen the new series?"

"Of Sebastian? Of course I have."

"And?"

"And what? They're wonderful."

"You don't think they're a little creepy?" The old man blinked. "I mean, seriously, can you tell me you're not worried that this series might be an epic fail?"

"I worry about that with each and every piece of work I handle, Morgan. I don't know what the general public will or will not like or accept. One day it's stark realism, the next painted soup cans or massive bright pink monkey wrenches. I know what I like and I like your mother's work. No, I love your mother's work and yes, this particular series is a bit more…imaginative than her usual style, but that's good. It shows she's willing and able to try something new. The photographs *are* as beautiful as any your mother has ever done and all the trademarks that make it a Christine Morgan Riley work of art are there, a world of light and shadow captured in a way that only she can."

Their eyes met but it was the old man who looked away first. "And there'll always be another series after this."

Morgan felt like he'd just beaten the old man with a sock full of sand. There were no bruises, no physical evidence of the attack, but Morgan had forced a confession that would not have come to light otherwise. Even her agent wasn't sure that photographs of a child-sized manikin was something the public was ready for or would eagerly accept the way they had his mother's other work.

Thank God the show was scheduled for after the holidays. At

least they'd all have a good Christmas and happy New Year...until First Friday.

"I'm sorry, William, I didn't mean to put you on the spot."

"You didn't, but I will be if I tarry any longer. I do have to leave in a bit. Just let me tell her you're here. Here, give me your topcoat and I'll hang it with mine in the office. It's warm as toast in there." The old man draped Morgan's coat over his arm and opened the gallery door. "You know, we both might just be moaning banshees about this and it'll turn out to be one of her best sellers. You never know, do you? That little manikin might make her another fortune. And me along with it. The little bugger does sort of grow on you." The old man winked. "I'll tell her you're here."

The metal door clunked against the frame as it shut and made a soft screech when his mother opened it and walked in – black slacks, white sweater and the asymmetrical hem of the smoke-gray open-front tunic fluttering behind her. Black and white and gray and—

"You cut your hair."

His mother stopped and ran a hand through the feathered layers, giving it a good muss that made it look even more stylish when she stopped.

"Don't you just love it? I should have done it years ago. This morning I let it air dry, can you imagine?" She smiled at him. "Well, what do you think?"

He'd never seen her with short hair. Even in the family albums going back to when she was a child, his mother's hair had always been long. It was strange, she still looked like his mother but...didn't.

Morgan jumped when she snapped her fingers in his face. "Hello?"

"Yeah, ah...it makes you look....um...."

"Younger?"

That would do. "Yeah. Younger."

"That's what my friend said...but I wasn't sure I believed him. You still look a bit stunned, dear, but you're reacting better than William did. I thought he was going to faint. He didn't tell you, did he?"

Morgan imitated the old man locking his lips.

"Good. I know it's a bit of a shock."

"A bit. He did tell me the gallery's set up."

Her smile was ambiguous.

"The opening's not for another three weeks and *we* usually only set up a day or two ahead."

"I know, but Gary and Wade are leaving for Florida tomorrow and won't be back until the Wednesday before the opening."

"That still gives us time."

"Yes, but I decided to have my Christmas party here. So it just made sense to set things up and leave them." She walked over to Morgan and took his hands. "But you can still come early and give the caterers a hand if you like."

"Great. Well, is there anything I can do now?"

"Yes, you can join me for Chinese food in the office to celebrate. I had it delivered, but first—" She pulled him toward the gallery door. "Close your eyes and don't open them until I tell you."

"Oooh, another surprise?"

"Don't be a smart-ass. Just close your eyes."

Morgan closed his eyes and felt the rush of warm air when the door opened. The old man was right, the gallery was as warm as toast.

"Walk slowly," she said, "and be careful. The two rows of display walls run from back to front—"

"Just like we usually set them up. Ow." She'd swatted him in the chest.

"Yes, but it's a bit different."

Morgan rubbed the spot under his breastbone. The setup couldn't be that different. The gallery was a 30' x 60' black box layout that could design a floor plan with modular art panels to whatever configuration an artist wanted. Morgan had been setting up her shows in the gallery since high school and the floorplan never changed: two rows of panels to create a central aisle, one side continuous, the other arranged with alcoves at the front and back that viewers could step into.

But there was a difference and he would have known that even if his mother hadn't mentioned it; he could tell by the sound his footsteps made against the gallery's hardwood floor as they walked down the middle aisle between the two rows of panels. The sounds were fainter near the back of the room, louder at the front.

"It's a modified V."

She slapped his chest again. Same spot. She could have been a sniper.

"I told you to keep your eyes cl— Oh. Just keep them closed for a few more feet, okay?"

When his footsteps were replaced by the sounds of traffic on Germantown Pike, Morgan knew they'd reached the front of the gallery, facing the double doors and glass-block windows. The sound reversed, sliding across his front and left side as she turned him toward the room and V-shaped display walls, so he'd have the same unobstructed view as anyone who walked into the gallery.

"Okay. You can look now."

Morgan took a deep breath and opened his eyes.

The one-hundred black-and-white photographs – 11 x 14 inches, white mat, black frame, non-glare glass – had been hung. The display's walls were laid out, front to back, in a modified V – he'd been right about that – wider at the back and tapering down toward a small round platform, like a miniature speaker's stand, between two matte-black bulletin sign holders.

The platform and signs faced the door and were the first things anyone would see.

The left sign read: THE SEBASTIAN SERIES / B&W initial print run 1-100. The one on the right held a poster-sized black-and-white photograph of his mother and the manikin, a red card tucked into the lower left-hand corner between the glass and frame.

NFS.

Not For Sale.

The pose was almost identical to the mother-and-son photograph she'd taken of the two of them when Morgan was five. The only difference between the two was that he'd been smiling.

His mother looked the same, except for the hair. In their photograph, him and her, her hair had been long and draped over her shoulder farthest from him to give balance to the composition. In this photograph, her hair was short, so she balanced the image by leaning her head against the manikin's.

"Well?"

Morgan nodded. William was right, there was nothing left for him to do.

Except be impressed.

"You did a great job."

"Thank you, but go take a look," she said. "And you might want to start to the left...although it really doesn't matter."

Of course, it mattered, or else she wouldn't have said anything, and as soon as Morgan saw the photographs he understood – the photographs were in a sort of chronological order. They started with the enlarged versions of the prints he'd seen on his mother's dining room table when he didn't immediately recognize what the small white thing hidden in the shadows and peeking out from behind the trunks of trees was. *Hide-and-Seek.*

He walked the circuit from left to right, moving around the gallery as if he was just someone who'd noticed the photographs and come in to take a look – not a fan or critic or collector, just someone who might look at the photographs and call them pictures. First he moved along the back wall (*Little Boy Found*, the cemetery photos), and next down the right side (*Autumn Song* – the manikin in a field of pumpkins and half-buried in a pile of leaves, standing at the window in his mother's living room, watching children come home from school). He turned right again at the platform, going up the right side of the center aisle (*Happy Halloween!*) and down the left (*We Gather This Day/Thanksgiving*).

He was in ten of the photographs – he'd counted – and his daughter was in fifteen. His wife was in one, from mid-chest down as she spooned food onto the manikin's plate.

"Well?" She moved closer, not to him but the photograph of her and the manikin, and ran her fingers down the glass over the manikin's cheek. "Do you think this will work for the party?"

"The party...."

She didn't ask about the photographs or whether he liked them or hated them or what he thought her friends/the critics/media/collectors/ et al. would say about them.

So he didn't tell her what he thought. He'd let all of the above do that.

"I think it'll be perfect."

"I do see a potential problem..." she said and Morgan shifted his weight forward.

"Yeah, I do, too, Mom."

Maybe she did know what people might think about *The Sebastian Series* and was worried. It wasn't too late, they could take the photos down and maybe she had enough shots of other things – trees, Hannah, bunnies – still on negatives that she could print out. He'd help her mat and frame and hang them.

She touched the glass again then looked at her fingers. "Do you think we should cover the photographs? I mean, the party isn't until Friday and I don't want things to get dusty and I don't want to have to come in early on Friday and dust."

As if that was a real possibility. She'd hire someone or ask him to do it.

Morgan took a deep breath. "You know the guys put in an industrial air purifier last year. I don't think you have to worry about dust."

"And the series?"

An afterthought but required, since, as she so liked to remind him... *had* reminded him, his opinion mattered to her.

"William and I talked about that when I arrived and I think he's right, you're giving people something new and different."

Nightmares.

"Did I hear my name being bandied about?"

The old man emerged from around the left display wall, buttoning a knee-length black-and-white-and-gray houndstooth overcoat – an animated Christine Morgan Riley photograph.

"No, I'd just asked him what he thought of the photographs and he never answered," his mother said to her agent but kept looking at him. "I think he's upset about something. Is it my hair? You don't like my hair?"

"Well, it's only natural. You did spring it on us."

"Do I need permission to cut my own hair? Morgan, answer me."

Morgan could feel the heat begin to creep upwards along his jawline. "I love it! I love the photographs. I think the series will be your best seller!"

They were both looking at him in stunned silence.

"Sorry."

"No need," the old man said and pulled back the layer of sleeves on his left wrist to look at his watch, a Rolex. Morgan felt his face cool. No wonder Ahern was concerned about the series failing; his mother's photographs had made him a rich man. "But it is getting late."

His mother glared at him. "Now see what you've done, you made William uncomfortable."

"How did *I*—"

"Nothing of the sort. Now, Christine, remind me again which image you want to use for the press releases and postcards."

The old man was very good at defusing familial bombs and Morgan wasn't the only one who noticed it. His mother walked over to him and bumped her short, feathered layers against his arm.

"I'm sorry."

"Me, too."

"I'm thinking about using this." She pointed to the photograph in the stand. "If you think people will recognize me with short hair."

Morgan laughed. He might have been forgiven, but she wasn't about to let him forget.

"I think it's perfect, Mom, really. When did you take it?"

"Oh, a few days ago…when I got my hair cut. I wasn't sure I liked it, to be honest."

"Well, then…."

"No, no…let's not start another donnybrook. At least not while I'm still here. So, first thing in the morning if you can fax me a copy, I'll save it to a JPEG and send it to the printers…and do you know how much easier it would be if you just installed Photoshop on your computer and made your own JPEGs."

"And it would be easier still if I started taking photographs with a digital camera, wouldn't it?"

Morgan backed up a step.

"Now, I didn't say that," William said.

"No," Morgan's mother said, "you didn't, because if you had I would probably start wondering why I need an agent if I could do this all on my own."

The old man looked at Morgan and nodded. "Sort of stepped into that, didn't I?"

"Up to the knee."

"Right. Well, I take it all back. Just send...FAX me the image and I'll do the rest like the good little agent I am."

His mother left Morgan and walked over to the old man and stood on tiptoes to kiss his cheek. "I have a negative and 8x10 you can scan in an envelope in my purse. Come on...Morgan, you, too. Dinner's probably getting cold. Would you like to stay, William? There's plenty."

"Tempting, but no thank you, I still have leftovers from Thanksgiving. My daughter had a twenty-pound turkey and about a thousand side dishes."

"Wow," Morgan said, "imagine that."

His mother shot him a *don't-you-dare* look and took the old man's arm as they walked back to the sales desk where she'd left her purse. Morgan followed and, even though the manikin had no face, could feel it watching him from the photographs.

Nightmares, definitely nightmares.

"There you are," his mother said, handing over a manila envelope, "and remember, I'll be sending a car for you on Friday. Party starts at seven, but I know you like to arrive early, so shall I have them pick you up at six?"

"As your agent I should discourage you from such extravagancies, but I won't. It will impress the hell out of my neighbors. All right, have a good dinner you two, and the next time I see you will be at the party. Fancy dress, is it?"

"No, it's a holiday party, not an opening. Wear whatever's comfortable and festive."

The old man looked as amazed as Morgan felt. "You're not going to take photographs?"

"At my own party? No, I want to enjoy myself, but you can take as many pictures as you like."

"Well, all right. I have a simply horrendous Christmas jumper I've been dying to wear."

"Perfect. Good night, William."

"Good night, Christine, Morgan."

"Good night, William," Morgan said, "and I think I have a sweater that might beat yours."

The old man made a finger pistol with his left hand and pointed it at Morgan. "I love a challenge. See you both Friday. Oh, and Christine, my daughter thanks you so much for hiring her for the party, she won't let you down…and I made her promise there'll be not a piece of turkey in sight."

His mother was laughing as she opened the office door, then immediately fanned the air as the captured aromas escaped. Morgan's mouth instantly began to water.

"Oh my God, I hope the purifier will get rid of this by Friday."

"It'll be fine and even if it's not, there'll be enough food to cover it."

"True." His mother took the upholstered executive chair behind the desk, leaving Morgan the wooden chair that had been painted to look like a tomato, and began unpacking the food containers.

"Oh, and don't think I forgot about you and Holly…I'm sending a car for you, too."

"Mom, you don't have to."

"I want to. I wish Hannah was coming. It won't be the same without her."

Morgan slid his chopsticks from their wrapper and broke them apart.

"I know, but she's really been looking forward to her friend's sleepover. And she'll be coming to the opening."

"Yes, she will and afterward you can take them both on the Art Walk. I haven't photographed at night using available light in a long time…it'll be fun." His mother picked up a container and handed it to him. "They're all dim sum. I know how much you love it."

"I do." Morgan took the container from her and pried off the plastic cover. The smell was unmistakable. Steamed pork buns. "But you don't."

"I like some of them."

Morgan finished the bun in two bites and opened another container. He didn't even have to guess the one, the name was written on the lid: soup dumpling chicken. He held the container out to her.

"All yours."

Morgan took her at her word and devoured the first over the bowl. It was delicious. His mother toyed with a fried sesame bun.

"I just wanted this dinner to be special for you. It is, isn't it?"

Morgan bit into the second dumpling and nodded.

"Good…because you deserve it. I don't say it enough, Morgan, but you are a good man and a good son and I think I've taken advantage of that for too long."

Morgan grabbed one of the paper napkins that came with the food and shook his head, but couldn't quite swallow the dumpling fast enough. "N'uh."

His mother smiled. "A poet. Go on, enjoy."

He did and was slurping down a second soup dumpling, letting her know how appreciative he was through sound effects, when he looked up and saw that she was still playing with the sesame ball.

"What's the matter, Mom, don't you feel well?"

"I'm fine." She smiled at him and Morgan knew there was more coming. "Oh, it's that…I seem to have lost my taste for Chinese food. Isn't that horrible?"

Morgan put down the chopsticks and crumpled the napkin in his hand after dabbing his mouth and chin.

"You should have told me. Are you sure you're okay?"

"I'm fine, but tastes change when you get older and.... I don't know...." She speared the sesame bun with a chopstick and sighed.

"We could have had something else, it's not like we have to get takeout every time."

His mother lifted the skewered bun like an hors d'oeuvre. "No, you're right and we'll decide what to get next time...but it will be a while. The next few months are going to be a little hectic, so I'll let you know, okay?"

"Okay."

"But since this will be our last Chinese night...." His mother saluted him with the sesame bun and popped it in her mouth. "Mmmmm."

It sure didn't sound like his mother had lost her taste for Chinese food.

CHAPTER SEVEN

I can't remember how many times I told Holly about not having to dress 'appropriately' for the party and she seriously almost lost it when she saw my ugly sweater – yeah, I wore a sports coat over it – but I think I almost had her talked into it until the limo showed up.

We were late because she had to change.

Twice.

* * *

"So, who do you think it is?"

Holly's head had been on a swivel since they arrived – late – and she had only fixed on the current topic – instead of the dark-wash jeans with rhinestone embellishments and metallic gold sweater she'd finally decided on – when his mother met them at the door.

Morgan shook his head and took a sip of mulled wine from the 'festive' red plastic cup.

"Oh, come on, you must have an idea."

It was his own fault, and some part of him had probably known it was going to happen, but he still had no idea how one innocent comment had escalated so quickly.

Or focused so intensely on one small pronoun.

All he'd done was tell his wife that his mother had gotten her hair cut and that one of her friends said he thought it made her look younger… and it started. First with questions that he had no answers for because his mother didn't say who her friend was or where they met or if *he* was a neighbor or another photographer or, or, or.

His lack of knowledge on the subject, however, didn't seem to faze Holly or slow her acceleration toward jumping to more and more uncomfortable and inappropriate conclusions about his mother's possibly intimate relationship.

Conclusions that Morgan continually rejected and tried not to think about, or become physically ill – no son wants to think of his mother *that* way – each and every time his wife brought the subject up.

Like now.

"What about him?" His wife pointed in the general direction of a crowd of people near the dessert table. "No, wait…the other one, in the llama sweater…the one with the blinking lights."

Morgan found the sweater in question – a real competitor to his own white snowflake-patterned green sweater draped with real gold garland and tiny silver bells – and the man wearing it.

He swallowed and lowered the cup. "That's her UPS guy."

"Well…?"

"No."

She sighed. "Well, he has to be here. I mean your mom would have invited him, right?"

"Probably."

"Okay." She nodded and turned away from llama sweater man. "Oh! What about the guy your mom's talking to? The nice-looking one in glasses, wearing a normal sweater."

"He's the art critic for the *Inquirer*…and the UPS guy would have a better chance."

"Okay, I'll keep looking."

Morgan waited until she'd walked away before answering. "Great."

As if he hadn't been doing that since they arrived at the party. And his mother hadn't lied; it really was a party and not a cleverly disguised premiere, even if a good number of the guests were critics, Arts and Entertainment editors, and reviewers.

It didn't even look like an opening, which, in keeping with his mother's style, tended to be monochromatic and a bit stark, much the way it had been when he'd last seen it four days earlier.

But not tonight.

The gallery had been festooned with garlands and tinsel and twinkling fairy lights, and the green-and-red-draped buffet tables were loaded with the kind of party food that looked right at home on the red plastic dinnerware and could be eaten without the need of utensils – chips, cheese, crudités with dip, five varieties of finger sandwiches, three kinds of mini tacos, cold cuts, rolls and half a table's worth of cookies, cakes and chocolates in the shape of reindeer. Besides the mulled wine, kept warm and replenished in two thirty-cup coffee urns, non-alcoholic cider flowed from a champagne fountain.

Christmas music played in the background just loud enough to be almost heard over the sound of voices and shuffling feet.

The gallery's maximum capacity, as posted on the sign near the door, was eighty-five, and that seemed pretty close to the number of guests his mother had invited. Some browsed the buffet, some took advantage of the metal folding chairs that had been placed around the room, and others wandered the aisles, pausing briefly in front of each mounted photograph to nod before moving to the next, the hors d'oeuvres plate and cup clamped firmly in their hands.

The dress code ran from the vast array of ugly/traditional holiday sweaters and slacks to suits and ties and festive dresses, but no matter what they wore, everyone had on a colorful tissue paper hat.

Even the manikin...although the paper hat was a bit much with the toddler-sized tuxedo his mother had bought for it. *Bought*, not found in any of the boxes of his old clothes. And he knew that because there was no picture of him, as a child, wearing one.

The manikin stood on the raised platform between the two signs, sparkling tufts of polyester 'snow' heaped around the tiny patent leather dress shoes on its feet, an empty Christmas cracker taped to its left hand. The red tissue hat, which presumably came from the cracker, on its bare, blank head matched the tuxedo's bow tie and cummerbund.

And his mother's flowing, bejeweled kaftan.

Morgan took another sip of the cooling wine and watched his wife disappear down the center aisle of photographs, but didn't look away fast enough. His mother saw him staring and said something to the critic that made him laugh – *no, not an art critic…too much conflict of interest* – and crossed the room toward him. Her hat was green.

Morgan finished his wine before she arrived.

"I forgot to give you this," she pulled another Christmas cracker from a hidden pocket somewhere in the kaftan and handed it to him. "For Hannah."

"Thanks." Morgan held on to it so it wouldn't crush in his pocket. He'd hand it off to Holly on her next *'Do you think it's him'* pass.

"Having a good time?"

"Yeah, it's great."

"Not too kitschy?"

"Just the perfect amount."

"Good, let's see if this pushes it over the top." Morgan watched her delve into her pocket again and take something out that she kept hidden in her closed hand. "I'm going to give these out tonight to everyone who's here and, if you think it's appropriate, to the gallery owners when I open the series. Hold out your hand."

Morgan put the empty cup between his teeth.

"Give me that." She took the cup and gave it to a middle-aged couple who happened to be walking by. "Would you mind tossing this for me, please? Thank you."

"Lovely party, Christine, and we love the photographs!"

"Thank you."

His mother waited until the couple left before turning her attentions back to him. "Hand. Out."

Morgan extended his hand and his mother put something in it, but kept her hand over it so he couldn't see what it was. The only thing he could tell was that it was small and hard and initially cooler than her hand but quickly warmed up.

"Do I have to guess?" he asked.

"No, but I don't think you'd be able to even with a hint." She glanced back at the photographs then turned to him and pulled her hand away.

It was a white enameled pin about two and a half inches long in the shape of a child with a head, body, arms, legs, but featureless, a blank…a miniature of the already pint-sized manikin.

"It's Sebastian," his mother said, as if he hadn't been able to figure that out. "Isn't it sweet? And look at the details on the hands and feet."

Morgan had to squint to see them, but they were there…tiny, almost imperceptible lines had been drawn on the hands and feet to denote the fingers and toes. There was a slight curve to the second line on the left foot…to show the crooked little piggy that didn't get any roast beef.

The detail was amazing and undoubtedly added to the overall cost of the pins, which couldn't have been cheap. Custom jobs never are and it took all his self-control not to ask how much the pin…pins, plural, had cost her.

It was something a banker would have done, so he nodded and even provided a soft whistle.

"Wow, Mom. This was a lot of work. It must have co— *Taken* a lot of time."

"Twelve days, would you believe that?"

"Wow, only twelve. Amazing."

"It absolutely is. The whole process is done by computers. I overnighted them a photograph of Sebastian, the company's in Pasadena, then Zoom-chatted with a designer and told her the details I wanted. They did it, sent a JPEG image for me to okay and that was it. I had them keep the file in case I decide to use these as promotional items but I'm still thinking about that. What do you think?"

What do I think? You don't want to know. "Why no clothes? Too much money?"

Shit. Almost made it.

She stopped smiling. "Trust you to focus on that, but no, the pricing was very reasonable. I'm sure you'd approve. But I decided against adding anything else because it would have been a distraction. This way it's just Sebastian."

"I didn't mean it the way it came out," Morgan said and, surprisingly, his mother smiled.

"I know, you worry about me but you don't have to. I promise you I'm fine and not spending money like a drunken sailor on leave."

"Okay, who are you and what have you done with my mother?"

She laughed so loudly that people turned around and laughed with her.

"Oh, Morgan, you are such a goof…can I ask a favor?" She closed his fingers over the pin. "Would you mind not wearing it until everyone gets theirs? I don't want to ruin the surprise."

"Not a problem, Mom." Morgan put the pin into his pants pocket.

"And don't worry, I'll send one home with you for Hannah. Now, if you'll excuse me, I have to get back to playing the hostess-with-the-mostest."

"Say hi to your friend for me."

He hadn't planned on saying that, it just came out, and the worst part was he couldn't think of anything to say after that.

As it turned out, he didn't have to.

"I already have," his mother said, "and he says 'hi' back."

★ ★ ★

In the dream, Morgan was walking down a long white corridor in a house he didn't recognize toward a pair of white-framed French doors when a red-lacquered music box on a low white platform began to play Beethoven's *Ode to Joy*. The music box was shaped like a little man with the top of the smooth head flipped back to expose the black-and-gray metal movements.

Black-and-white-and-gray-and-red.

Ode to Joy ended and began again, ended and began again by the time Morgan reached the doors and pushed them open. The sky was pale gray, the ground hidden by a thick white mist that rippled like water against Morgan's legs as he walked toward another set of mist-ripples coming toward him. While the music box played on and on, something moved at the center of those ripples…something small and white that smiled at him as it lifted its arm and—

—drove a bright white knife into his belly.

Sebastian, NO!

Morgan's eyes flew open. The room wasn't white, it was dark, and there was no corridor or French doors, only dark-blue blurs that slowly solidified into recognizable objects: the edge of the mattress, the bedside table that held the lamp, the projection clock (12:53) and his cellphone in its charging station.

He was in bed, next to his wife, and it was still night. It was a dream… so why did he still hear *Ode to J*—

A second jab – his wife's elbow – cleared his head. "Are you going to answer that?"

"Hello?"

"I'm so sorry to call, Morgan, but they simply won't believe that I'm fine."

Morgan sat up, shivering as his legs and feet left the comfort of their heated blanket for the room's pre-set night temperature of 63°.

"Mom?" Morgan felt his wife turn toward him. "What's wrong?"

"Oh, dear…I woke you up, didn't I? Of course, I did, look at the time. I'm sorry, but they said they'd call you if I didn't and I thought it would be better coming from me."

The chill deepened across his back when Holly sat up and released the heat trapped beneath the blankets. "What happened? Is she all right? What happened, Morg?"

Morgan turned on the lamp, squinting against the sudden glare, and shook his head. The digital numbers on the clock changed. 12:54.

"I don't know," he whispered and stood up, felt his muscles tense in preparation because no one – especially his mother – calls at 12:54 except in an emergency. *But she's calling, not the police, not the hospital…my mother is calling and she sounds okay, so it can't be that bad…maybe she just had a flat tire or her car wouldn't start or…or….*

12:55.

Morgan took a deep breath.

"Oh, dear, I woke up Holly, too. Tell her I'm sorry and that I'm fine. *Perfectly* fine. I've been trying to tell the Emergency Room doctors that, but—"

It wasn't just a flat tire.

"You're in the hospital?"

"She's in the hospital?" His wife moved to his side of the mattress. "What happened? Is she okay?" Morgan put the phone on SPEAKER and held it between them. "Christine, are you okay?"

"I'm so sorry I woke you, but as I just told Morgan, they were going to call and I thought it would be better if I did so you'd know I'm fine. I just had a little accident, that's all. A deer ran out in front of the car and I swerved to avoid it and hit a tree. I don't think the Land Rover's too badly damaged."

"You drove?" Holly shouted into the phone. "Why didn't you hire a car like you did for us?" She looked up at Morgan and leaned back. "Sorry, that's not important."

It wasn't, but apparently his mother thought it was. "I only live five blocks away, that would have been an indulgence…but maybe I should have." Holly nodded but didn't say anything. "But I'm fine."

"Then why are you in the hospital?"

"I just bumped my head when the car hit the tree, but you know how thorough hospitals are when you have good insurance. They want me to stay overnight and then run some tests in the morning, but, as I've told you…and them…I'm fine."

"Christine, what hospital are you in? Do you want one of us to come?"

Morgan knew Holly wasn't just volunteering him for the mission. She would go and sit with his mother all night if that's what was needed. She was a rock in a crisis and always just a bit ahead of him. It might have taken him another two seconds before he asked those same questions.

"Absolutely not! Don't even think about coming down, it's late and visiting hours are over. Besides they'll probably be waking me up every five minutes to check that I haven't slipped into la-la land." Morgan heard the muffled sound of a man's laughter in the background. "Tomorrow will be fine. I'm at Chestnut Hill Hospital and we're still waiting for a room— What?"

Morgan turned off the speaker and walked across the room, began pacing from the bed to the door to the master bath and back again, bed, bath, bed, bath to work the cramps out of his legs. "Mom, is that the doctor? Let me speak to him."

He heard the man echo the same thing through the phone.

"It's not necessary," his mother said, and Morgan wasn't sure which of them she was speaking to.

Not that it mattered.

"Mom." "Mrs. Riley."

"Fine, but—"

Morgan heard the faint sound of a voice over the ocean in a seashell sound as his mother muffled the phone and he stopped pacing. He was standing by the window. It had started snowing, the flakes shimmering in the glow of the security lights.

"Mr. Riley, this is Dr. Wilson, I treated your mother when she came into the E.R. She did sustain some injuries to the left side of her—"

"I told you not to scare them." His mother's voice was in the background now. "Morgan, I'm fine!"

"She is fine," the doctor said, "but according to the first responders she seemed altered at the scene and somewhat disoriented."

"I just hit a tree, for God's sake."

The doctor cleared his throat but not quick enough to cover the laughter. "Your mother did sustain some injuries to the left side of her face and head, which is why we'd like to keep her overnight for observation and run some tests in the morning."

The doctor had spoken slowly and deliberately and Morgan knew it wasn't entirely for his benefit.

"But she'll be okay."

"We'll know more in the morning, Mr. Riley."

Morgan started pacing again. He hadn't expected to get an answer, not with the ever-present specter of a possible malpractice lawsuit looming overhead, but it would have been nice.

"I won't be your mother's attending physician, but I will make sure they get my notes before I leave my shift. I'll hand you back to your mother now, Mr. Riley, and try not to worry."

"Morgan, I'm fine."

"I know." Morgan walked to the closet and slid back the door to his side, began by pulling the jeans he'd worn earlier out of the hamper and tossing them over one shoulder. He heard his wife yawn as he took down a half-zip sweater, hanger and all, and slid the door shut. He dropped both on the closed toilet seat and turned on the bathroom vanity lights as he closed the door. "I'll be there as soon as I can."

"No, we're fine."

Morgan stopped. "We? Who was in the car with you?"

"What? No one. Morgan, please don't come. You won't be able to see me anyway. Visiting hours aren't until—" There was a pause and then a woman's voice answered. "—eleven and they're taking *me* to my room, so everything's fine."

"I'm still going to come."

"I don't want you to."

"I don't care."

Morgan unbuttoned his flannel pajama top in the moment of silence that followed.

"Fine, but be careful, it looks like snow."

Holly was back under the covers when he walked back into the room.

"You know you might not be allowed to see her tonight."

"I know," he said and tossed the phone next to him on the mattress when he sat down to put on his socks and boots. "But it's not like I'll get much sleep tonight anyway and I'll be there in case…."

"Nothing's going to happen, Morg, your mom's a tough lady and she sounded fine."

…we're fine… "Yeah, but, you know."

"I know."

Morgan was double-knotting the laces on his left hiker when *Ode to Joy* began again. It didn't sound anything like a music box.

"I'll get it." Holly yawned as she picked up the phone. "She's probably going to tell you not to come. Period. The Great Oz has spoken. … Hi, Christine, it's Holly. Morgan's just about ready to leave and…. What? … Oh. Okay…. What? Right, okay…I'll tell him. 'Bye."

She handed Morgan the phone.

"Is everything okay?"

"She wants you to bring her camera."

"What?"

Holly rubbed the sleep out of her eyes. "You mother wants you to stop by her place and get her camera and bring it to the hospital."

"That's nuts."

His wife didn't disagree with him. "Yeah, but you know your mother." Yawn. "She probably got inspired and…." She sat up and gave him a quick kiss before burying herself under the covers again. "Drive carefully and give me a call when you get there."

"I'll text."

"'K." Her voice was already drifting away. "She said the camera's in the living room. Turn off the light, okay?"

Morgan stood up to turn off the light and tuck the quilt around her shoulders. She was already asleep and snoring gently before he reached the door.

Morgan tiptoed down the hall even though his daughter was sleeping at a friend's house and wouldn't know her grandmother had been in an accident until she got home – and maybe not even then. He needed a lot more information before he could try to answer any questions Hannah would have.

As well as the ones he already had.

What had the doctor meant by *altered*?

Why had his mother said *we* if she'd been alone?

"Crap."

Morgan took a deep breath. Her *friend* had been in the car with her and was probably at the hospital, which explained why she didn't want him to come. It wasn't the ideal setting for introductions…but what if the guy had been hurt?

"*Shit!*"

That was a whole other can of legal worms Morgan didn't want to even begin to think about, so he went back to a simpler question: Why the *hell* did she want her camera?

⋆ ⋆ ⋆

The answer became obvious when he pushed back the semi-private room's privacy curtain.

She wasn't alone.

Morgan let the curtain fall shut behind him. The glow from the half-round nightlights above each bed was more than enough to let him see the extent of her injuries.

And why she'd wanted the camera.

His mother was on the bed nearest the door, a blanket pulled up to her chin, another doubled over her feet, two thin pillows beneath her head. A thick pad, secured by tape, covered the left side of her forehead from temple to midpoint, the white gauze a stark contrast to the bruise – black and gray – that spread across her left cheek to the point of her chin. The right side of her face was untouched.

The heart-shaped icon on the monitor above her bed blinked slow and steady. She was asleep.

The monitor above the second bed was dark.

It was tucked into the middle of the bed with a pillow under its head, the arms outside the covers, flat against the mattress, and wore a child-sized hospital gown decorated with spaceships. There was a small stuffed bear caged beneath the fingers of its right hand and a large adhesive pad with smiling happy faces taped to the right side of its head.

She wanted the camera for that. *Sebastian in the Hospital. Sebastian Gets a Boo Boo.*

"Did you bring it?"

He turned too quickly, startled, but managed to catch the camera strap before it slid off his shoulder. "I thought you were asleep."

"Just resting my eyes." His mother raised the bed until she was sitting up. "Give that to me before you drop it."

Morgan walked to the bed and handed her the case, glad to be rid of the responsibility. The camera inside was priceless, only because it was old, outdated, and would cost a small fortune to repair, if there was anyone around who still could do the work.

"Thank you." She ran her hand over the case and smiled. "You didn't have to come, but I do appreciate it."

Morgan kept his back to the other bed and what was in it. "How are you feeling?"

"I have a headache, but otherwise I feel fine."

Morgan nodded. "A headache, but you feel fine."

"Yes."

"No. No, you don't. You can't because you were in an accident and were disoriented and probably still were when you had them put that thing in the next bed. What the hell is wrong with you? You could have died, do you know that? I know you didn't want me to come but I needed to be here to see for myself that you were okay…and you asked me to bring your camera for another photo op. Jesus Christ, why didn't you just ask your friend to—

"Mom?"

She'd hugged the camera case to her chest, rocking slowly back and forth, tears glistening on her cheeks…but the flashing heart icon above her bed remained slow and steady.

"Jesus Christ, Mom, what's wrong? Are you in pain? Let me get a nurse."

"No." She grabbed his arm when he reached for the call button. "No, I'm.… I was going to say I'm fine, but you're right, I could have been killed. I guess it just hit me, is all."

"I'm sorry, I shouldn't have said that." He took her hands and tried to rub some warmth into them. "I was just scared."

"I know and I'm sorry." She took a deep breath and pulled her hands away. "Could I have a tissue, please?" Morgan grabbed the small tissue box from the bedside table and held it for her. "I don't know what they make hospital tissues from, but I swear they leave in the bark." She wiped her eyes and cheeks, the left one more gently, then smiled at him. "They gave me something for pain and that's probably the only reason I—"

Her voice broke as she leaned forward to bury her face in Morgan's chest, sobbing almost uncontrollably as he wrapped his arms around her. And pushed the help button.

"It was all my fault."

"The accident? No, it wasn't. There's black ice all over the road. I hit a patch and—"

"Not that. I shouldn't have had him in the front seat. I never do that, but it was late and I was tired...I should have gotten a car to pick us up. I shouldn't have listened to him, but he wanted to drive around and see the Christmas lights...like we did when you were little. I know how dangerous it is to put a child in the front seat, that's why I always make Hannah sit in back." Her fingers clawed through his sweater. "I swear I do, always. You believe me, don't you?"

Morgan heard the squeal of rubber-soled shoes pounding down the hall toward them.

"Of course I do, Mom, I know that." Morgan leaned down and put his lips next to her ear. "Mom, who was with you?"

"No one."

The squealing sound was closer.

"Mom, I know you had someone in the car with you. Was he hurt, is he here in the hospital?"

His mother turned her head toward the other bed. "Yes, he's hurt."

"Mom, look at me, this is serious. Who was in the car with you?"

"He hit the dashboard and maybe the door, I don't know, but I saw him. The headlights were still on and the light filled the car and I saw him. His head cracked like an eggshell." His mother touched her right temple. She was still looking at the manikin. "I should have laid him down on the backseat and buckled him in like I always do. It was my fault, all my fault. I could have killed—"

The squeal was replaced by the sound of the privacy curtain being pulled aside as light flooded the room.

"Is everything all right, Mrs. Riley?"

Morgan stood up and backed away from the bed to give the nurse room.

"Oh, yes," his mother said and dabbed her eyes with the tissues. "I'm just blathering. I think whatever you gave me is making me a little crazy."

She looked at Morgan and smiled. Morgan nodded but didn't return her smile.

"I'll let the doctor know. Can I get you anything? Would you like another freezer-pop?"

His mother laughed and even that didn't sound right. "They've been giving me these wonderful little popsicle things. Made with real juice. I'm going to get some and you'll have to for Hannah…when it gets warmer. Thank you, Denise, but I'm fine. Just a little sleepy."

"Well, that's to be expected, so why don't I just check your vitals now so I don't have to wake you."

"For the next ten minutes." His mother turned to Morgan and winked as the nurse wrapped a blood pressure cuff around her arm. "The fun never stops."

His mother sounded fine now, normal…as if everything she'd said before the nurse came in never happened.

Maybe it was the medication. Morgan remembered the sensation of his head floating above his body the one time he was prescribed codeine after a tooth extraction.

"Everything looks good, Mrs. Riley," the nurse said. "Are you sure I can't get you anything?"

"No, I'm fine."

"Good. And it looks like your little man is doing fine, too." The nurse looked toward the bed behind Morgan, but her eyes never left his face. "Why don't you try and get some sleep."

Subtle, but direct. Morgan nodded as the nurse left the room. Message received.

"I'll see you in the morning, Mom."

"Throw this away for me, will you?" His mother handed him the tissues. Morgan tossed them into the small, lined wastepaper basket next to the bed then leaned down and kissed the top of her head.

"I didn't mean to upset you, Mom, and the nurse is right, you need to rest. Do you want me to stay?"

"In that?" They both looked at the room's recliner/visitor's chair. It was just slightly bigger than Morgan's and he'd fallen asleep in his many, many times. "No, go home. I'm not sure when they'll spring me from this joint. They said they want to do some tests but…."

"Let me ask the nurse and I'll be right back, okay?"

"Okay."

Morgan left the room to the soft whirr of motors as his mother lowered the headboard.

The nurse who'd come into his mother's room was keyboarding information into a computer when Morgan reached the circular station opposite the elevators.

"Just give me a second..." she said.

"Take your time."

"Done." She tapped two keys and stood up. "Is she asleep?"

"Pretty soon. She wanted to know when she'll be able to leave tomorrow...later today, I mean. And she said something about having tests?"

The nurse picked up the metal chart holder on her desk and opened it, shook her head. "Your mother was given some tests today and you'll be able to discuss the result of those with Dr. Costa, who will be taking over your mother's case, but I don't see any other tests listed here." She closed the file and set it back on her desk. "Your mother gave us the name of her primary care doctor and the hospital contacted Dr. Han and sent him the results as well."

"Will he be coming in to see her?"

"I don't know, Mr. Riley."

"Ok." He'd call Han in the morning. "So I'll be able to take her home...?"

"Visiting hours starts at eleven and you're more than welcome to come then, but I don't know when your mother will be released. That's up to the doctor after he evaluates her in the morning."

"Rough estimate?"

The nurse shook her head and Morgan should have known better than to ask. Nurses might know more about a patient's minute-by-minute status, but they weren't allowed to give opinions or answer questions relating to that status. Only doctors could do that.

"Sorry."

She nodded.

"Is there anything else, Mr. Riley?"

"Yeah." Morgan leaned forward and watched her step back an equal distance. She didn't know him except that he was the son of one of her patients. "The doctor said my mother was…disoriented when they brought her in?"

"According to the information given to us, yes."

"Well, right before you came in, she was saying…she wasn't really making much sense."

The nurse reopened his mother's chart. "Her vitals are good, but the medication your mother was prescribed can cause some strange reactions. I've already informed the doctor about it."

"Oh. Good. Thanks." Morgan took two steps away and one back. "One more thing. Was somebody else brought in with my mother?"

Because the chart was already open and in her hands, the nurse looked down. "No, just your mother and Sebastian."

Sebastian. They knew his name.

"That's another thing," Morgan said and waved a hand in the direction of his mother's room. "Why?"

The nurse closed the chart and put it away. "We know your mother's work and if you look around you'll see quite a few of her photographs in the lounge areas. That's not to say that we don't treat every patient equally and with the utmost care…."

"But she's famous."

The nurse gave him a one-shoulder shrug. "But she was agitated when she came and seemed terribly concerned about it, so…." She shrugged the other shoulder. "We had the room so it wasn't like we were taking a bed from a critical case and it calmed her down and that was the most important thing. She did mention something about taking pictures of us with him for a gift shop calendar."

"Photographs."

"What?"

"Nothing. Thanks. Really, thank you for taking care of her. I'll just go tell her I'm leaving."

His mother was asleep when he got back.

Moving slowly, Morgan walked to the bed and stood looking down at her. She looked so peaceful he didn't want to take the chance of waking her with a good-night kiss or accidentally come in contact with the wound on her forehead.

Jesus Christ, he never even asked about that.

"Sh…." The truncated word sounded like something you'd whisper to a restless baby, but the intent remained the same.

He'd asked about her friend and the damn manikin but not once had he asked his mother, the ER doctor, or the nurse about the wound on her head or what other injuries she had. She'd seemed fine and perfectly lucid and rational…until she broke down and started talking about that damned manikin.

Morgan turned and covered the space between the two beds on tiptoes.

The manikin looked jaundiced in the nightlight's glow as Morgan reached down and peeled back one side of the Happy Face bandage. It came away easily. Adhesive didn't stick well to smooth plastic.

"Ouch."

Morgan didn't try to suck the sound back even when his mother muttered, but he did hold his breath until he heard her breathing slow back into a sleep rhythm. He'd stood at his daughter's bed enough nights to recognize the sound.

His mother was right, the plastic forehead had cracked like an eggshell. There was no telling what caused the impact crater to the right side of the smooth forehead, just above where an eye would be, if the manikin had a face, and would have proved fatal in a real child that size.

Morgan ran his thumb over the damage and felt some of the smaller cracks shift under the slight pressure. He had no idea if it could be fixed – who the hell fixes manikins? – or if his mother would have to go out and buy a brand-new little Sebastian II.

Or just scrap the whole series along with the broken Sebastian I. With photographs, of course.

Sebastian: The End.

It had a nice ring to it.

⋆ ⋆ ⋆

My mother wasn't crazy.

CHAPTER EIGHT

You know, some of my favorite things to play with when I was a kid were empty film canisters. Really, and, there were a lot of them around the house…she wasn't as big into recycling back in the eighties…so I took them.

I was the king of film canister rockets.

No, they're easy to make. All you have to do is put a little water in the canister, drop in an Alka-Seltzer tablet, snap down the lid, put it lid-side down on the ground and stand back. My friends and I had a regular fleet of rockets.

Three canisters taped together, one on top of the other, was about the limit, but you had to remember to only use one tablet. I remember my friend Bob put in two tablets and the lid blew off before he could set the rocket down.

That was funny.

It's weird, I'd forgotten all about those. I'll have to show Hannah.

What? Oh, yeah, sorry. I don't know why I got off on that topic. So, before I went back to the hospital, I spoke with my mother's primary care doctor, which was an education in itself, believe me. He had seen her charts and he concurred with the findings…no intracranial bleeding which was great, but apparently one of the tests indicated that she might have suffered a micro-stroke either after or possibly before the accident.

He explained it to me, but to be honest all I heard was the word stroke.

He told me not to worry though. He'd adjusted her medication, had her on herbal supplements and her numbers had improved greatly, once she'd stopped eating sodium-heavy foods.

She hadn't lost her taste for Chinese food, after all.

Too little, too late.

Sorry.

I got to the hospital at three that afternoon. She had called me and told me not to show up until then, because she was going to be busy all morning. Now, if someone who had just been in an accident – and had sounded like a crazy person the night before – said that to you, what would you think?

More tests, right? You would have thought they were running more tests on her because they'd discovered something was wrong, right? Right…that's a normal reaction and one which will instantly elevate a person's anxiety level. So, when she hung up, I called the hospital and asked them what tests they were going to perform on my mother. They said there were none scheduled.

My mother didn't lie…she never mentioned the word test, *I just…I just assumed that's what she meant.*

She never lied to me.

Never.

Then they told me that the attending doctor on her case had signed her release that morning – probably around the time I called – but she'd asked and been given permission to stay and take photographs.

Mystery solved.

Of course I was relieved but still a little…I don't know what…loopy. Yeah, that's a funny word, isn't it? I didn't get a lot of sleep when I got home. In fact, I slept in the recliner…tried to sleep, but every time I closed my eyes I kept seeing her in the hospital bed with her face all bruised and that bandage….

I called her a couple of times before I headed out, but it went straight to voicemail and even that wasn't unusual. She always turned her phone off when she was working.

I brought her the camera, so I don't know why I was…why it bothered me. I knew she was going to take photographs; I just didn't think she'd make a day of it, especially not after the accident. Maybe it wouldn't have happened if it was just another photoshoot – but it wasn't and she'd been hurt and I'd just learned about her high blood pressure and I was worried about her. All I wanted to do was get her home and sit down and just talk, to ask her why she hadn't told me about her condition. I was her son. I needed to know that.

She should have told me.

Maybe I could have done something.

It was an accident.

★ ★ ★

Morgan knew she wouldn't be resting, that would have been too much to hope for, but he had expected her to be dressed and impatiently waiting for him. When he hadn't been able to reach her, he'd called the hospital and asked one of the nurses on her floor to let her know he was coming.

Whether or not his mother actually received the message was another thing. It seemed reasonable to assume that she had, until Morgan pushed aside the privacy curtain and found her standing on a chair next to the window. She was dressed in pale blue hospital scrubs – and photographing the manikin, still wearing a child's hospital gown and bathrobe, from overhead.

Morgan had noticed everything – the clothes, the manikin, the chair – and yet somehow missed the fact that the camera strap hadn't been around her neck. Somehow he missed that.

"*Mom!*"

If the strap had been where it was supposed to be, the camera wouldn't have fallen from her hands and shattered when it hit the hard, sterile floor.

The lens broke off on the first bounce; the F-stop and focusing rings detached on the second. The third bounce sprung the back of the case open and the camera disemboweled itself, the exposed film spooling out onto the floor like a brown and black ribbon of intestines.

It was over in a matter of seconds, but the sound the camera made when it hit kept reverberating inside Morgan's head.

"Oh, God, Mom. I'm sorry."

For a minute she just stood there and looked at the broken camera, then at her hand.

"Help me down."

He crossed the room slowly, picking his way through the debris field in case there was a chance, however miniscule, that something could be salvaged. His mother was still holding out her hand, still looking down at the broken camera.

"Mom, I—"

"Just help me down, Morgan."

She gripped his hand tightly as she stepped off the chair and let go so quickly Morgan could feel the blood rush back into his fingers. She didn't move and Morgan couldn't. He was waiting for something… accusations, rage, grief…anything besides the absolute and thundering silence that filled the room and kept him locked in place.

When she did move, bending to pick up the camera with its dangling roll of exposed intestines, Morgan's lungs sucked in air he'd unconsciously denied them.

"Mom, I'm so sorry."

She nodded, just nodded, and began winding the film back onto its misaligned spool.

"We've been all around the hospital this morning. The doctors and nurses were wonderful with him. I…got some amazing photographs in the children's ward. You should have seen them, Morgan, it didn't seem to matter that they were in hospital beds or wheelchairs or had IVs taped to their arms. The minute they saw Sebastian in his little hospital gown and bandaged head they knew he was one of them. There was one little boy in the pediatric oncology ward…he was so weak, but when I wheeled Sebastian up to his bed, he reached out and touched the bandage on Sebastian's head and asked if he was going to be okay. The photograph would have been—"

His mother shook her head and tried to close the camera back, only to have it spring back open. The latch was sprung.

"You can always come back, I mean after the camera's repaired."

"The little boy is dying, Morgan, he won't be here even if I did come back."

Morgan took a step toward the door and heard something snap under his shoe. *Shit.*

"I'll go over to your place and grab one of your other cameras and be right back."

The silence returned and for a moment Morgan let himself believe that she was considering his offer.

"No."

"Why not? Look, we can stay here as long as you like and take more photographs."

His mother looked up at him. "You really don't understand, do you? I photograph moments. Each photograph I take is a single moment in time and when the shutter closes, the moment is gone. Time goes forward, Morgan, never backward. Even if you brought me another camera, I could never photograph those moments again. It's impossible."

"I understand," he said even though he really didn't. "It won't be the same, but Sebastian's here and the kid is still alive...."

Too much, and he didn't need to see the look on his mother's face to know that.

"I didn't mean it the way it sounded."

"I'm sure you didn't. Here." She handed him the camera body as she walked over to the manikin and took it by the shoulder. "Would you mind cleaning this up while I get him dressed? You can use the bag they put my things in."

"I could go home and get you some clothes."

Maneuvering the wheeled platform around the camera fragments, his mother picked up the miniature tuxedo from the bed closest to the window and pushed the manikin into the bathroom. A child's parka and a fuzzy hat in the shape of a bear were still on the bed.

"That would be a wasted trip. I'll be fine in this. Excuse us."

She started to close the door behind her.

"Why didn't you tell me you had high blood pressure?"

The door stopped and she looked at him through the opening. Her face went red, intensifying the white of the gauze pad on her forehead and deepening the bruise on her cheek. Black-and-white-and-red.

"Why would I?"

"Because I'm your son and I love you." It might have sounded better if he hadn't been standing among the broken camera pieces, but he meant it. "I shouldn't have had to find out about it from Dr. Han."

"So much for doctor-patient confidentiality." She took a deep breath and the red flush began to drain away. "You don't need to worry, Morgan, I'm taking my medication and—"

"Not eating Chinese food."

Her lips twitched into what might have been a smile, but it was so quick Morgan couldn't be sure.

"Yes. And you're right, I should have told you, but I didn't want you to worry. I'm fine and we're on top of it. I promise."

The door closed.

Morgan was crouched, putting pieces of the broken camera into the plastic drawstring bag containing his mother's neatly folded party clothes, an assortment of 'personal care items' that every patient gets and discards immediately upon arriving home, and a get-well card from the hospital, when his mother's agent walked in.

"What happened? Is that…."

Morgan looked down at the shattered lens in his hand.

"Oh, my God."

"It was an accident," his mother said as she opened the bathroom door, pushing the manikin into the room ahead of her.

The old man raised one hand to his mouth, the other to the center of his chest and Morgan got to his feet, ready to catch him if he passed out. But William surprised him and remained upright.

"Look at you," William said, his back straightening as he lowered his hands to take hers. "Are you all right? I mean, of course you're not, but…are you?"

"Just four stitches," she said and Morgan realized another thing he'd forgotten to ask her. "A little bruised, but not broken. Never broken. I'm fine, but Sebastian…. Oh, William, his poor little head."

His mother leaned her head against the old man's chest and began crying.

"It's all right, Christine, it's all right. Shh. I got here as fast as I could. I was on a call to London when you rang this morning. Hush now, we'll see to Sebastian, don't worry. He'll be fine. Shh, hush now."

Morgan bent down and finished picking up the pieces. He felt like an interloper.

Still holding the old man's hands, his mother tried to steer him toward the visitor's chair. "I'm fine, William. Sit down, you look like you're about to have a heart attack. You're right. I'm sorry, I shouldn't have broken down like that."

The old man held her out at arm's length and smiled. "You're entitled after what you've been through. And I'm serious, don't worry about Sebastian, I know a lot of sculptors who might be able to help. You'll see, he'll be ready for his close-up, Mrs. DeMille, in no time."

"We'll see. Did you find all the pieces, Morgan?"

"I think so." Morgan stood up and handed her the bag.

She took it without opening it. "You don't happen to know any good camera repairmen, do you, William? Never mind. Morgan, would you mind seeing about my release papers? I think you might have to sign something."

"Sure."

Morgan could hear them talking – his mother about the manikin and the old man telling her not to worry – when he left the room, and imagined he could still hear their voices while he waited his turn behind a middle-aged couple at the nurses' station. A nurse pushing a wheelchair nodded to Morgan as he passed.

"How may I help you?"

"My mother said there were papers I needed to sign for her release?"

"And your mother is…?"

It was almost refreshing that she didn't know. "Christine Riley, room 312."

The nurse looked down at his computer, then back at Morgan. "No, you don't have to sign anything, Mr. Riley, it's all been taken care of."

"Is she good to go home?"

The nurse nodded to something over Morgan's left shoulder. "I think she is."

His mother was sitting in the wheelchair as the nurse pushed it down the hall toward the elevators. Her agent walked a few steps behind, one hand carrying the hospital tote, the other against the manikin's back, propelling it forward.

The manikin was wearing the parka and hat, and the empty camera case was over the old man's shoulder.

Morgan fell into step behind them.

"There wasn't anything I needed to sign."

"No?" When they reached the elevators, the nurse leaned around the back of the wheelchair and pushed the down button. "Well, I thought there would be. I guess you really didn't need to come after all."

"Christine, what a thing to say." The old man shook his head. "Don't mind her, Morgan, she must have hit her head harder than we think."

His mother laughed. "You're right, I'm sorry, Morgan, I didn't mean it the way it sounded. And I am sorry. About the papers."

But she wasn't about wishing he hadn't come and he accepted that. If he hadn't shown up, playing dutiful son, the camera would still be in one piece.

When the elevator doors opened the nurse wheeled his mother in and stepped to one side, holding the doors until her agent and the manikin got in.

"But you needn't stay, Morgan, William will drive me home. We need to talk business."

"Of course, yes, of course I will." The old man turned the manikin around to face the front of the elevator and took his place behind it, keeping a hand on its shoulder to hold it steady on the ride down. "But don't worry, Morgan, I won't tire her out, and I'll make sure she's fine before I leave."

"Are you getting in?"

Morgan had been standing there waiting for someone to ask and it almost didn't matter that it was the nurse. Nodding, he stepped in and took a place to the left of the manikin and old man, hugging the wall and watching the floor indicator above the doors as they closed, the way people do when getting into elevators with strangers.

"I might know a man who can fix this," William said, lifting the bag, "a mechanical genius with his hands."

"We'll see. I spoke with the administrator this morning about the possibility of doing a calendar for the hospital and, fortunately, I took a few rolls before the accident, so there may be enough. There's one of Sebastian with a little boy in the cancer ward that might be too much, but I'll let you decide."

Morgan could feel his mother's stare and forced himself to watch the yellow number three over the doors morph into a two. His mother could be cold, hard, funny, delightful, silly, generous, practical, stoic, patient, indifferent and loving…but he'd forgotten just how cruel she could be when it suited her.

"It might be," the agent part of the old man said, "but I'll take a look at the print. But, and you hear me now, Christine Morgan Riley, not until you're healed and a hundred percent. Besides, you've already got one calendar slated so there's no rush. Got a name for it yet?"

M for Mezzanine.

"I was thinking *Sebastian and the Children of Hope*…with the hospital's name. Will you email the permission forms to the hospital? One of the volunteers came with me and took down the children's names, which will make things easier."

"Your mother thinks of everything, have you ever noticed that, Morgan?"

The doors opened to the Lobby and Morgan stepped out first. "Yeah, hard not to."

At the main entrance, William left the manikin next to the wheelchair while he went to get his car and pull it around to the patient pick-up/drop-off zone. The nurse stood behind the wheelchair, making small talk and asking questions about Sebastian that his mother was only too happy to answer.

When the car arrived, the old man got out and opened both the front and back doors on the passenger side. His mother thanked the nurse as she got out of the wheelchair and, after explaining what had happened to her camera, apologized for not being able to take his photograph with Sebastian.

"Maybe next time," the man had said, "but make sure you only come as a visitor, okay?"

His mother laughed and promised and waved as the nurse pushed the wheelchair back into the hospital, but wouldn't get into the car until she made sure the manikin was lying down across the backseat and securely strapped in.

Morgan flinched when his mother slammed her door shut.

"She'll be fine, Morgan," the old man said, walking around to the driver's side. "I'll make sure of it."

"Thanks, William."

Exhaust plumed in the frigid air as the car pulled away and flared red when the brake lights came on.

"Morgan."

His breath made smaller clouds when he squatted down in the street next to her door. "Mom, I'm so sorry about what happened."

"I know, but I need you to do something for me. I'm not sure where the Rover is. The police were there, so could you check with them and find out where they put it? And if it's not completely totaled, have it towed to Skytop Rover in Philadelphia. That's where I always take it, so they have all my information."

"Sure."

"Thank you. Okay, William, let's go."

Morgan stood up as the car pulled away and watched until it left the parking lot.

His mother never looked back.

CHAPTER NINE

You know how people are always saying 'if I'd only known...' after something happens?

If I'd only known it would be the last time I saw him or her, I would have told them how much they mean to me.

If I'd only known my favorite restaurant was going to close, I'd have gone more often.

If I'd only known that girl in high school liked me, I would have asked her out.

If I'd only known getting my mother a digital camera would end her career, I never would have done it.

Words to live by, right? But that's all they are, just words...just something people say. A catchphrase.

If I'd only known.

'If I'd only known' this or 'If I'd only known' that, things would have turned out differently.

Maybe.

If I'd only known what was going to happen, I'd have gotten my mother a spa coupon...something she'd like and maybe use, but more likely would stick in a drawer until it expired and she'd throw it away without thinking about it.

That would have been a good present, but guilt's a wonderful motivator. It can move mountains and heal wounds and let you make the biggest mistake of your life without realizing it.

You feel guilty enough and you start thinking, 'I need to fix this. I need to make this right,' and you go out and do something and it works! You fixed it. You made it right.

Except you didn't.

God, if I'd only known.

* * *

Compared to Halloween, his mother's Christmas decorations were remarkably conservative. White twinkle lights framed the roofline and porch and outlined the windows hung with fresh evergreen wreaths on red-and-green plaid ribbons. A larger wreath decorated with holly sprigs and a bow of the same plaid ribbon covered the upper half of the front door.

Electric candles flickered in each window below the wreaths and bordered the front walk.

A lone snowman stood in the middle of the front lawn.

It was medium-sized with branches for arms and wore a battered black top hat with a sprig of holly in the brim and had a bright red scarf wrapped below its slightly lopsided head. The snowman was real, his mother couldn't stand plastic snowmen – which seemed a bit hypocritical now that Morgan thought about it – and did without when the weather didn't cooperate. Instead of coal, his mother had taken rocks she'd found in the woodlot behind the house and painted them black for eyes, the wide smile and five buttons down the front.

The only concession his mother had made to authenticity was the plastic carrot for its nose. There were too many hungry squirrels in the neighborhood.

The carrot, along with the painted rocks, battered hat and long red scarf, sat in a box labeled SNOWMAN in his mother's mudroom.

Morgan recalled them making snowmen each year and had seen pictures his father had taken of him and his mother before the time he could remember. They made one every year when the snow got deep enough. He'd keep watch and build it back up when it started to melt until there wasn't enough snow left and all he could do was watch it melt away until it was gone.

And then he'd have to wait until spring when a daffodil would appear in the exact spot where the snowman had stood.

As if by magic.

His father told him that was the snowman's spirit coming back to let Morgan know it was happy. For the longest time, after he realized it wasn't magic or the remnants of a frozen soul, he thought his father had planted the daffodil bulb where the snowman would be built. He was surprised to find out it was his mother who thought of it.

He would have done the same thing for Hannah, but even though they often built a snowman on the narrow front 'lawn', any daffodil he'd plant beneath it wouldn't have survived the lawn service's first spring mowing.

The auxiliary road and cul-de-sac had been cleared and someone had been duly diligent with a snow blower and/or shovel to clean off the communal sidewalk, the front walks and each driveway.

Morgan had blessed the Good Samaritan(s) when he pulled into his mother's drive and silently wished them a very merry Christmas when he got out of the car and heard the soft, comforting crunch of ice-melt under his boots.

He'd called his mother when he left Phoenixville to let her know when to expect him and chatted a few minutes about road conditions and Hannah's first crack-of-dawn Christmas. His mother had laughed and he'd laughed and it was nice, congenial, the kind of conversation distant relatives or not-so-close friends would have.

The kind of conversation he and his mother had been having since she left the hospital.

Nice, polite and distant.

Even though she'd been the one who dropped the camera, an accident that wouldn't have happened if she'd just put the strap around her neck like she always did, they both knew who was really responsible.

If he hadn't shouted at her and if she hadn't been standing on a chair the day after crashing the car into a tree, none of it would have happened.

But it had and they both knew it was his fault.

Morgan put the black plastic bag of presents next to the tower of presents already in the vehicle's storage space and swiped his foot across the electronic actuator. He watched through the rear window to make sure nothing got crushed as the liftgate closed.

The backseat was reserved for the manikin.

His mother had met him in the hallway and handed him a bulging black garbage bag, tying the red drawstrings into a bow as he held it. Another bag, equally bulging, sat open on the floor just inside the front door.

"Take this out and I'll finish putting the rest of the gifts.... What are you staring at?"

He didn't have time to make up an answer so he just told her the truth.

"You."

They hadn't seen each other since the hospital parking lot so for some reason, probably based on knowledge gathered from movies and television shows where a character is beaten to a bloody pulp in one scene and is fine the next, he'd thought her face would have miraculously healed.

And it might have, but Morgan couldn't tell.

She looked like a model.

If his mother had worn makeup before, beyond the lipstick and mascara she complained about but begrudgingly put on for interviews, openings, and the Christmas party, Morgan hadn't noticed. Now it was hard not to notice the perfectly applied foundation and delicate peach blush on her cheeks where there'd been only pale skin and a deep purple bruise the last time he saw her. The gold eye shadow was an almost perfect match for the gold lamé headband she wore across her forehead and had tied over her left ear.

A scar was harder to cover with makeup.

"You look...great."

His mother smiled and tugged at the headband. "Thank you. I just felt like getting dressed up a bit. I had time this year, so I figured why not?"

Of course she had time *this year* – this year there hadn't been the mad rush to get to her house and back again so Hannah wouldn't have to wait to open her gifts. *This year* his wife and daughter wouldn't have to stay in their pajamas and robes and he wouldn't have to change back into his. *This year* his daughter wouldn't have to wait to open her gifts from Santa until his mother had gotten the photographs she wanted.

This year there'd be no 'just look at your present, don't open it yet', no tension, no muss, no fuss, no waiting.

This year his mother'd had time to put on makeup.

This year….

"What are you doing out there?"

She stood at the top of the porch steps, scarf fluttering in the wind, arms wrapped around the gold satin poinsettia on the white sweater.

"Just admiring Frosty," he said. "Did you plant—"

"Well, admire him from inside, I don't need two snowmen. Come on, let's get going."

Morgan nodded and jogged, carefully, up the walk. He stamped his feet up the porch steps to get the circulation flowing and made sure he'd wiped most of the salt melt out of the non-skid treads before he walked into the house.

The second bag was tied and waiting for him.

Morgan was reaching for it when she called him from the living room.

"Come in here for a moment. I need your help."

The Christmas tree next to the fireplace was massive, covered with familiar ornaments from his childhood and strings of twinkling multi-color fairy lights. Open boxes and packages, gifts from friends and neighbors, sat propped up on the plaid tree skirt, letting whoever came in – him, this time, *this year* – see what she got.

What *they* got.

Mixed in among the bath salts (safe gift for the elderly), latest *New York Times* bestseller, cookie tins (closed), scarves and sweaters were toys and children's books and clothes and a stuffed canvas autograph dog, the kind Morgan had seen sold for graduations and kids' birthdays.

The manikin stood next to the tree dressed in a pair of dark green corduroy pants and nutcracker vest over a holiday-red turtleneck… nothing fancy, just the kind of thing a kid would wear to visit family. One stiff arm was outstretched and rested on the handlebars of a tiny Amish scooter decorated with a large red bow and gift tag.

To Sebastian, From Santa.

Morgan watched the flashes of color from the fairy lights – red, green, blue, yellow – dance across the hard plastic face.

"You fixed the head."

His mother walked in from the dining room, carrying two 8x10-inch framed and matted photographs. "What did you say?"

Morgan pointed. "I said you fixed the head…from the accident."

His mother gave him a brilliant, perfect imitation of a model's smile, where nothing moved except the lips and then only enough to give the impression of happiness.

"Oh, yes. Didn't I tell you? A woman William knows…an artist who works primarily in polymers. I think she did a marvelous job."

"Looks it." Morgan walked over to the manikin and ran his thumb over the spot where the crack had been. The plastic was smooth against his skin.

"Don't!"

Morgan pulled his hand away as if he'd been scalded. His mother closed the distance between them and handed him the photographs, forcing Morgan to step back in order to take them. "Sorry, but the polymer is still very fragile. It feels solid, but it's still curing or whatever they call it, so it's best not to touch it."

"It's a really good job." He looked down at the area where he thought the damage had been and couldn't see so much as a faint demarcation line between the original plastic and the repair work. "What did she do – fill it and then, what, polish it smooth?"

"I really don't know." His mother took Morgan's arm and pulled him toward the dining room. There were rolls of holiday wrapping paper and a container of bows and gift cards still on the table that she hadn't put away and two medium-sized gift bags, their tags already made out. The snowman bag was to Hannah, the silver bag with gold snowflakes was to Morgan and Holly.

Both were from his mother, not Santa.

"Which one do you think Hannah would like for her room?"

She held up the photographs. One was from Halloween and showed Hannah in her witchy costume kneeling next to the blank-faced clown and holding out a piece of candy; the other was from Thanksgiving. In it, Hannah sat on the edge of his mother's chair holding *The Wind in the Willows*, while the manikin looked on.

Morgan knuckled the Halloween photograph.

"That was my choice, too, but I wanted to make sure." His mother handed him the Thanksgiving print. "You can put yours in the bag, if you would. There's already tissue in it."

"Can I ask you a question?" Morgan separated the silver and gold tissue paper and slipped the photograph into the bag.

"Of course."

"Why did you buy a scooter?"

He watched her fold the blue and silver tissue down over the Halloween photograph.

"Isn't it adorable? I originally thought about getting a bike, but—"

"It can't bend its legs," Morgan finished for her.

"Exactly. When I bought it, I thought it would make a wonderful December photograph for the Sebastian calendar, but now it's just décor. Why don't you take these and the last bag out to the car while I get Sebastian ready and then come back."

His mother walked with him to the hall and continued to the coat rack, where she took down a child's snowsuit while he picked up the bag of presents.

When he got back, the manikin was wearing a neon-blue no-pull dog harness over its snowsuit, an embroidered name patch SEBASTIAN sewed to the front of the padded chest piece. Morgan was familiar with the design. Most, if not all of the HOA-mandated thirty-pound-maximum canine companions that were walked around the development wore them.

"Why is it wearing a dog harness?"

His mother put a knitted blue hat on the manikin's head and looped a matching scarf around its neck before wheeling it toward the front door. "Well, after the accident…. Oh, I didn't tell you, Skytop Rover called and I should be getting Old Faithful back by mid-January, and they'll have a loaner for me on the 27th."

Morgan nodded. "Good. About the harness...?"

"Sorry, got off track. Well, as I began to say, after the accident I realized it could happen again so I started looking around for a car seat that would keep Sebastian safe but allow him to...stand upright, which makes it easier for me. Anyway we...I was watching television and saw a commercial for a harness clip that attaches to the latch plate of a seat belt so I ordered a harness that fit Sebastian and it works perfectly. We tested it out in Evelyn McIlveen's car and believe me, the way Evelyn drives I was more than satisfied.

"Are you ready?"

Morgan nodded.

"Good. Let's go."

His mother left the manikin to grab her long parka and purse off the coat rack, then handed Morgan the purse while she put on her coat and zipped it up. In previous years she would have handed him the camera bag, too, but not *this year.*

* * *

It wasn't a manikin, but it was close enough that when his daughter pulled it from the layers of tissue paper that covered it, Morgan had to swallow a mouthful of non-alcoholic eggnog before he sprayed it down the front of the Fair Isle sweater his mother had given him.

His mother had gone to a lot of trouble making the faceless cloth doll look like Sebastian. It had on green slacks, a red turtleneck and the same color vest but without a nutcracker. With it in the box was a snowsuit, boots and knitted hat and scarf just like the manikin's.

It made Morgan's flesh crawl. Hannah *loved* it and kept repeating how *much* she loved it, and how it was the best present she'd ever gotten in her *whole* life...even better than the coral and pink and purple bike Morgan had stayed up half the night to put together and that she had been riding around the condo, his wife told him, until they got back.

And she opened up the Sebastian lookalike, the best present ever.

Morgan finished off the eggnog and tried not to look at the bike that sat, forlorn and forgotten, near the back of the tree with the first batch of Santa presents.

The manikin stood next to his mother's chair in *front* of the tree.

"I love him! Thank you, Grammy!"

His mother took it as graciously as she took any accolade, with well-practiced humility.

"One of my neighbors made the outfit. She's a fantastic seamstress, makes costumes for Stagecrafters and a number of other community theaters. The doll's an Amish poppet I got—"

"While you were buying décor?" His wife looked at him and cocked her head. Morgan shook his. "Later. Sorry, Mom, you were saying?"

"As a matter of fact, I did see similar dolls while I was there, and I knew how much Hannah loved Sebastian, so I wrote a letter to Santa and asked him to bring my only and beloved granddaughter her very own little Sebastian. And I think it looks quite a bit like Sebastian, don't you?"

"A volleyball looks like Sebastian."

His wife nudged his leg. His daughter giggled. And his mother ignored him.

"So, Hannah, what are you going to call your new baby?" his mother asked and added quickly, "But it can't be Sebastian. There's only one Sebastian, just like there's only one Hannah in our family."

His daughter's face scrunched up in thought. "I dunno. What'd you think, Daddy?"

Morgan studied the dregs in his glass as if it would give him an answer – the eggnog was almost the same color as the manikin – and shrugged.

"What about…Junior?"

"What a good idea!" Holly sounded relieved. She knew him too well.

"Oh, absolutely," his mother added. "I think that's perfect."

Morgan leaned over his knees so his face was almost level with his daughter's. "What about you, Hannah-Banana? You can call it SJ, for Sebastian Junior."

He watched his daughter's face as she thought about it, imagining the tiny micro-gears and circuits opening and shutting inside her skull as they contemplated the possible moniker. The smile was slow in coming, but when it finally came, he slowly released the air he'd trapped in his lungs.

"Yeah!" Turning in place, she held the doll toward the manikin. "What do you think, Sebastian?"

Playing along, his mother leaned down and put her ear next to the manikin's head. "He thinks that's a really good name. And says you should thank your daddy for coming up with it."

Hannah looked over her shoulder. "Thank you, Daddy."

Morgan watched his mother put her hand against the back of the manikin's neck and tip it forward on its base.

"Thank you, Daddy," she said in a high, childish voice.

Hannah laughed out loud and Morgan felt the eggnog in his stomach curdle as his mother leaned the manikin back but didn't move her hand away.

"And I want to thank you all again for the wonderful gifts." She nodded to the open boxes stacked neatly to one side of her chair. "I love them…especially this."

She lifted her hand and rattled the five charms on the Pandora charm bracelet Hannah had chosen and given her: a camera, a pumpkin, a dangling snowflake and two initials – S and H.

"It makes me sound like sleigh bells!"

"We can get more charms," Hannah said, coming over to admire the bracelet again. "There are about a million of them."

"That many?" His mother sat back. "Well, we'll have to see, but I think it's perfect just as it is. I guess we should start cleaning up."

"In a minute," Morgan said. "We're not done yet."

His mother looked around at the carnage of shredded paper and empty boxes that littered the family room floor.

"We're not?"

"There's one more gift. Hannah, would you get it please?"

His mother's eyes widened as Hannah, still clutching the faceless doll, ran to the back of the Christmas tree for the present Morgan had put there before leaving that morning and sworn Hannah to secrecy. He didn't think she'd be able to do it, but even though she knew what it was – Grammy's BIG surprise – his daughter hadn't so much as looked at it since his mother's arrival.

Of course, having more gifts and a miniature Sebastian to keep her occupied might have had something to do with it.

"For me?" his mother said when Hannah handed her the box wrapped in smiling snowmen. She looked at the gold-trimmed gift card – *To Mom, Love Morgan* – then looked up at him. "Not from Santa."

"No," Morgan said, "not from Santa."

"Should I be worried?"

"No."

"Can I shake it?"

"No!"

"Ah, special and fragile. The plot thickens."

Hannah was bouncing on her toes. "Open it, Grammy. Open it, open it!"

"Do you know what it is?"

"No!"

"I guess I should open it." She looked at Hannah. "Do you think I should open it?"

"*Yeah!*"

"Hannah, inside voice."

"Yeah."

"Well, you'd better help me."

"Okay."

"No." Holly beat him to it. "This is Grammy's special gift from your daddy, you just watch, okay?"

"'K."

Morgan leaned back in his chair and ran his thumb across the glass's embossed holly pattern just to have something to do as his mother, under his daughter's watchful eye, ripped apart the smiling snowmen.

"It's a digital camera!" Hannah shouted a split instant before the wrapping paper had completely revealed the shiny cardboard box underneath. "Just like mine!"

"Oh, Morgan."

"Hannah!" Holly said, and this time it was Morgan who nudged her leg. "It's okay, Hanny-Bananny, you kept it a secret for a long time and I'm proud of you. Mom, I know you said you never wanted one but I thought you might like to use it, just for pictures, until we get your camera fixed. And it's not like Hannah's."

They'd gotten Hannah a little inexpensive point-and-shoot when she went to sleep-away camp the year before. "This is a professional model. Go on, take it out of the box. It's sturdier than it looks."

His mother opened the box as if she expected something to jump out at her.

"It's very light," she said when she finally lifted it out. "I always thought they'd be heavy, like a real camera."

"It is a real camera, Mom. And I charged it and put in a 32 GB Class 4 SDH…. It's all ready to go. All you have to do is turn it on and start taking pictures."

"Yeah! Take a picture of me and SJ!" His daughter ran to the tree and struck a pose. "Cheddar!"

His mother put the camera back into its box and his daughter stopped smiling. It was the first time her grandmother had ever refused to take a picture of her and she didn't understand why.

Morgan did, but it was a rather esoteric explanation for an eight-year-old.

"Grammy needs to read the instructions first," his mother said, "but I will take a picture before I go home. Promise."

Morgan felt Holly take the glass from his hand. "I'll get you some more…or would you rather have coffee? Hannah, why don't you go into the family room and turn on the Disney channel? We can clean up later."

"Can Sebastian come?"

His mother looked at the manikin and nodded. "Yes, I think Sebastian would like that. Oh, Holly, don't forget this!"

Morgan watched his wife take the calendar his mother had given them, the first copy of *The Sebastian Series.* He'd flipped through the months after unwrapping it and recognized most of the photographs from the Christmas party/pre-gallery show. For December his mother had used a photograph of the manikin in footed pajamas standing in front of the fireplace. There were no stockings hung from the mantel, no garlands or twinkling lights, but Morgan doubted that anyone would look at the striking black-and-white photograph and not think December.

And come January 1st his wife would take down last year's Christine Morgan Riley calendar – *Tree Shadows/Sunsets* – from the front of the refrigerator and put the new one up so Hannah could keep track of the days with the new *Sebastian* magnet Santa Claus had given her.

"Have fun, you two," his mother said as his daughter pushed the manikin into the family room, its stuffed replica securely tucked under her arm.

Holly followed Hannah. "I'd better go check on dinner."

"I am overwhelmed, Morgan," his mother said when they were alone. "You really shouldn't have."

Morgan hoped she meant that in appreciation for his having done something so unexpected and generous and not as a condemnation. You *really* shouldn't have!

But since he wasn't sure which it was, he simply nodded and began to recite what he'd learned from his Google research of the Canon Power Shot ELPH and which had been corroborated by the Best Buy sales associate.

"It's really pretty simple, actually. Just point and shoot, the software does everything else. You don't even have to use the viewfinder." He pointed at some random space above the camera. "Just flip out the LCD monitor…or you can use the viewfinder, if you're more comfortable with that. It has 20 megapixel resolution with an option that allows you to switch orientation from portrait to landscape. You can also shoot videos."

"So it's just like my phone."

Shit.

"Well…." *Shit. Shit. Shit.* "Sort of, but—"

"And I suppose I will be able to transfer pictures from it to my computer."

Shit. Shit. Shit. Shit. Shit. Shit. "Yes."

"Thank you, Morgan. It's a very thoughtful gift."

It was the exact same thing she'd said about the alpaca-wool slippers Holly had given her. Morgan took a deep breath.

"It's been rated the top-of-the-line model, Mom, and it can do anything your old camera could...and more. Very few professional photographers use non-digital these days."

His mother looked down at the camera. "I'd be surprised if they did. Taking pictures is easy, I sometimes do that with my phone. For fun. But let me ask you this, would any picture I took with this camera be *mine*?"

It was a loaded question and Morgan knew that, but his mother just sat there and waited for him to step into the line of fire with an answer. *Shit. Shit.*

"Of course it would."

"Oh, Morgan." Obviously he'd given the wrong answer. "It would be the camera's picture. Some of my best photographs are of things I didn't notice when I took it, but show up when I develop the film. Would that happen with this camera or would its computer compensate for human error?"

"Mom, it's not A.I. You can still make plenty of mistakes, believe me. But the beauty of digitals is that you can erase whatever doesn't work or enhance an image. I can download a photo editor program and—" *I should not have said that.*

"And have a picture that anyone with the ability to press a button could have taken."

And I probably shouldn't say this either, but...what the hell.

"Mom, that's bull and you know it. I can take a picture with that camera and it would just be a picture, maybe good, maybe bad, but a picture. But, if you take one, it will scream Christine Morgan Riley. It's your talent that people see, Mom, the way you see something and are able to capture it so others see it, too. And that doesn't depend on a camera. I will continue to look for a replacement SLR for you, but in the meantime...."

She nodded. "In the meantime."

"It's just to play around with. And this way you can still take Christmas pictures."

His mother smiled and Morgan felt the muscles in his neck tighten.

"Well, I suppose it might be better than my phone and it would be ungracious of me not to use it, so...." She pulled out the remarkably thick owner's manual and opened it. "Let me just peruse this for a bit."

"Okay." She hated it. Absolutely and unconditionally hated it. Period. Morgan stood up.

"I think I'll get some coffee. Would you like some?"

She didn't look up. "No thank you, dear."

"Okay, then I'll just leave you to it."

"Umm." His mother turned a page. "Fine."

Shit. Shit. Shit. Shit. Shit. Shit.

Morgan detoured through the family room to check on his daughter, who was happily settled into a corner of the couch/recliner munching an oatmeal-raisin-chunky peanut butter breakfast cookie, the faceless doll sitting on one side and the faceless manikin standing at the other. They were all watching a Disney Christmas special.

"How's it going in here?"

His daughter nodded without looking away from the antics of the dancing snowman on the screen.

"Okay then."

Morgan left the family room and headed for the kitchen. At least his daughter was happy with her gifts. *Shit. Shit. Shit. Shit.*

"Shit, shi—"

He found his wife crying by the sink.

"Hon?"

He got within two strides of her when the cloud of onion gas enveloped him and forced him back. "Why aren't you using the food processor?"

She grabbed a dish towel and wiped her eyes. "It turns them to mush and you know grated onions make better potato pancakes."

Morgan walked over to the breakfast nook to grab a napkin from the tabletop dispenser and used it as a face mask. "Right, tra-dish-HON!"

He thought he'd done a pretty fair impression of Chaim Topol's Tevye but obviously it had lost something in the translation. His wife sniffed and went back to grating onions.

"My grandmother said if you don't shed a few tears making latkes no one would smile when they eat them."

"Your grandmother was a sadist." Morgan wiped his nose in sympathy and tossed the napkin into the trash. "But you can't argue with the results."

Holly sniffed again. "So, your mother…?"

Morgan knew he could play dumb and pretend he didn't know what she was asking about, but that suddenly felt like too much effort.

"She absolutely hates it."

"Oh, Morgan." His wife's red eyes were a perfect complement for the look on her face. "I'm sorry."

"Yeah."

"Did you tell her that you're still looking for a new non-digital?"

"Yes, but…." Morgan held his breath as he grabbed his mug off the drainboard and hurried over to the Keurig where he dropped in a butter rum pod. He usually didn't like flavored coffee, but it was Christmas, after all, and a bit early for the real stuff. "It's a gift. It's just a Christmas gift, and when— *If* I can get her camera repaired, she'll stick it away in a drawer and that'll be that."

"Okay." Holly nodded and went back to grating and weeping while Morgan watched the stream of coffee fill the mug. Dinner might still be a good many hours away, but part of his wife's grandmother's tradition was the onions had to be grated as soon as the last present was opened and set aside to rest until they were needed. Holly never asked why, but that's what she did each and every year.

"Need any help?"

Holly sniffed. "Not right now. Why don't you go in and keep your mother company? You know, relax a little."

"I can do one or the other," Morgan said, "but not both at the same time."

Holly gave him a red-eyed glare.

"I'll see if Hannah needs anything then start cleaning up."

"Sounds like a – *sniff* – plan."

Considering she'd woken them up just before the crack of dawn that morning, his daughter had lasted a lot longer than Morgan thought she would, so he wasn't surprised when he walked back into the family room and didn't immediately see her.

Cartoon reindeer danced across the television screen as Morgan walked over to the couch and looked down. His daughter wasn't awake and she wasn't alone.

They were stretched out on the couch. Hannah was on her left side, back pressed against the cushions, her arm thrown over the manikin's chest as it lay beside her on its back, a throw pillow under its raised head, the faceless Amish doll crushed between them.

The manikin's stand and wheeled base were on the floor next to Hannah's shoes.

If it had just been Hannah on the couch he would have smiled and maybe tossed the afghan over her and left. Hell, if it had been her and the Amish doll, he would have probably done the same thing. But there was something about the way the manikin's head was positioned, the slight turn to the right toward his sleeping daughter, that seemed calculated and deliberate.

And made Morgan's skin crawl.

The coffee mug was full when he got back to the kitchen. "Come with me."

Holly blinked back the tears. "What's wrong?"

Morgan handed her the dish towel as he grabbed her arm. "Just come with me."

He let her go when they reached the family room and nodded toward the couch. "Hannah's asleep. Go look."

"She probably needs it." His wife immediately lowered her voice to a whisper as she crossed the room. "Oh, isn't that sweet?"

Morgan walked up to the couch just to make sure she was seeing the same thing he had a moment before.

She was.

"How can you call that sweet? It looks..." —*unnatural*— "...creepy."

"Maybe a little, but it's just a doll. How do you think she got him up there? He's pretty heavy."

"It," Morgan corrected. "*It's* pretty heavy. And I don't know and I don't care!"

They were talking too loud. Hannah mumbled and pressed her face against the manikin's neck, hugging it closer. Morgan reached out to knock the thing away from his daughter when his wife grabbed his arm and pulled him out of the room.

"Holly!"

"Shh!" She didn't let go of his arm until they were in the hall. "It's cute, Morgan, adorable even. I need to wash up and get my phone...or better yet...did you say the camera you gave her is all ready to go?"

"Yeah, but she hates it. What about our daughter and that...thing?"

"Hold that thought," Holly said and hurried toward the living room trailing the scent of onions behind her. "Christine? Christine, grab the camera and come here. You need to see this."

There was more to the conversation that Morgan couldn't make out, but a minute later the two of them were walking toward him – his wife with a smile that would have made the Cheshire Cat jealous and his mother with somewhat of a bewildered look but holding the camera... with the strap around her neck.

That in itself was a Christmas miracle, so Morgan didn't have a word big enough for what happened next.

They parted a few feet in front of Morgan, his wife heading to the kitchen while his mother tiptoed into the family room.

"Two points," his wife whispered to him as she walked by. "Go look."

Morgan poked his head around the corner of the doorway and saw his mother stalking the couch, using the camera's viewfinder instead of the view screen. He'd remind her of that feature later, but he sure as hell wasn't about to bother her now. She was using it like a *real* camera.

His mother was coming around to the front of the couch when she saw him and motioned for him to stay where he was.

She took five pictures – Morgan counted the electronic shutter clicks – before tiptoeing across the room.

"The manual said I can change lenses," she whispered. "Is that right?"

Morgan nodded.

"Wonderful. I think I may have a close-up lens that will fit. If not, I'll just buy a new one. Morgan…." Her voice softened. "Thank you. I can be a…. I love it. Thank you."

Morgan watched her take a few more pictures, not photographs, then walked back to the kitchen to heap praise and adoration upon his wife and bask in her wisdom.

Which he was sure she wouldn't let him forget.

Morgan was dunking his second Nyakers gingersnap into his reheated cup of coffee when Hannah burst into the kitchen.

"Come on! Grammy wants to take a picture of us by the Christmas tree! She took pictures of Sebastian and me when we were asleep! Cookies! Can I have some for me and Sebastian? Thank you. Hurry up, she wants to take pictures!"

Then she was gone and the Nyakers tin was down two more cookies.

Morgan popped the sodden gingersnap into his mouth while Holly squirted lemon-scented dish soap into her hand and elbowed the sink faucet on. He'd had more years of conditioning than either his wife or daughter, but they'd caught on quick enough – when Grammy wanted to take pictures, you didn't waste time explaining the difference between pictures and photographs or—

He looked down at his jeans and sweater. The sweater was fine – his mother had given it to him – but the jeans…and his wife's and daughter's outfits….

"Should we change?"

His wife stopped moving and gave him a deer-in-the-headlights stare. "Oh, my God...should we?"

"*Mom! Should we cha*-nge*?*"

His mother was standing in the kitchen doorway. "I was coming in to sneak a cookie. I love gingersnaps. What did you say?"

"Here." Morgan held out the tin and watched her sneak two. "I was just wondering if we should change. For the photo— pictures."

"Oh, good heavens, no. This is just for fun." She bit one of the cookies in half. "'Urry up."

Morgan brushed off the front of his sweater and looked back at his wife. She'd pulled off her apron and was drying her hands on it.

"Go. I'm right behind you."

Morgan entered the living room to a real flash and electronic click.

Hannah and the manikin, and doll, were standing in front of the tree in a holiday parody of *American Gothic w/Doll* – the obligatory Christmas family picture, suitable for framing and sending to relatives across the country, or used as the calendar image for December.

"Now...with everyone. Morgan in the back, Holly...you know, like last year. Hannah, move your dolly, I mean SJ, to your left...your other left. Perfect. Okay, everybody. Say cheddar!"

"Cheddar!"

Some things never change.

—flash—tick—

And some things do.

"Very nice." His mother nodded then turned the view screen toward them. "This has better resolution than my phone."

It should, it's a camera. "You know, you can change it to black-and-white...." Morgan reached for the camera but his mother pulled it out of reach.

"I know, I read that in the owner's manual. It's amazing the things it can do."

"Isn't it though?" His wife kicked his ankle, possibly harder than she needed to, but he got the message. "It is a good little camera."

"It is and again, thank you. Now, enough chitchat. Okay, now everyone get on the floor.... Oh, just like that, Holly, perfect. Morgan, do you see what Holly's doing? Do the same only in the opposite direction. No, legs to the left, right arm out...straighter, sit straighter. Good. Hannah, hmmm...let's see. Get on your knees in the middle between your mom and dad and put Sebastian next to you. Let me just check."

His mother looked at the view screen, not through the viewfinder just as if she'd been using a digital camera for years. It might not be the same camera and she might only be taking pictures, but she was still Christine Morgan Riley, photographer.

"Oh, I like that. Very nice symmetry. Now, on the count of three. One...two...three."

"Cheddar!"

"Yes! Now Holly, turn Sebastian toward Hannah. Hannah, turn toward Sebastian and the two of you turn toward each other. Good. One...two...three."

"Cheddar."

—flash—tick—

"I know what I said and...I need to apologize for that, too, but I wish you'd given me this first so I could have taken pictures of everyone unwrapping their gifts."

Morgan heard his wife sigh. "We could rewrap some. I still have paper and bows."

"Oh, no, that isn't necessary," his mother said, and Morgan started counting. *One. Two. Thr—* "Well, maybe just a few."

Yup, some things *never* change.

CHAPTER TEN

No, I didn't go to the gallery opening. Got a bug at work and didn't want to give it to anyone, so I stayed home.

I heard it was great and the Art Walk, yeah, I love those and really hated to miss that…and the opening, of course, but Holly and Hannah really had a good time and told me all about it.

Remember when I was talking about 'if I'd only known'? Yeah. If I'd only known that was going to be her last opening, I would have…

…I guess I wouldn't have been sick.

⋆ ⋆ ⋆

"Are you sure you don't want us to stay?"

Morgan tugged the afghan out of the way as the recliner raised him from the lie-flat position to a semi-upright one. He'd been coughing around the house since Wednesday and came home complaining of a headache and sore throat. He had no fever – his wife checked – but still felt chilled despite the afghan and sweat suit he'd changed into after taking a hot shower.

"No, no, I'll be fine. I'll just veg out in here and relax. I'm probably on the downhill side and should be fine by tomorrow."

"Well, we'll see. I don't like leaving you alone when you don't feel well. Maybe we should stay home."

"No." Morgan coughed into the afghan. "I'll be fine. Really. Besides, the car's already here and if you didn't go Hannah would miss out on the experience. How many more times will she get to ride in a limo?"

If his mother hadn't hired another town car to pick them up for the opening, if his staying home meant Holly would have had to drive herself and their daughter through the dark and frigid January night, he would have had a miraculous recovery.

"I'll be fine.... Was that the doorbell?" Morgan raised the recliner into a full sitting position and lowered the footrest. "Did you hire a babysitter for me?"

Holly laughed. "I think they're called home-care specialists for someone your age, and that's a good idea...but I didn't. Be right back. *Hannah! Two minutes!*"

Morgan looked up at the ceiling as the sound of his daughter's footsteps thumped overhead. It was a big night for her as well as his mother and a part of him would have liked to have been there to see her basking in the glory as she stood next to her photographic doppelganger.

But not a big enough part.

"Okay, Miss Hannah, tell your daddy bye and we'll head out."

His daughter came wearing her hooded parka and carrying the faceless Amish doll, dressed in its miniature snowsuit and knit cap, under one arm. Hannah and Holly were also appropriately dressed for the occasion, for the Art Walk, not the opening.

"We're going, Daddy." Hannah said and tried to jump into his lap for a quick cuddle.

"No, Hannah." Holly came in holding an insulated bag and TV tray. "Daddy's sick."

"I'll be better soon," Morgan said and held out his hand, fingers pressed together. "Finger kiss."

His daughter laughed and clasped her fingers together, making kissy sounds when their fingers met.

"Okay, you two, enough. Hannah, go potty and wash your hands. And then we're off."

"'K...bye, Daddy!"

Morgan watched her leave and felt a pang of guilt.

"Bye, baby, have fun. So," he looked up at his wife, "who was at the door?"

"DoorDash with your dinner." She handed him the bag and unfolded the TV tray, setting it up in front of him.

"Chicken soup?"

"Close." She took the bag back and opened it…and the minute she did Morgan knew what it was.

"Chinese food."

"Ding, ding, ding, ding, give that man a cigar! Hot-and-sour soup, brown rice and those little crispy bits you like so much. And almond cookies if you think you can handle it."

Morgan looked at the unopened containers and nodded. "Thank you."

"Oops, almost forgot." She put the fortune cookie down next to the soup and kissed the top of his head. "Enjoy. And don't feel you have to wait up for us. You're sick, remember."

"Yeah," Morgan said. "I'll remember."

After a few more thumps – his daughter running down the hall – the front door opened and closed and – *Bye* – he was alone.

Morgan pushed the afghan off his legs and took off the sweatshirt. If he was lucky he would get a chill and maybe a cold. He deserved it for lying to his wife and daughter, but he'd made up his mind at Christmas to miss the opening. It wasn't as if he hadn't already seen the show – that he hadn't even been asked to help set up – he had, at the Christmas party, and after the week he'd had at work the last thing he wanted to do with his Friday night was wander in and out of galleries on an Art Walk…but – and his imagination had worked overtime on this one – the idea of seeing the terrible look of anticipation in his mother's eyes that he had, at last, found either a replacement or someone to fix the camera he'd broken – by accident but not his fault – really did make him feel sick.

Hannah and Holly would enjoy it and deserved to go, but he was going to sit this one out, and not even the possibility that his mother might actually have introduced him to her *friend* had been enough of an incentive.

Besides, there'd always be another opening. That was the one thing he could always count on.

Morgan pulled the tray back toward him and opened the fortune cookie first.

It was blank.

CHAPTER ELEVEN

I never did find a decent replacement for the camera. I can't tell you how many websites I checked out…and I did find listings for non-digital SLR film cameras…but they were either in pretty bad shape or cost prohibitive. No, cost wasn't the main concern, but to pay a few thousand for a camera that was older than the one she had didn't seem like a sound investment.

Jesus…I do sound like a banker, don't I?

Guess she was right.

Sorry…off track again. To be honest, when she used the digital at Christmas I thought she was just being gracious, or maybe it was her way of letting me know she'd forgiven me…a little…but I didn't expect it to last. I figured that once she got home she'd put it back in its box and stick it on a shelf or in a drawer and wait for me to find a new camera.

But then she sent me a JPEG file of images and I thought, 'Oh my God, she's using it! I did it. I fixed it.'

There were thirty photos in the file and a one-line message: Hope you like them. Mother.

What I'd told her at Christmas was true, it didn't matter what camera she used, hell, she could have used her cellphone for that matter, because it was her gift, her talent that shone in those photos. They were as good as any of her previous work, but they were different.

The photos were in color and that was a whole new…aspect of her work that I had never seen. No one had and it was…different. You didn't have to think about what you were seeing, didn't have to wonder if there was something hidden in the shadows…it was all there.

And they were wonderful, don't get me wrong, but it was…different.

It would have been easy to change them into black-and-white images. It's one click on any photo editor program. But she didn't use it.

I asked her about that, why she hadn't saved the images in black and white, when I called and told her how wonderful I thought they were and she told me she'd only taken them for fun and wouldn't be showing them to anyone except family, so it didn't matter.

They were just pictures, not photographs.

And I believed her. Why wouldn't I?

My mother wasn't crazy. She was...just my mother.

★ ★ ★

They always started planning their annual Easter trip to Longwood Gardens in the gray months before even the vaguest suggestion of green appeared and ice occasionally encased bare, winter-scarred branches.

It didn't matter if the trees were in full foliage and heavy with the scents from a thousand acres of flowers, or if most of the trees were still bare, with the floral displays limited to the arrangements in the Exhibition Hall, and the tulips, snowdrops, crocuses and daffodils that had been planted along the walking paths. What mattered was that each year they continued the family tradition that had been started by Morgan's great-grandfather, a local businessman. He decided after a rather heated discussion with a fellow church member that he'd had enough hypocrisy from self-proclaimed Christians who only showed up on major holidays but still felt entitled to foist their personal beliefs on others. His mother had only been four the first time her family had gone to Longwood instead of Easter Service, but she remembered wearing a bright white dress and holding the man's hand as he explained how they honored God more by walking in a garden than sitting in some dark church.

Morgan didn't know if that had been the reason his mother had never been a churchgoer, but Easter was always spent at Longwood.

Plus, it was a wonderful place to take photographs...something of which his mother had, over the years, taken full advantage.

While Morgan couldn't remember his first few Easter visits, he had an extensive photographic record from the time he was an infant (*First Easter in the Gardens*) through adolescence (*First Love* with his first girlfriend, Rowan Something-Irish), marriage (*To Have and Hold*) and all the way to Hannah (*First Easter in the Gardens II*).

His mother loved Longwood and Longwood loved her, giving her free access to the grounds throughout the year. They also hosted occasional small private showings of her work that featured the gardens, and which could only be purchased in their gift shop.

He'd only ever missed two Easter visits: when he was eight and had strep throat, and that morning.

The storm arrived just after they'd finished their own tradition of pink and lavender scrambled eggs with turkey bacon and toast cut into the shape of bunnies. Morgan was still at the table drinking coffee and watching his daughter search for the eggs – the two dozen they'd dyed the night before and an equal number of plastic ones filled with jelly beans – when the kitchen lights flickered and a crack of thunder rattled the dishes waiting to be washed.

"*DADDY!*"

Hannah appeared in the kitchen before the echoes died, eyes wide, her right hand clenched around the handle of the empty painted straw basket that had been filled with an obscene amount of mandatory candy and trinkets earlier that morning, her left gripping a neon-blue plastic egg.

A floppy pink rabbit with plaid ears and an insipid smile was tucked under her right arm. It was a much more expressive replacement for the faceless doll she'd gotten for Christmas.

"It's only thunder, baby," Morgan said as another loud rumble moved overhead and rain began lashing the windows. "It was pretty smart of the Easter Bunny to hide all those eggs inside, wasn't it?"

His daughter looked up when the lights flickered. "Uh-huh."

Morgan had been watching the storm's progress since it was first mentioned on his weather app.

Living in a condo development did have its drawbacks, but there were still enough places on their small, fenced-in micro backyard for Mr. E. Bunny to hide eggs. Of course, that was in good weather. It was a known fact that rabbits, especially magical ones that delivered baskets filled with candy, hated getting wet, which was why the eggs had been hidden inside.

His wife had waited until their daughter had left the room to search before applauding.

The roll of thunder that followed the flicker came later and was definitely softer. "Hear that? Storm's moving away. I think it'll just be rain from now on. So, back to the hunt."

"Okay," Hannah said, but kept glancing up at the ceiling as she left the kitchen.

Morgan pulled out his phone and checked the weather radar. The screen was in shades of green, dark green and really dark green as an undulating red and orange band, flecked with yellow, moved slowly… very slowly…from left to right. The tiny red dot that was Phoenixville was almost hidden beneath a yellow splotch.

He minimized the scale.

Chestnut Hill was a yellow ribbon on a larger red/orange background.

"Found another one!"

Morgan closed the app. "Yay! Where'd you find it?"

"Beneath the cushion in Grammy's chair."

Morgan put it there when he heard the first thumps coming from his daughter's room.

"Wow. That is one sneaky Easter Bunny!"

"You do remember where you hid them all, right?"

"Most of them." Morgan looked up as Holly came to join him at the table. She was nibbling one of the six-packs of Dove chocolate bunny ears Mr. E. Bunny had left on her pillow. "There's nothing I like better in the morning than a good cliché."

She smiled and took off an ear tip.

"Ouch."

"And just remember that!"

Hannah came back in before Morgan could come up with a witty retort. "I can't find any more."

"How many have you got?"

She did a quick count of the eggs already in her basket. "Twenty-three."

"I think the Easter Bunny hid at least thirteen more eggs. You'd better keep looking. What's that over there? No...there."

Morgan kept pointing until she found the lime-colored egg he'd hidden behind the open vertical blinds in the family room. There was so much rain hitting the sliding glass door it made the morning light dance across her face. Holly stretched and nudged the yellow egg that had been sitting under the trestle table leg out into the middle of the kitchen floor.

"Oh! What was that? And I think I see another one in the laundry room." Morgan cleared his throat and held up three fingers. "I mean I think I see *three* eggs in there. What a clever bunny."

Their daughter darted into the small alcove. "Where?"

"Where?" his wife whispered.

"Just keep looking," he said. "If they were snakes they would have nibbled your toes and your nose."

"Found them! But there are only two."

Morgan nodded. He'd look later. "Okay, but I'm sure there are still some left."

When their daughter walked toward them, his wife crossed her arms, hiding the candy, and licked her lips.

"Where do *you* think I should look, Daddy?"

She'd asked similar questions before, but this time it felt like it had a sharp edge to it, almost as if she knew, without a doubt, she was speaking to Mr. E. Bunny himself. And it hurt. His baby, his little girl was inching her way out of childhood and there was not a damned thing he could do about it.

Next year or the year after that there'd still be Easter eggs to find and plates of cookies for Santa but the magic would be gone.

The sharp edge hurt like hell.

Morgan shrugged. "I don't know. Did you look under things? In things? Behind things? You know how sneaky the Easter Bunny can be."

His daughter gave him a side-eyed smile.

"Yeah," she said, "I know. Think there're any upstairs?"

He was going to but hadn't gotten the chance. "I don't think so."

She nodded and walked out of the kitchen. "Okay."

His phone buzzed and began playing *Ode to Joy* as Holly unfolded her arms and looked at the glistening lump of melted chocolate covering her hand. Morgan picked up the phone – it was his mother – and hit ACCEPT.

"Quality chocolate has a low melting point," he whispered to his wife. "Hi, Mom. Hoppy Easter."

His father's traditional greeting.

"Happy Easter, Morgan." And one his mother never thought was funny. "Have you been watching the weather reports? It's a one hundred percent chance of rain…heavy at times, one to three inches here in the city, probably the same where you are…with some possible flooding to the south."

She was watching the Weather Channel. Morgan leaned back and watched his wife walk to the sink and attempt to scrape the chocolate off her fingers and hand into a bowl. One simply does not wash Dove chocolate down the drain.

"Winds out of the Northeast reaching forty miles an hour, with gusts to sixty, and, oh this is new, the possibility of freezing rain or sleet by evening. Ah, spring." His mother took a deep breath. "Doesn't look like a good day to visit Longwood, does it?"

"Not at all," Morgan said.

"Do you think Hannah will be too disappointed?"

Morgan glanced into the living room where his daughter had just found the green plastic egg he'd hidden under the leaves of the Chinese peace lily. "I think she'll be okay."

"Well, tell her we'll go to Longwood when it's sunny. Besides, it might not be open to the public today. I don't think anyone in their right mind would want to tramp around the grounds in this kind of weather."

"Good point. Okay, I'll tell her we'll go some other time. Holly said the lamb should be ready around five…."

"Don't hate me."

Morgan sat up. "That sounds ominous. Why would I hate you?"

"Because I'm not coming to dinner."

"Why not?"

"Look outside. The weather is terrible. I don't want to drive in it and I certainly don't want you to. If anything happened to you I could never forgive myself. So, with that in mind I accepted an alternate invitation to dinner."

Morgan turned around and looked at his water-blurred reflection in the sliding patio door.

"From your *friend*?"

If she caught the inflection in his voice, she ignored it. "With a *lot* of friends, Morgan. Rob and Chas, they live in the blue Federal, always host an Easter open house for the neighbors and this year I'm going. In fact, they called and told me they'd come pick me up in their kayak if the cul-de-sac flooded. Isn't that sweet?"

"Adorable."

"Tell Hannah I'll drop off the basket the Easter Bunny left here for her sometime next week. Oh, and I got you and Holly some of those See's Candies cream eggs you like."

"Thanks."

"Give everyone our love." She laughed. "Sebastian and mine."

"Okay."

"I love you, too."

Morgan swiped his phone off and watched another blurred reflection join his in the rain-splattered glass. Holly had finally given up and washed the remnants of rabbit ear off her hand.

"What's wrong?"

"She's going to have dinner with the neighbors." Morgan grabbed his coffee cup and carried it to the sink. "Doesn't want to drive in this or have me come get her."

"Well, bless her for that." Morgan poured out the coffee and turned on the hot water. The rising steam smelled like mocha. "I mean it, Morg. I'm glad you.... I mean, I'm sorry she won't be here, but maybe it's for the best. It is pretty awful out there. And this way we'll have more lamb chops."

"Yeah."

"Is her friend going to be there?"

Morgan turned off the water and set the cup in the drainboard. "I didn't ask."

"Morgan, you know—"

"*Dad!* I only found five!"

Morgan looked at his wife and shook his head…and wasn't sure if it was because there were still six missing eggs scattered around the condo… or if it was to warn her to drop the subject about his mother's friend.

But whichever one it was, Holly seemed to understand.

"I'll be right there, Hannah-Banana," he said and walked out of the room.

CHAPTER TWELVE

Hannah has three Sebastian scrapbooks now, did you know that?

My mother did the first one by herself, and they worked on the second together when Hannah was older. She just finished the third one as a class project about her family.

It's got most of the same things as the first two…photos and articles, mostly about my mother and her career, although there are some pictures of us from the Inquirer's *Arts and Entertainment section. There's a really nice one from last Halloween of Hannah walking up to a house next to the hand truck.*

What? No, but you can see my hands and a leg, I think.

The project got an A.

Me? No, I never kept a scrapbook. My job was to go through the paper and cut out every article and picture about her for her scrapbooks. I don't know how many, I never counted. I'll ask William what he thinks I should do with them.

No, I stopped doing that when the Inquirer *went digital…I don't know, maybe fifteen or sixteen. I know people thought she was a bit of a Luddite because of her often-publicized views on modern technology and photography, but she knew her way around computers and it was just as easy for her to go online and cut-and-paste those articles and pictures without my help.*

I guess I'll have to look for those files, too.

★ ★ ★

Morgan swallowed the bite of the cheesesteak he'd Grubhubbed to help get him through the final edit of the company's financial prospectus before its debut at the Board of Directors meeting in the morning, hit SAVE, and raised his hands over his head à la Rocky Balboa.

"Finished! *Yes!*"

His shout echoed out through the empty office loud enough to make Steve, the night maintenance worker who was wiping down the teller stations at the other end of the building, give him a thumbs up.

Morgan waved back and picked up the rest of his sandwich. He hadn't seen Steve come in or he wouldn't have been quite so enthusiastic, but he'd finished, it was done, and now he could go home and sleep through the night without worrying about it.

Whew.

Settling back in his chair, he took another bite of the *wiz wit* and smiled at the latest travel brochure his wife had surreptitiously slipped into his briefcase that morning. She hadn't said anything about the two weeks of overtime he'd had to put in on the project, or the time and a half compensation that came with it. She had, however, begun casually but constantly talking about the possibility of them taking a really *nice* family vacation that summer.

There were also nightly threefold options in full color that ranged from Disney Family Cruises to the Caribbean to spending a week on horseback herding cattle at a Wyoming dude ranch.

It didn't take much detective work to figure out which option Holly coveted, although Morgan thought Hannah would probably prefer the dude ranch.

Tonight's brochure was about digging for dinosaur bones in some place called Fruita, Colorado.

Decisions, decisions.

Morgan swallowed and was going in for another bite when his cellphone, still in office mode, buzzed itself toward the corner of his desk. Although Holly had been saint-like in her acceptance of his nights spent in the office, she usually called around this time to ask how much longer he'd be and if he thought he'd be home before Hannah went to bed.

Most nights he made it just under the wire, but tonight he'd be home in time for a bowl of ice cream in front of the TV and a bedtime story. They were on their third re-read of *The Wind in the Willows.*

After wrapping the remains of the cheesesteak in its white paper sleeve, Morgan wiped his mouth and fingers and shoved everything back into the delivery bag before tossing it into the trash basket behind his desk and reaching for the phone. Steve would take care of it when Morgan left.

The Caller ID wasn't his wife's.

"Hi, Mom, what's—"

"Help!"

Morgan only realized he'd gotten to his feet when he heard his desk chair hit the wall behind him. It must have been loud because Steve was hurrying across the office toward him.

"You okay, Mr. Riley?"

Morgan shook his head. "Mom, what's wrong? What's the matter?"

"You gotta help." Her voice sounded strange…muffled but high-pitched like a frightened child.

"Mom!"

"Mr. Riley?" Steve was standing at the door of his office. Morgan shook his head and grabbed his coat off the back of his chair and set it spinning. "Unlock the front door for me, please."

The man raced to the door and held it open as Morgan struggled into his coat. The day had been unseasonably hot and muggy, but the night air felt cold after the stuffy office and he shivered.

"Mom, talk to me. What's wrong?"

"Mama fell down! She won't wake up!"

"Who fell down, Mom? Mom!"

"Mama fell down and won't wake up! Help me! You gotta help me wake Mama. Help! Mama, wake up!" Her voice got loud and more frantic. "Mama! Come quick and help her! *Help her! Morgan!*"

The line went dead as Morgan reached his car.

"Hope it's nothing serious, Mr. Riley." Steve had followed him out to the parking lot.

"Hope so, too."

"Is there anything I can do?"

"No…yes, just turn off my computer. Thanks."

Morgan didn't turn on the Bluetooth until he was out of the parking lot and on the main road.

"Nine-one-one, what is your emergency?"

"My mother fell and…she doesn't sound right."

"Is she conscious now?"

"I don't know."

"Is she breathing?"

Jesus, she could be dead. "I don't know."

There was only the slightest hesitation in the dispatcher's voice. "Could you check for me, please?"

Morgan took a deep breath and realized he was doing the same thing he'd seen so many characters on TV do. "I'm not with her. She called me while I was at work so I don't know how she is. I'm driving over to her house now."

"You're doing fine, sir. Can you give me your mother's address, please?"

Morgan gave it twice, slowing down the second time and enunciating carefully.

"Thank you, sir." There was a momentary pause where all Morgan could hear was the pounding of his heart. "An ambulance is on the way."

"Good. Thank you." Morgan hit the horn when the car in front of him didn't move when the light turned green. "Jesus."

"Are you all right, sir?"

"What? Yeah!" He hit the horn again. "I'm fine!"

"Sir, do you think you should pull over? I can have officers at your location in a matter of minutes and they can transport you."

Morgan understood what the operator was saying and slowed down. "No, it's okay. I'm okay."

"I'm sure you are, sir, but I don't think your mother would be very happy if you got in an accident."

"I know." Morgan loosened his grip on the steering wheel and felt the muscles in his shoulders relax. "I'm sorry. I didn't mean to yell."

"Completely understandable, I just want to be sure you make it to your mother in one piece."

"I know. I'm okay, really. Thanks."

"Is there anything else I can do for you?"

He slammed on the brakes when a car pulled out in front of him and hoped the 9-1-1 operator didn't hear it. "No. Thank you."

"What's your name?"

"What?"

"What's your name, sir?"

"Uh, Morgan. Morgan Riley. My mother's Christine Riley... the photographer."

If the dispatcher knew his mother's name and reputation she never let on, but it made him feel better to have said it. He knew it wouldn't make any difference, but there was always the chance that the ambulance would get to his mother quicker if they knew she was famous.

"Okay, Morgan, how far away are you from your mother's house?"

Morgan looked up at the road sign as he drove through an intersection just as the light turned red. "Maybe ten minutes. There's not a lot of traffic right now."

"Okay. Can you do me a favor, Morgan?"

"Okay."

"Good. I want you to take a deep breath and hang up the phone and then I want you to concentrate only on your driving. Don't worry about your mother; the ambulance is almost there. Can you do that for me, Morgan?"

"Yeah. Okay. Thanks."

"I was just notified that the EMTs have arrived at your mother's house."

"How is she?"

"I don't have that information, Morgan. I'm sorry."

Morgan couldn't remember from the TV shows if the 9-1-1 operators didn't have that information or weren't allowed to give it out.

"Okay. Thank you."

"You're very welcome. Be careful, Morgan."

Morgan nodded and pressed down on the accelerator as he disconnected the Bluetooth.

"Just let her be okay. Please, God, just let her be okay."

★ ★ ★

Just let her be okay.

Just let her be okay.

Just let her be okay.

Just let her—

Morgan turned the car into the strobing red-blue-red-blue lights that filled the cul-de-sac and washed over the faces of the crowd, neighbors and strangers, who had heard the sirens and come to investigate. The ambulance was in the driveway, its back door open. Two police cars were parked in the center of the cul-de-sac, doors closed. Another police car was parked diagonally across the entrance. Four officers lined the sidewalk in front of his mother's house, keeping the crowd back, a fifth got out of one of the cars as Morgan drove around and pulled into the curb.

The officer motioned for Morgan to lower the window as he walked toward him.

"Do you live here, sir?" The officer was soft-spoken and polite, but kept his hand pressed against the top of the driver's-side door when Morgan tried to open it.

"No, but—"

"Then I'm afraid you'll have to move your car."

"But I...I called 9-1-1. I'm her son."

"Come with me." The officer stepped back and opened the door for him. "The paramedics are with her. I'll take you in."

Morgan nodded and let the officer escort him through the crowd to the house. Morgan recognized the voices that called out, neighbors' voices telling him his mother was going to be fine and that she was a strong woman and not to worry. Other voices prayed.

Just let her be okay.

"It's the son," the officer said as they climbed the stairs to the front porch. Not *her* son, just *the* son. Detached. Impersonal.

The man on the porch wasn't in uniform, but he acted like he was. "Come with me, Mr. Riley," he said and walked with Morgan into the house as far as the hallway. "Mrs. Riley's son is here."

Another woman's voice, not his mother's, answered. "Okay."

Morgan walked into the living room alone.

Just let her be alive.

Two paramedics were in the process of lifting the collapsible gurney for transport, the man had his back to Morgan, the woman faced him. The man's body screened the blanket-covered shape on the gurney.

"On the count of three," the woman said. "One. Two. Three."

"She's dead," Morgan whispered and was surprised at how easy it'd been to say it out loud. "Is she—?"

The gurney's foldaway legs extended and locked into place with a loud snap. The shape under the blanket moved.

"—alive?"

The female paramedic smiled at him and leaned forward. "Christine, your son's here."

The shape under the blanket twitched and made a sound that was halfway between a groan and a draining garden hose. "Suhbaazznn?"

"That's right, Christine, your son. He's here."

"Suh-baaz. Zznn." Her voice was low and raw. She didn't sound like herself…or like the voice on the phone.

"That's good, Christine, that's very good." The woman motioned Morgan to come closer, but he couldn't move. "It's okay. Let her see you."

The male paramedic nodded and stepped around to the side of the gurney to give Morgan room. "Christine, look who's here."

"Suhbaazznn?"

Morgan took a step closer and saw the dark stain on the carpet in front of her chair a moment before the urine stench enveloped him. God, how long had she been lying there before she called him for help?

"Mama fell down and won't wake up! Help me! You gotta help me wake Mama."

Morgan covered his mouth, pressing hard the same way the officer had pressed his hand against the car door – to keep it shut.

She looked small and frail under the heavy gray blanket they'd fastened over her, her face so pale it almost looked translucent above the foam neck brace. A gauze pad, smaller than the one she'd had in the hospital, covered her left eye. The only light in the room was from the reading lamp on the table next to her chair. His mother would have wanted more light, maybe had him hold a reflector to brighten the face of the woman on the gurney, or maybe she'd want the shadows to deepen around the hollows in the face so the glint in the right eye would be the only spark of white – black and white and gray – and she'd have asked him to bring her camera and not remembered that it was broken.

That he broke it.

By accident.

But if it hadn't been and if his mother wasn't the woman on the gurney, she would have taken a photograph in black-and-white-and-gray. Morgan felt the cellphone in his coat pocket and pressed his hand tighter against his mouth.

"Suh?"

"It's okay," the woman paramedic said, "talk to her."

Morgan lowered his hand and tried not to breathe too deeply. "I'm here, Mom."

"Nnn…. Suh! Baaz! Znn!"

"Do you have any idea what she's trying to say?" the man asked.

Morgan shook his head. "No. What happened to her?"

"We don't know—" Just like the 9-1-1 operator, they knew but couldn't tell him because they weren't doctors. More protocol bullshit. "—but she's stable and she has a strong pulse. It's lucky you called us when you did."

His mother looked at him. "Suh-baaz-znn."

"She called me." Morgan touched the blanket over her right arm. She closed her eye. "I mean I called 9-1-1 but she called me first and she wasn't making any sense. Why is she wearing an eye patch?"

The woman's lips tightened. "A precaution. Well, whatever the reason, you called and got your mother help." *—Help her! Morgan!—* "We don't think she'd been down very long when we arrived."

"But what happened?"

"They'll be able to give you a complete update at the hospital, sir," the man answered, "but now we have to get her in the ambulance. Move back, please."

The man moved to the foot of the gurney, the woman to the head, and together they pushed his mother into the hallway. Morgan followed on the right side, so she could see him.

"You'll be okay, Mom."

She stared at him, the right side of her forehead wrinkling. Only the right side.

He didn't need to wait for an update from a doctor and even though the paramedics would have sidestepped the question if he asked, Morgan knew what happened. He took a deep breath.

She'd had a stroke. The paramedics covered her left eye because she couldn't see out of it. *Jesus.*

"Et suh-baaz-znn."

"Mom, I don't understand."

She closed her right eye and opened it, the wrinkles deepening. Maybe she knew what had happened to her...maybe she knew what was happening when she called. *Help me! Come quick and help her! Help her! Morgan!*

Morgan lifted the blanket and took her hand, gasping at the strength when she gripped it. The paramedics stopped, giving them a moment.

"I know, but you'll be okay, Mom."

She squeezed his hand tighter. "Et suh-baas-zn! Maa-ggnn et suh-baas-zn."

Shit. He understood her.

And pretended he didn't.

"I love you, too, Mom."

She pulled her hand away. "*Et ch—gak—znn! Et ch—gak—znn! Maa-ggnn! Et ch—gak—znn!*"

"We have to go, sir."

Morgan nodded and moved out of the way.

"It's okay, Christine," the male paramedic said and put her hand back under the blanket. "We're going to take you to the hospital. Try to rest, we're going to take good care of you."

Morgan followed the gurney until the officer standing in the hall stopped him.

"Let them do their job, sir. Do you want to ride with her in the ambulance?"

His mother began yelling when they were halfway down the front steps— "*Suh-baaz-znn! Suh-baaz-znn!*" —and managed to pull her hand from the blanket again. It clutched at the air above her as if she was trying to grab something. Morgan saw the looks on the faces of the crowd in the rotating flashes of blue and red. Shock, concern, horror.

His mother couldn't see them and that was a blessing. The shame of having her friends and neighbors see her like that might have killed her.

And maybe that would have been a blessing, too.

Morgan closed his eyes – *I didn't mean that, just let her be okay* – and when he opened them the paramedics were loading the gurney into the back of the ambulance while the officers moved the crowd to the opposite side of the cul-de-sac.

"*Maa-ggnn! Et ch—gak—znn!*"

Morgan! Get Sebastian.

"Sir?" Morgan jumped. He'd forgotten the officer standing next to him. "Do you want to ride in the ambulance with your mother?"

"No, I'll drive. I can drive."

"I think it might be better if I drove with you. My partner can pick me up at the hospital. How would that be?" The officer didn't wait for an answer. "We know your mom. My partner and I patrol this neighborhood and she had us pose for a couple of pictures with Sebastian last fall. Sebastian's reaching up, you know, toward the teddy bear my partner is holding…it's one of the teddy bears we carry with us, you know to help calm kids down. Your mom had me kneel beside him with my hand on his back, you know, like I'm comforting him or something. She sent a copy to the station and our sergeant put it up in the lobby. It's a really great picture."

"Photograph," Morgan corrected and watched the woman paramedic close the ambulance door with his mother and her partner inside and run around to the driver's side.

"What?"

"My mother takes photographs," Morgan said, "not pictures."

"Oh. Right. Photograph." The officers on the street waved the ambulance off. "We were the first on the scene and were inside with your mom when the paramedics showed up. The poor guy jumped a mile when he saw Sebastian standing there dressed in pjs and a robe like he was a real kid. Tell the truth, I almost did the same thing."

"It was there?"

"Yeah, standing next to her. I don't know what happened, but maybe she tried to pick him up and.... I was surprised at how heavy he is. But I'm sure she'll be okay. She's a strong lady. Whatever happened to her, she still had the wherewithal to open the front door for us."

"The door was open?"

"Yeah, wide open so we could get to her faster. And the fact that she was able to do that is a good sign."

Mama fell down and won't wake up! You gotta help me wake Mama.

Morgan winced at the sound of the backup alarm as the ambulance reversed out of the driveway. The woman didn't turn on the siren until they cleared the cul-de-sac. He could still hear it even after it disappeared.

"We'd better get going," the officer said. "You ready?"

"Just let me turn off the lights and lock the door."

"We can do that for you."

"It's okay, I'll do it."

A second officer was walking up the front path. "I'm so sorry about your mother, Mr. Riley, but I'm sure she's going to be fine. And don't worry, we'll keep an eye on the place until she gets home."

"Thank you. I'm just going to turn off the lights."

The sound of his footsteps followed him into the living room. He stopped at the edge of the large wet spot on the carpet in front of his mother's chair. Her cellphone was face down on the table. One of the paramedics, or maybe the officer, had picked it up and put it there, the same way they moved the manikin back behind the chair to get it out of the way because it'd been standing there next to her when the officers arrived.

If she'd been strong enough to walk all the way to the front door, open it, and walk back again, then why did she call him? His number was first on her speed dial, but why didn't she call 9-1-1 herself?

Mama fell down and won't wake up! Help me! You gotta help me wake Mama.

Because she'd had a stroke and wasn't thinking rationally.

Morgan decided to leave the reading lamp on so the house wouldn't look as empty from the outside as it felt on the inside, and used his key to lock both the door latch and deadbolt.

As he crossed the porch, he heard a child crying from one of the neighboring houses.

"Yeah, kid...I know how you feel."

CHAPTER THIRTEEN

I only got to see her for a few minutes that first night and then only when they wheeled her past the waiting room in the ICU ward. She was under sedation, but they let me hold her hand. I told her I'd see her later and that I loved her, but I don't think she heard me.

Maybe she did.

It felt like I was in a dream I couldn't wake up from.

I stayed to talk to the doctor...well, listened mostly, and it wasn't good. I was right, it was a stroke. The doctor said they'd run more tests in the morning, but the preliminary diagnosis was that my mother had suffered a right hemispheric CVA...a stroke that affects the left side of the body as well as affecting speech, memory, sight and cognitive ability. The tests were to determine the severity of the damage.

Sounds like I know what I'm talking about, doesn't it? Don't be that impressed.... I Googled right hemispheric CVA when I got home.

The doctor told me she was breathing on her own and had responded to questions and those were the things I was supposed to focus on.

Good advice. Of course, then the doctor started asking me questions that I couldn't answer. Had I noticed any change in my mother's behavior? Had she recently changed the dosage of her blood pressure medication? Had she complained about headaches recently? Or fatigue? Or blurred vision? Dizziness? Difficulty speaking?

Had she been hallucinating?

What was I going to say?

The truth was that I didn't know and I told the doctor so.

Some great son, huh?

Fortunately, if you want to call it that, the hospital still had her records from the December accident, so there was that.

The doctor told me to go home and get some rest. My mother was being monitored and the hospital would call if anything happened. Of course, everyone knows what that means, but we all pretend we don't.

Hospitals are for hope.

Maybe I should have stayed, but I went home and I don't even remember driving or calling Holly. I just remember getting into the car at the hospital and the next minute I was carrying a hot twenty-ounce cup of Wawa coffee into the condo and it was after midnight.

Of course, we told Hannah…but only that her Grammy was sick and had to go to the hospital for a few days. We decided not to go into too much detail until we had more information. No, I don't think that was wrong. What good would it have done if I told her the truth?

Look, I know Hannah never got to say goodbye, but she's just a baby… my baby…even if she is outgrowing Santa Claus and the Easter Bunny. I just wanted to protect her a little while longer.

Was that so bad?

⋆ ⋆ ⋆

It's like déjà vu all over again.

The line had always made Morgan smile and sometimes even laugh out loud, depending on who'd said it. It was funny, unless the feeling of having already experienced the present situation was walking back into your mother's hospital room after a hiatus of a mere five months.

Then it wasn't so funny.

Of course, there were enough differences that made it feel like a whole new experience.

The previous time, she'd only been in for a bump on the head and a photo opportunity.

This time….

This time the room was smaller and windowless, a no-frills, efficient, utilitarian cubicle crowded with monitors and equipment dedicated to the care of one and only one patient. There hadn't even been a chair for him to sit in until a nurse brought one and placed it at the foot of the bed.

The last time Morgan had visited his mother in the hospital, she was still his mother. This time she wasn't. They had her propped up with pillows in a semi-upright position so she wouldn't aspirate into her lungs. Her left arm was taped to a board to keep it from curling into her chest. Her right arm, resting on the top of the starched white sheet and gray blanket with an IV needle taped to the inside of her elbow, twitched every six to nine seconds.

Morgan had counted.

The bed vibrated every three minutes and lasted for ten Mississippis, and each time it did, the left side of her face, from the beige eye patch to the drooping corner of her mouth, would tremble. The nurses had tied an adult bib around his mother's neck to catch the drool.

The bib was white with blue trim that matched the vinyl backing. His mother's gown was white with a gray diamond pattern. The room was white. The floor was pale gray. The pillows behind his mother's disheveled hair were white. The machines surrounding the bed were black and white or gray and white.

The only colors in the room were on the monitor over the bed – green with a small beating red heart next to it (pulse), white (temp), red (SpO^2), green (RR), two colors for blood pressure: yellow (SYST) and green (DIAS), ending with red (MEANmmHg?) – and in his hand.

He hadn't planned it, but even his outfit, white shirt, black windbreaker and gray slacks, followed the color scheme…and made the bright yellow construction paper card he was holding stand out all the more.

Morgan brushed his fingers across the flower and unicorn stickers his daughter had used to decorate the front of the card, careful not to get near the block-letter GET WELL GRAMMY message outlined in red glitter glue. Hannah had written the message inside the card – *WE LOVE YOU! From Hannah and Sebastian* – with an aqua felt-tip pen.

He and Holly had discussed whether or not to tell their daughter, and, in the end, agreed on a kid-friendly version: Grammy got sick and had to go to the hospital, but the doctors were taking good care of her and she was going to be fine. He'd been able to make it sound like he believed it because he'd already said the same thing to his wife and his mother's agent and his manager.

And maybe if he said it to enough people, he'd start to believe it himself.

Hannah had only asked one question he hadn't prepared for. "Who's taking care of Sebastian?"

But his wife answered without missing a bit.

"He's with a babysitter," she said. "Now, why don't you make Grammy a get-well card? That would make her so happy."

If anything could, it would be that, but Morgan had his doubts when he arrived at the hospital. She'd had a restless night and had to be given a light sedation to help her sleep.

He'd been there for almost an hour and she was still asleep.

Morgan leaned forward over his legs and tried to arch the tightness out of his back and shoulders. He could stay there all day if he needed to. His manager told him to take off as much time as he needed and not to worry about the meeting; he'd already printed out the report and, after thanking Morgan for the amount of time and effort he'd spent on it, sent along his and the branch's best wishes for his mother's quick recovery.

Recovery, maybe, but it wouldn't be quick. The vascular neurologist in charge of his mother's case was not particularly optimistic. His mother's condition was grave – the adjective, not the noun. She'd suffered a subarachnoid hemorrhage stroke caused by an arteriovenous malformation, AVM, and was, at the moment, paralyzed on her right side, which may or may not be permanent. She might not regain her sight in her left eye, she was having some difficulty swallowing, and had limited speech capability, but there were indications that his mother's cognitive functions, beyond the obvious damage caused by the stroke, were close to normal. She responded to questions put to her as best she could, and was cognizant of where she was and what had happened to her.

Of course, they needed to run more tests to be sure, the doctor assured him. Morgan had nodded and agreed, and silently prayed to God the doctor was wrong. His mother was Christine Morgan Riley, the photographer. She needed her hands to hold a camera and focus it. She needed her eyes, both eyes, to judge depth and distance and see the shapes and images hidden in the shadows. Without those two things she'd be nothing.

And, if the doctor was right and she knew what had happened to her....

"God...." Morgan didn't know what to ask so when the bed started to vibrate again, he began to count and had just reached eighty-nine Mississippis when his mother opened her eye.

"Hey, Mom...." He stood up and her eye tracked him as he walked to the bed and leaned down. "Hi."

She blinked and the right side of her mouth twitched, tried to form words while the left side hung slack and motionless. A bead of drool slipped down her chin. Morgan lifted a corner of the bib and wiped it away.

"It's okay, Mom."

Her eye widened. "Suh-baaz-*znn*?" *Sebastian?*

It would have been easy to think that the doctor was wrong and she didn't know what happened to her this time, and thought she was still in the hospital from bumping her head when her car slid on black ice. It would have been so easy to accept that she was only asking about the manikin because in a minute she'd ask Morgan to run home and get her camera because she had an idea for the Sebastian series.

It would have been easy if it was true.

Morgan straightened the damp bib and kept the smile on his face, pretending he didn't know what she was asking about, and *that* was easy.

"Shh, don't try to talk, Mom. I know you're scared and have a million questions, but try to relax, okay?" When his lips started to quiver, he let the smile go. "Everything's going to be fine."

The right side of her forehead furrowed. "Morr-ggnn." *Morgan.*

"Yeah. That's good, Mom. Say my name again."

"Suh-baaz-znn?"

Morgan sat down and took a deep breath. "My name, Mom. Say *my* name."

She lifted her chin. "Suh-baaz-znn."

Morgan could still feel her watching him when he glanced at the monitor over the bed: heart rate 93bpm, blood pressure 160/100…and he had no idea what the normal range was for a seventy-two-year-old woman who'd just suffered a stroke. Somehow, in all the excitement, he'd forgotten to Google that tiny piece of information.

"Morr-ggnn."

But he wasn't about to pull out his phone and do it now.

"Morr-*ggnn!*"

97bpm 165/110

Morgan met her eye and held his breath, waiting for the sound of footsteps from the hallway. The last time she'd been in the hospital he'd upset her enough to trigger an impromptu visit from a nurse. This time all he heard were the beeps and whirrs of the monitors from the other rooms.

"Morr-ggnn?"

"Yes, Mom?"

"Suh-baaz-znn!"

99bpm 170/110

"Mom, please, you have to calm down."

97bpm 165/110

"Look! Look what I have." Morgan lifted the card for her to see. Her eye followed the movement. "Hannah made this for you. It's a get-well card. We told her you were sick but that's all. We'll explain more to her later. And look at this…."

He opened the card to show her the inside. "Do you see what it says right here? Her handwriting's getting better, but…I'll read it for you. It says, 'We love you from Hannah…and Sebastian'."

His mother's eye widened. "Suh-baaz-znn."

Morgan didn't react as he stood and looked around the room. "There's not a lot of places where I can put this up. Oh, how about here?"

Morgan walked over to the room's dry erase board to the right of the sliding glass door. On it, written in black, were the names of the patient (C.Riley), the attending physicians (Menlow/Dias/Han) and AM nurse (Stella). Morgan slipped the card into the lower left corner of the board.

"There." Morgan walked back to the bed. "How's that?"

"Morr-gun."

Her hand trembled as she lifted it toward him and twitched when Morgan took it, cupping it between his and careful not to raise it too high.

94bpm   163/110

"I'm here, Mom, I'm here."

"Morr-gun." Her fingers closed gently over his. "Morr-gun, airs suh-baaz-znn."

Morgan, where's Sebastian?

Morgan shook his head and lowered her hand back to the mattress. "Just rest, Mom."

"Morr-gun…."

96bpm   164/110

"Morr-gun, *ing* suh-baaz-znn."

Morgan, bring Sebastian.

Morgan watched the monitor.

"*Morr-gun,* ing suh-baaz-znn!"

99bpm   175/114

"Mom, calm down."

102bpm   175/116

"Ing suh-baaz-znn!"

101…100…99…97bpm   172/113

He looked at her and clenched his jaw to keep the words he wanted to yell at her from escaping. *No! Stop asking about that damn thing. I can't bring it. I* won't *bring it. You're in Intensive Care, Mom. You had a stroke and if you don't calm down, you're going to have another one!* Stop asking about that damned manikin!

His jaw ached when he finally relaxed the muscles.

"Morr-ggnn, ing suh-baaz-znn. *Naaw!*"

Morgan, bring Sebastian now.

Morgan shook his head. "I don't understand what you're saying, Mom. I'll be right back."

"Morr-an? *Morr-an!*"

A buzzer went off in the room as Morgan stepped into the hall. Two nurses and an orderly were running down the hall toward him.

"My mother's awake."

One of the nurses stopped while the others entered his mother's room. "Why don't you go down to the waiting room? I'm sure the doctor will want to talk to you after he sees your mother."

Morgan nodded and continued to nod until he reached the elevator and rode it down to the main lobby. He briefly thought about getting a triple-shot Americano until he saw the line at the coffee kiosk, and quickened his pace past the gift shop's window display featuring a selection of faceless Amish dolls.

The waiting room was moderately full, no surprise there. Not in the mood to join the throng of anxious and worried strangers, Morgan stayed just outside the entrance so the doctor wouldn't have to waste time searching for him, and turned on his cellphone.

There were three text messages (one from his wife – *Call when you find out anything* – two from work, both from his manager – one to tell him the report looked great and thank him, and one offering prayers for his mother's speedy recovery) – and three voicemails from his mother's agent.

"Morgan. It's William. Ahem. I've been trying to call your mother since last night and she's not picking up. Did I do something to offend her? Call me."

"Morgan. It's William. Ahem. I just stopped by your mother's house this morning and a neighbor told me what happened. Oh my God, Morgan, how is she? Call me."

"Morgan. Call me."

While Morgan was weighing the options of returning the call now or waiting until he got more information, the phone vibrated in his hand and *Ode to Joy* began. It was William Ahern.

Morgan swiped left.

"Morgan!"

Shit.

Morgan put the phone back into his pocket as the old man detached himself from a chair along the side wall and rushed toward him. He looked the worse for wear and that was something Morgan had never seen. Usually the epitome of professional fashion, William's tan three-piece linen suit was so wrinkled it looked as if he'd slept in it, the brown moiré tie pulled loose and dangling from the open collar of a shirt that probably cost more than three of Morgan's own dress/casual shirts combined.

William might not be his mother's *friend*, but he loved her and no matter how lost and disheveled he looked, his grip was firm and strong when he took Morgan's hand.

"I'm sorry, Morgan, I know it's not my place to be here, but the hospital wouldn't give me any information when I called so I thought…."

"It's all right, William. Please sit down." Morgan let go of the old man's hand and took his elbow, steering him to the chair he'd just left and taking the one next to it. "I just left her and she's…she was awake. I'm just waiting for her doctor now. I was about to call you."

Lying was getting much easier.

The old man leaned back against the chair and took a deep breath. "Oh, thank God, thank God. I didn't know what to think. What happened?"

"Mr. Riley?"

They both looked up. The doctor wore a white lab coat over green scrubs. His name was printed on the lab coat over his heart. Morgan stood up to take the doctor's hand.

"I'm Dr. Dias." They shook hands quickly, like boxers touching gloves. "I'm one of the neurologists working with your mother."

William cleared his throat and stood up. "If you'll excuse me, I think I should go. But if you could let me know how she's doing, Morgan, I would appreciate it."

Morgan stopped the old man before he could walk away. "This is William Ahern. He's my mother's agent and friend. Is it okay if he stays?"

"That's up to you, Mr. Riley, but I'm fine with it. We can talk here or someplace more private if you'd rather."

"Here's fine." Morgan sat down and watched the old man do the same. "How is she?"

The doctor grabbed a chair from the row opposite and pulled it into the aisle halfway between Morgan's and the old man's. "First let me say I'm a great admirer of your mother's work. I was fortunate enough to meet her a few years ago at an opening in Philadelphia and was immediately taken by the strength of her personality."

"Thank you." He didn't know what else to say to a statement like that.

"She's going to need that strength, Mr. Riley, and it will be up to you to remind her of that."

"You don't have to worry about Christine," William said, "she's a fighter. I'm sorry, Morgan, I shouldn't have interrupted."

Morgan patted the old man's knee. "That's okay…and he's right, she is a fighter."

"That was evident when I walked in. I gave her a light sedative to help her rest. Did something happen while you were with her?"

Yeah, she wanted me to bring her damned manikin to the hospital.

"Yes, she was trying to talk but I couldn't understand what she was saying."

The doctor nodded. "It's a form of non-fluent aphasia where your mother understands what's being said to her but can't communicate in return."

"Oh my God, Morgan."

"But will she be able to?" Morgan asked. "I mean, I know it'll take time but…will she?"

"Yes, there's a good chance. As I said earlier, your mother's a very strong-willed lady…but it will take time, Mr. Riley. Your mother suffered a hemorrhagic stroke to the right side of her brain, which impaired her left side coordination and movement."

"Oh God. Oh God."

Neither Morgan nor the doctor looked at the old man.

"Right now we don't have a long-term prognosis, but once your mother is strong enough to begin physical and speech therapy we'll have a better idea. We are going to run more tests to assess the scale of her impairment and will be monitoring her closely to insure she doesn't suffer a second stroke."

"God, Morgan."

Morgan held the old man's hand as the doctor continued as if William was the family member and he was just a friend who'd come by for moral support.

"I know how frightening this sounds and I won't lie and tell you, either of you, that this is going to be an easy road. It's not. Mrs. Riley is in for the fight of her life, but she'll have the easy part compared to her family and friends who have to sit on the sidelines and just wait it out. I've seen both sides, so I know. Just stay positive and give her time and believe with every fiber of your being that she is getting the best care possible. Because she is."

Morgan met the doctor's eyes and nodded. He believed the doctor about the care his mother would be getting, but he also believed what he'd read the night before that the five-year survival rate for hemorrhagic stroke patients was only 26.7%.

Good ol' Google.

"Thank you, Dr. Dias. Can I go back up and see her?"

"You can," the doctor said, "but she might be asleep. And right now it's very important that your mother get as much rest as possible. We'll evaluate her in the morning and if we think she's a good candidate we may start her on some limited physical therapy."

"So soon?" The old man clutched Morgan's hand. "The poor woman's just had a stroke, for the Lord's sake!"

"It's called inpatient rehabilitation, William, and it can start as early as twenty-four to forty-eight hours after a stroke." The old man and the doctor stared at Morgan. "I did a little research at the office. Sorry, Dr. Dias."

"Don't be," the doctor said, "the more informed family members are about what is happening to their loved ones the easier it makes my job. Just be careful about believing everything you read; there is a lot of misinformation and some of it pretty frightening."

"I looked at WebMD."

"That's a good one, but if you ever have any questions or need to know more information, I will be happy to provide whatever answers I can."

In other words, stop looking for trouble. Morgan nodded.

William was gazing at the doctor as if he'd suddenly sprung a halo. Or horns.

"About my going to see her…?"

"Of course you can, but if she's asleep…."

"I won't wake her, I promise."

They stood together and the doctor gave them a moment's privacy by moving the chair he'd been sitting in back across the aisle.

"I'd love for you to come along, William, and I know you've been waiting down here, but they only allow one visitor at a time."

"No, no, no, that's not an issue. You need to be with her, she's your mother and you only get one of those in your life…but if she is awake, give her my best and tell her I'll pray for her. Unless you think that will upset her and then don't mention it."

"Given the circumstances, I don't think she'll mind." They shook hands and the old man's grip was weaker this time. "And I'll put your name on the visitors' list, but right now I think you should go home and get some rest. You look a little rough around the edges."

"Thank you, Morgan, and I will get some rest." William let go of Morgan's hand in order to tighten the knot of his tie back into its proper position and smooth down his hair. "But not yet. I still have a bit to do for your mother's Philadelphia opening." He extended his hand to the doctor. "Goodbye, Dr. Dias, and thank you for allowing me to sit in."

Morgan watched William try to brush the wrinkles out of his coat as he walked away before following the doctor back to the elevator banks.

"I won't come with you," the doctor said as Morgan got out on the ICU floor. "I still have rounds, but remember what I said: just give her some time. I can call you when I get the test results or we can speak the next time you're here."

"I'll be here tomorrow after work."

"Fine. See you then."

Morgan nodded to the doctor as the elevator doors closed and prayed his mother would be asleep when he walked into her room.

She was.

Thank you, God. I owe you one.

CHAPTER FOURTEEN

Three days.

That's all it was, just three days.

★ ★ ★

A nurse was standing next to the bed when Morgan walked in, giving his mother water by dipping a long-handled sponge into a cup and then placing the sponge tip into his mother's mouth, where she would suck it dry. Repetitive motion back and forth, back and forth…like watching a greedy baby bird feed with a malformed beak.

A towel, tucked behind her shoulders, covered the front of his mother's hospital gown to soak up the water that dribbled from the left side of her mouth.

Morgan stood in the doorway until they noticed him.

The nurse smiled.

"We have her on a saline drip to keep her hydrated, but that doesn't help with dry mouth, does it, Mrs. Riley?"

His mother grunted and opened her mouth, accepting the saturated sponge when it arrived. Morgan watched the muscles in her throat flex as they tried to remember how to swallow.

His mother grunted three more times before turning away from the sponge. A droplet of water fell onto the towel and disappeared.

"Done?"

His mother faced the nurse and blinked.

The nurse put the sponge into the cup and the cup onto the rolling cart behind her before removing the towel from around his mother's neck.

"Done." The nurse used a corner of the towel to wipe off his mother's mouth and chin. The bib his mother wore that morning was pale yellow with a darker yellow trim.

"Can't you give her ice chips?" Morgan asked.

"Soon," the nurse said, whose name Morgan didn't think to check on the dry-erase board. "We just have a little work to do first, don't we? Now, is there anything you need, Mrs. Riley?"

His mother blinked twice. When the doctor called the night before, he'd said her cognitive functions were better than any of them had hoped for and Morgan had just seen proof of that. One blink for yes, two blinks for no.

"Okay, then, I'll leave you two alone."

His mother's eye watched the nurse leave. "Mor-gan."

Morgan pulled the chair close to the bed and sat down. "Hey, that's good, Mom. You sound better."

Her head bobbed in what might have been a nod and she tried to reach up before Morgan took her hand and put it back down on the mattress.

"What?"

She sighed – that didn't need a second-guess translation – and shifted her eye to the left, repeating the motion twice before looking at Morgan and giving him a half-face frown.

"What?"

"I."

"I.... Oh." Morgan squeezed her hand gently. "It's an eye patch. The doctors covered your eye."

"C?"

"Can you see?" One blink. *Truth or lie?* Morgan glanced up at the monitor. 98bpm 162/110. *Truth.* "I don't know...but I think they said you may have scratched it—" *And lie.* "—so they covered it to give it time to heal."

She nodded.

95bpm 162/110

"I think the eye will be okay."

93bpm 160/110

"Um-is?"

"What?"

She took a deep, rattling breath. "Paa-is."

Promise.

"I'm not a doctor, Mom. We'll have to wait and see, but you're already doing so much better. The doctor said you're a real fighter."

"Ha."

"Do you remember anything, Mom?"

She blinked twice. "Na."

"You called me. Do you remember doing that?" Blink. Blink. "You sounded strange and you weren't making much sense. Were you alone when you…got sick?"

Blink. Blink.

"Who was with you?"

The frown deepened and the numbers on the monitor inched upward. "Suhbaazinn."

Morgan sat back. "It's okay, Mom, it's okay. The important thing is that you knew something was wrong and you called for help. You're on the mend but it's going to take some time before you're better. Just time and rest and you'll be…."

As easy as lying had become, Morgan couldn't make himself tell her that she'd be fine or back to normal or taking photographs or able to see out of both eyes and walk…so he lied about something else.

"I may have found a new camera for you. It's a few years newer than the one…your last one and looks to be in good condition. I've been emailing the owner."

He hadn't been looking for a new camera, hadn't so much as thought the word *camera* until that moment.

"But don't get your hopes up. Still…." Morgan lifted his hands and crossed his fingers. "You never know."

A bead of drool slipped from his mother's mouth and fell onto the bed. Morgan looked away.

"So, is there anything I can bring you?"

"Suh-baaz-inn."

Jesus, not again. "I have a couple books on tape you might like."

"Mor-gan airs suh-baaz-inn?"

Morgan, where's Sebastian?

"I was looking at Amazon and I can get *The Wind in the Willows* as a download. I can get a copy and bring over my tablet."

"Suh-baaz-inn."

"There's one narrated by Sir Derek Jacobi. You remember how much you liked him in *I, Claudius* and—"

"Mor-gan ing suh-baazinn! I nee im!"

Morgan, bring Sebastian! I need him.

99bpm 163/114

"No."

Her eye widened. "Wa?"

Morgan stood up and walked over to the bed, holding onto the raised bedrails as he leaned forward.

"This isn't like the other time you were in the hospital, Mom, you won't be able to get up and take photographs even if I did find a camera. You had a stroke, Mom, and you're in the ICU and you're partially… you wouldn't be able to hold a camera even if you had one. So there's no way I'm going to bring that thing in here."

Her eye glistened but not with tears.

"All ill-mm."

Morgan stood up. "What?"

She closed her eye, squeezing it tight, and took a deep breath. When she opened her eye again it was dry.

"All. Illam. A-yet."

Call William. Agent.

"No, it's okay. He was here and wanted me to tell you…to give you his best."

"Ees eer ow?"

He's here now?

"No, he—" *Had to leave to work on one of your openings.* "—left. The poor man looked exhausted."

She closed her eye. "'K."

Morgan sat down and waited for her to open her eye, shifting his gaze between her face (that looked peaceful, finally) and the monitor (97bpm 160/110). When her heart rate dropped another point Morgan cleared his throat.

She opened her eye.

"I guess you're tired."

Blink.

Morgan stood up. "Okay, I'm going to head out."

Blink.

He walked over to the bed and kissed the right side of her forehead. "I have a morning meeting, but I'll come see you after work."

Blink. Blink.

"You don't want me to stop by?"

Blink. Blink.

Morgan gave the monitor one more look – 93bpm 160/100 – before walking to the door.

"I love you, Mom."

She didn't blink. "Mor-gan."

"Yes?"

"Ont um ak."

Don't come back.

"Right." He winked. Once.

★ ★ ★

Morgan didn't say anything about his mother's parting comment when he got home, because it wasn't anything that he hadn't heard before. It happened with less frequency than it had when he'd first moved out and had what he'd considered at the time a broader and more erudite view of the world compared to his mother's.

He couldn't remember how many times a 'discussion' would end with his mother telling him to leave and never come back.

And he wouldn't…until the next Monday when he and his mother would have Chinese food as if nothing had happened.

Until the next time.

So when he got home and his wife and daughter asked how Grammy was, Morgan told them the truth: It would take some time before she came home, but she was on the mend.

Lying might be easier, but telling the truth, sometimes, was simpler.

"Your mom is going to be okay, isn't she?" Holly asked after dinner when their daughter was upstairs doing homework and any truths could be kept secret between them.

"The doctor says she's strong and you know Mom. She wouldn't let anything as mundane as a stroke do her in."

They were sitting on the sofa recliner in the family room, watching TV, which limited the items she could hit him with. The throw pillow barely grazed his arm.

"Morgan! That's a terrible thing to say. Don't joke about it."

Morgan handed the pillow back to her. "Sorry, but I think she'll be okay. It won't be easy for her, but I really do think she'll be okay."

"Good." She hugged the pillow to her chest and turned toward the TV. "You're a hero, Morg, you saved her life. If you hadn't gotten to her in time, we wouldn't be able to joke about it."

"I know, but she called me. I just called 9-1-1."

"And that probably saved her life. So just accept it. You're a hero… mine, Hannah's and your mom's."

"Fine, I'm a hero, but if you start singing 'Wind Beneath My Wings' I'm leaving."

"Heroes never accept credit."

"No," Morgan agreed, "heroes don't…but they do accept Butterscotch Dilly Bars." He turned toward her. "Hint. Hint."

"I don't think we have any left. It was our turn to host the Brownie meeting the other night, remember?"

Morgan didn't remember because that was the night he became a hero.

"No Dilly Bars? Hero sad."

"I should have known I'd regret that." Holly lowered the footrest on her section of the recliner and stood. "Okay, one box of Butterscotch

Dilly Bars coming up, hero. Hannah! I'm going to Dairy Queen, want to come along?"

"Yeah!"

Morgan checked the ceiling for cracks as the sound of his daughter's thundering steps echoed across the upstairs hall and down the stairs.

"Shoes!"

The thunder reversed direction and, after a moment of silence, resumed all the way into the family room. "Ready!"

"Okay, Let's go."

"Can I get a large Wonder Woman Cookie Collision?"

"You can get a mini." His wife followed their daughter through the sliding patio doors and turned around. "Anything else we need?"

Morgan shook his head and snuggled down. "Hero thanks you."

She grunted and sounded almost exactly like his mother. "Be right back."

Morgan waved as she closed the door.

And was asleep before the next commercial.

CHAPTER FIFTEEN

You know, a few years ago my wife and I were watching a movie on Netflix...I can't remember the name, but it was a romantic comedy with a bunch of big-name stars – but in one scene an actor is talking on the phone in a London flat and there's one of my mother's framed photographs on the wall behind him.

It's the one of me standing next to my father's casket at the funeral. Every time the camera turned back to the actor, there I was, looking over his shoulder. It just looked like that because in the photograph I was looking down at the casket.

I called her and told her about it and she said something like 'oh, how nice'. There are so many of her photographs around they're probably in a lot of movies and TV shows. They've became part of the collective background.

Which is not a bad legacy, when you think about it.

So anyway, the next day I get into work and there's a massive and I mean massive *wicker basket sitting on my desk – TO MRS. RILEY – filled with individually wrapped whale-shaped iced cookies that looked identical to the whale-shaped balloon that was tied to the handle. 'Get Whale Soon'. Cute, huh? Everyone in the branch signed the card.*

I couldn't wait to show her.

Remember what I said about thinking there's always going to be a next time?

★ ★ ★

The balloon danced at the end of its blue ribbon as Morgan left the elevator. One of the whale cookies had slipped to starboard on the ride up and required a bit of straightening so that it could show off its purple-white-icing smile. Everyone he'd passed in the lobby had smiled and the two nurses he'd shared the elevator with thought it was both 'adorable' and '*so* cute'.

His mother might take one look at it and roll her eyes...eye, but if nothing else the helium whale would add a little personality to the otherwise austere room.

"Mr. Riley...."

Morgan smiled at the nurse manning the station and held up the basket. "Got a delivery to make."

"Mr. Riley, wait, please."

The balloon drifted toward the ceiling as he stepped into his mother's room. "Look what the office sent you."

"Hello, Morgan."

William stood from the visitor's chair and walked through the spot where his mother's bed should have been but wasn't. The whale balloon caught a current of air and bounced against the side of Morgan's head when Morgan lowered the basket.

"Hi, William. Is Mom still in PT?"

The old man watched the balloon. "They took her."

"Okay. Did they say when they'd be bringing her back?"

"Do you mind if I sit down, Morgan?"

"No, not at all."

Morgan looked for someplace to put the basket before finally giving up. He couldn't remember if there'd been a bedside table in the room or not, because there wasn't one now. Maybe they were moving her to another room, in which case he'd just hang on to the basket and deliver it there.

"Are you okay, William?"

The man looked up at Morgan and shook his head. "I stopped in this morning to see her. Oh, God, Morgan."

"I know."

"I'd tried to prepare myself, you know how one does, but I couldn't. I didn't realize how bad it was until I saw her...but Christine was still there...." He tapped the middle of his chest. "Inside. She tried to speak, I mean, she did speak, but I couldn't understand what she was saying. I should have tried harder and maybe this wouldn't have happened. God, Morgan, she tried so hard to tell me something and I couldn't...."

"Don't do this to yourself, William."

"And who else should do this? It's my fault, Morgan, if I hadn't come and given her my bloody phone...."

When the balloon's ribbon brushed against his check, Morgan grabbed it and held it away from his body. His mother had taken a photograph of him holding a balloon on a windy autumn day when he was five.

"Why did you give her your phone?"

The old man blinked at the question. Just once. "She wanted it. I hadn't turned it off like you're supposed to in a hospital so when it rang, some other client, I took it out and swiped left and was about to turn it off when she...your mother said something and, Morgan, she held out her hand.

"For the life of me I still didn't know what she wanted but she kept looking at me and then at the phone...just the one eye...."

"William."

"Yes, sorry, so I mean eventually I figured it out and handed it to her. Morgan, then she gave me the look...you know the one I mean, the one that says, 'you can go now, I'm busy'."

Morgan nodded. He'd seen that look all his life.

"So I stepped out of the room and...." He shook his head. "I don't know what she was going to do... I thought... because she had the use of her right hand, I thought she was going to try and tell me something by writing it out. I don't know, I wasn't thinking very clearly, but if that was the case, she wouldn't have wanted me to leave. Maybe she wanted to say... I don't know, but there was no message from her. Maybe she was going to, but..."

William pulled his cellphone from his pocket and ran his fingers gently over the shattered screen.

"It happened so fast, Morgan. An alarm went off and then these nurses and a doctor came running into her room and I followed...tried to follow but this one nurse told me to stand back and give them room and then they took her.

"I found this on the floor."

Morgan was suddenly aware of the weight of the cellphone in his pocket.

"William, where's my mother?"

The old man looked up but another voice answered.

"Your mother's in surgery, Mr. Riley."

Morgan didn't recognize the doctor standing in the doorway, but he was so young the scrubs and surgical cap he wore looked like a costume.

His mother would have taken a photograph.

"What happened? Why didn't someone call me?"

"It's my fault," William whispered. Both Morgan and the young doctor ignored him.

"We did."

Morgan shifted the basket and touched the phone through the pocket. "I turned it off before I left work because the hospital...."

The balloon brushed against his face. Morgan wound the ribbon around his hand and broke it. The balloon drifted up to the ceiling, where the air current pushed it into a corner.

"What happened?"

"Your mother had another stroke."

"Oh God, it's my fault."

"*William!*" Morgan took a deep breath and exhaled. "Not now. Please."

Morgan nodded to the doctor. "Your mother's blood pressure suddenly spiked – It wasn't your fault, sir – and she presented with symptoms of a subdural brain bleed. Upon examination the bleed proved significant enough to require a craniotomy to relieve pressure on her brain. She is still in surgery. When the nurse on duty saw you, she informed Dr. Dias and he sent me to give you an update."

The last few words were thin and raspy as he ran out of air. He took a deep breath.

"If you and Mr. Ahern would like to go down to the surgical waiting room on the mezzanine level, Dr. Dias will be down to speak with you when the surgery is completed."

"How did it happen?"

"Dr. Dias will explain everything when the surgery is completed. Try not to worry."

Morgan carried the basket by the handle and heard the cookies shift each time he took a step.

There were already four people in the elevator – two in scrubs, one in a lab coat and a weary-looking woman in a blue smock – when the doors opened. They backed up to make room but only Morgan and the basket got on.

"William?"

"I'll talk to you later, Morgan. I…can't."

The doors closed.

When the doors opened onto the mezzanine, Morgan stepped aside to let the woman in the smock get off and found himself following her to the surgical waiting room.

Dr. Dias was waiting for him in green scrubs and matching surgical cap; sweat darkened the color across the man's chest and forehead. His skin felt damp when they shook hands.

"Mr. Riley, please sit."

Morgan sat and put the basket on the floor next to him. It was too cheerful for the quiet room. Thank God he'd gotten rid of that damned balloon.

"How is she?"

"Stable and in recovery. We'll be monitoring her closely until she comes out of the anesthetic and then we'll see where we go from there." He pulled off his cap and wiped his face with it. "I don't know what happened, Mr. Riley, and my intern told me what Mr. Ahern said, but I can assure you his presence did not cause this. In fact, up until the moment it happened, your mother seemed fine. She spent a restful night and was alert this morning. Her blood pressure was within normal parameters both before and after her physical therapy session and she was even able to take a few sips of water orally, which is a bit of a milestone. Everything looked good. But let me assure you, Mr. Riley, that if there had been the slightest indication that something like this was going to happen, you would have been called immediately and Mr. Ahern would not have been allowed to see her."

Morgan nodded and waited for the shoe to drop. That sounded like a preamble; the rest was coming.

"When your mother's blood pressure suddenly spiked, she was rushed into the O.R. where I performed a craniotomy, at which time I was able to get the bleeding under control. I also discovered a clot which I removed with a small suction tube, after which I gave your mother a dose of Alteplase to prevent another clot from forming."

The doctor's voice remained calm and steady with no inflection or emotion to betray anything but practiced professionalism.

"Then she's okay?"

"She's stable, Mr. Riley. We won't be able to ascertain if any further damage has been done until she's awake."

"Of course."

"When your mother was admitted you signed an authorization allowing for emergency surgery should it be needed, is that right?"

Morgan nodded even though he couldn't remember half of everything he'd signed that night.

"Good." The doctor stood up and shook Morgan's hand. "I gave the volunteer at the reception desk both your name and your mother's patient number." He nodded toward the reception desk next to the door. The woman sitting behind the counter was the same woman Morgan had followed from the elevator. "She'll inform you when your mother's out of recovery and give you her room number. In the meantime, you can check your mother's status on the electronic tracking monitors around the room."

Dias pointed to one of the half-dozen suspended monitor screens around the room. The constantly rolling display – white on a black background – showed a patient's name, alphabetized by last name, their room number and current location. Morgan had to wait through two cycles before the Rs appeared.

Rigby, F #214-CD/S2.

Rivera, J #424/R3.

Riley, C #411/R1.

"Thank you."

"I'll be in touch, Mr. Riley, and help yourself to the coffee and snacks. If you'd like to grab dinner, the volunteer can give you a voucher for the cafeteria and tell you the quickest way to get there if you haven't been before. I think the floor line color is aqua or turquoise…I get those two confused. I'll be in touch, and try not to worry."

Morgan waited until the doctor had left and the volunteer was talking to a new arrival before pulling out his cellphone and furtively checking to see if anyone else was using theirs or if the smaller, more secluded waiting room, unlike its bigger public cousin downstairs, was a NO PHONE ZONE.

There were more than twenty people sharing the wait-space with him, including the volunteer, half of whom had their phones out and were either texting or speaking in hushed tones because, unlike downstairs, there was no wall-mounted TV running a game show or twenty-four-hour news channel. There was little to distract from the rolling displays on the monitors except the magazines in the side-by-side wall racks. Everyone was quiet and still, getting up only to use one of the designated restrooms or to check out the coffee and pastries or exchange one magazine for another or to step onto the wide mezzanine balcony for longer conversations.

Morgan held up his phone as he walked by the volunteer to let her know where he was going and why. The volunteer nodded.

Three people were already in the corridor talking quietly on their phones. Two, a man and a woman, were leaning against the waist-high glass block wall, well apart from each other and looking down into the lobby as they spoke. The third person, a woman, stood at the far end of the hall, her back turned toward the lobby.

Morgan found a spot on the wall equidistant from all three and turned on his phone. When it powered up, he selected MESSAGES and began texting Holly. He didn't feel like talking.

At hospital. Mom had emergency surgery. Is in recovery. Don't know what time I'll get home.

What happened? She ok?

Don't know.

Do you want me to come down?

No. It's okay. Don't tell Hannah.

I won't. You sure you don't want me to come?

I can drop Hannah off at the Goodmans'.

No. May be a long night. I'll call when I find out anything.

Okay. Give her our love when she wakes up.

Morgan looked at the last message until the colors reversed and imprinted itself on his eye. He had to blink twice before he could see the screen well enough to answer.

Will do.

Do you need anything?

No. Thanks.

I love you, Morg. Stay strong.

Always. Love you, too.

Morgan put the phone away but stayed at the wall, arms resting against the chilled chrome railing, and watched the ebb and flow of the crowd below him. It reminded him of the ant hill he and his father had accidentally broken open one summer while they were digging a new rose bed. While most of the ant-people wore street clothes, there were a number in scrubs and lab coats scurrying back and forth across the lobby. With the exception of those lined up at either the franchised coffee/pastry kiosk or main reception desk and the dozen or so taking advantage of the color-coordinated seating, everyone was moving back and forth across the lobby to the elevator bank or stairwell or gift shop, some coming in, some going out.

The patterns changed constantly and there was always something that caught Morgan's attention long enough to make him forget about the waiting room and its monitors…

…and the shape that suddenly appeared next to him and cleared its throat.

"They just called down from recovery." The woman in the smock smiled at him. "Your mother's regained consciousness."

"Thank you."

The woman smiled and walked away.

Morgan took a deep breath and thanked God, Dr. Dias, and his mother, in that order, before taking his phone out.

Mom's awake. More later.

♥♥♥♥☺

Morgan gave the volunteer a wink and heard her giggle as he headed over to the refreshment table for a cup of coffee and helped himself to a whale cookie from the basket to celebrate.

He didn't think his mother would mind.

Morgan was contemplating stealing a second one when Dr. Dias walked in.

It was the way he walked in that made Morgan set the coffee down and get to his feet.

"She's dead, isn't she?"

The doctor cleared his throat and looked Morgan in the eyes. "Your mother made it through surgery with no complications and was taken to recovery, where she began to regain consciousness. I don't think she was fully awake when she suffered a massive stroke. She.... Your mother was still on a ventilator and CPR was immediately started. I was paged and arrived to find your mother unresponsive with no pupil response. We attempted to restart your mother's heart while continuing CPR after each attempt but despite our best efforts we were unable to revive her. I'm so very sorry, Mr. Riley."

"I don't under...." Morgan shook his head to try and clear it. It felt like it was filled with cotton. She was dead. His mother was dead. He licked his lips and tasted vanilla icing. "Okay."

The doctor nodded. "I'm so very, very sorry, Mr. Riley. Would you like to see her?"

She's dead.

"See her?"

"If you feel up to it. It might help, she looks very peaceful."

She's dead.

Morgan left the basket on the snack table and threw the coffee into the trash before following the doctor back to the elevators and up two floors to a quiet, carpeted hallway lined with closed doors.

Each door had a letter on it instead of a number. The doctor stopped in front of the door marked D.

"Take as much time as you need," he said and opened the door just enough for Morgan to see the lower half of a bed and the sheet-draped shape that lay on it. "There's a call button on the wall if you need anything. When you're finished, just tell the nurse on duty. Again, I am so very sorry, Mr. Riley."

"Thank you."

The carpet swallowed the sound of the doctor's steps as Morgan walked in and closed the door behind him.

It was a nice room, much nicer than the last one his mother was in. It was large and airy, the walls painted a pale gray and a series of small black-and-white framed landscapes – pictures, not photographs, and not his mother's – along the back wall took the place of a window. The recessed lighting over the bed was just bright enough to make a positive identification.

There were no shadows, no curious angles, nothing otherworldly or surprising, nothing that when someone looked at it would be recognized as a Christine Morgan Riley…except her body.

They'd covered her with a light gray blanket that had been pulled up to her chin. Her head, wrapped in a pale blue scarf to hide the surgical scars, rested on a white pillow. Someone had taken off the gauze eye patch and both of her eyes were closed.

Dr. Dias was right; she looked peaceful.

Dead.

My mother is dead.

It didn't seem possible.

The knock on the door was very soft but it still made Morgan jump.

"I'm so sorry to disturb you, Mr. Riley," the nurse said, "but I just wanted you to know that I have your mother's things, if you'd like them now. Or I can come back later."

Morgan was grateful she hadn't used the term *personal effects. Your mother's things* sounded less final somehow.

"No, it's okay, I'll take them."

The nurse stepped into the room and handed him a white plastic bag with the hospital's name printed on the side in blue, the same kind of bag they used in the gift shop.

"I'm so sorry for your loss. Stay as long as you like."

She was gone before he got a chance to thank her.

The bag held only the robe and slippers she'd been wearing when the paramedics took her away. The robe and slippers had been washed and smelled of lavender. The pajamas weren't there, but they'd been drenched in urine and probably had to be cut off her body in the E.R. Not much to save after that. The card his daughter made was in a clear plastic envelope.

Just three things to take home.

They didn't even include the personal care items...not that his mother had used anything except the long-handled sponge that she'd sucked water from. Although they could have included the bib she'd worn, washed and folded, of course, as a souvenir.

"See this? My mom wore this in the hospital before she died. Think I'll use it the next time we have ribs."

Morgan closed the bag and walked over to the bed, gently brushing his fingers against her cheek. He expected it to be hard and cold the way his father's had been in his casket, but her skin was still soft and just a little cool. He tucked the blanket in around her shoulders.

Now he was supposed to say goodbye. In every movie he saw or book he read, when someone died their loved one always said goodbye. A final kiss on the brow was optional.

Morgan couldn't do either. Not here, not now.

He'd said goodbye to his mother a million times and she to him and it always meant *'I'll see you later.'*

They always said goodbye, except the last time. The last time, yesterday, she'd said *don't come back* and he said *right.*

Morgan left the room and closed the door as quietly as he could behind him.

The nurse who'd brought in the bag of his mother's *things* was standing at the end of the hall with another woman. The woman was dressed in street clothes – dark blue slacks and a pale blue blouse. The nurse held a clipboard. The woman's hands, clasped at her waist, were empty.

The woman wore a hospital ID on a lanyard around her neck – E. Stanton. The plastic cover reflected the light as she extended her hand to Morgan.

"Mr. Riley, I'm Eva Stanton, the hospital's bereavement counselor. Here's my card." Morgan had been wrong; her hands weren't empty. "I met your mother back in December and she mentioned you and your family. No one can prepare for something like this, so if you or your wife or daughter would like to talk, I would be honored to help. I am so very sorry for your loss, Mr. Riley. Your mother was an amazing woman."

After a brief handshake, E. Stanton turned and walked away, leaving Morgan with the nurse.

For some reason, the nurse wasn't wearing a name tag, so nothing reflected the light except the clipboard when she held it out to him.

"Would you mind signing this after you read it? It states that you received your mother's belongings."

Things had become *belongings*. Reality. Check.

Morgan laced his arm through the bag's handles and took the clipboard, signed his name without reading it and handed it back. The no-name nurse took the clipboard and folded the page over before handing it back.

"This is for the release of your mother's…of the deceased to the funeral home. Do you have one in mind?"

"Munn Family Funeral Home and Mortuary. We have a family plot at Graybryer Memorial Gardens." He had no idea why he'd thought it important to add all the details, but he couldn't stop himself. "It was one of her favorite places to photograph."

The nurse gave him an indifferent smile.

"That is a lovely place." She handed him back the clipboard. "There are three copies for you to sign. One is for you, the other for the hospital and the third will go with your mother."

Morgan signed – all three copies – and handed the clipboard back. The nurse folded back the first paper he'd signed then slipped one of the release forms out and handed it to Morgan.

"The hospital will contact the funeral home if you like."

"No, I'll do that."

"When you do, tell them to call hospital extension 913 for any other paperwork that is required."

Morgan folded the piece of paper and put it in the bag with his mother's robe and slippers and get-well card. "Thank you."

The nurse nodded. "If there's anything else you need, Mr. Riley, please feel free to contact the hospital. I am so very sorry for your—"

Morgan nodded but left before she could finish. It was rude and disrespectful and his mother would have been appalled by his behavior. But he was never going to see the nurse again or, if he was lucky, the hospital, and at the moment he just couldn't take another dose of detached sympathy.

He'd be facing plenty of that soon enough.

CHAPTER SIXTEEN

No, I didn't cry.

I don't know why, I just didn't.

I had too much to do, okay? I had to go home and tell my wife and hold her while she cried…and she cried enough for the both of us so I didn't have to. That's why.

What? Yeah, I cried when my father died, but I was younger then and all I had to do was grieve and hurt and feel sorry for myself. That was my job.

Of course I loved her, why would you even ask that? The thing is….

The thing is, I don't feel anything.

I know she's gone and I miss her, but it's all just words. It's like there's a hole inside me that keeps getting bigger, and the bigger it gets the less I feel. I know I'm sad and I know I'm grieving, but it's in the abstract…like the sadness and grief are photographs and I'm just looking at them.

You're right, my mother would love that.

We decided to wait and tell Hannah when she got home from school the next day. She was already in bed when I got home and I didn't want to wake her with news like that…it was the same reason I didn't call my mother's agent even though I knew he'd probably be awake. He'd left a voicemail on my phone, probably asking how she was, but I couldn't tell him over the phone.

I wanted to give them both one more night.

★ ★ ★

Morgan didn't get the chance to tell him. All he'd done was walk into William's office and close the door and the old man broke into tears.

He didn't even get to say, "I'm so sorry, William."

The only thing he was able to do was stand silent and watch the old man dab at his eyes with an increasingly soggy wad of tissues.

"She's gone. Oh, God, she's gone. I knew it the second you walked in. Oh, my God, Morgan. Was it.... Did she suffer?"

Morgan hadn't asked and Dr. Dias hadn't said anything, but it seemed too cruel to say that. "No, I don't think so."

"That's a blessing then, but...I can't believe she's gone. Your mother was such a force of nature."

"I know."

Morgan walked to one of the chairs facing the desk and sat down while William took deep breaths and composed himself. Or tried to.

"I'm so sorry, William." It almost felt good, in a strange way, to be the one saying it instead of the one it was said to. "It happened last night, but I thought it might be easier to tell you in person."

"Something like this is never easy, but thank you." William deposited the wad of tissues in the wastepaper basket behind him and pulled out a linen handkerchief to blow his nose. "I just pray it was peaceful."

I hope so, too. "She just slipped away."

The old man smiled, briefly. "A lady always knows when it's time to leave the party and your mother was a lady. I'm sorry, Morgan, I shouldn't have gone on like this, and I think I knew something was wrong when you didn't call." He took a long, rattling breath. "But she's at peace now. How will we get on without her?"

"As best as we can. What else can we do?"

William folded the handkerchief and put it on the desktop. "You're right, that's exactly what we do. Your mother was the strongest woman and most dedicated artist I've ever had the privilege to know and if she were here right now, she'd be kicking my butt from here to Tuesday for acting like this. So...what can I do to help?"

"I don't know what plans you had but would you contact her publisher and galleries?"

That seemed to be exactly what William needed to hear. Special friend or whatever he'd been to her, the transformation from grief-stricken man to power agent was almost magical as his fingers began tapping the keyboard of his laptop.

"Of course. I'm sure there are a number of galleries that will offer to send photographs to the service, but I'll keep the number low. I don't want this to look like a retrospective of your mother's work."

"Perfect."

William, all business now, looked at Morgan over the laptop screen. "Where will it be?"

"Graybryer Memorial Gardens."

William nodded. "Right, the Munn family…good people. And that's such a beautiful place. Your mother took some of her best-known photographs there."

"I know."

"And the service will be in the chapel?"

"Yes. I'm going over there at ten to make the arrangements."

William looked at his Rolex and nodded. "Might I make a suggestion, if it's not too presumptuous?"

Morgan nodded.

"When you select your mother's casket, try not to pick something too bold. Not black and definitely not white. I don't think Christine would have appreciated that. Maybe something in the gray scale to emulate her work?"

"I'll have to see what's available, but that's a good idea." It was a great idea and just the thought of picking out a casket for his mother, regardless of color, made his stomach twist into a knot.

"Subtlety was her forte…until Sebastian. There's nothing subtle about the photographs she took of him, except those first ones. After that your mother wanted the world to see him in all his glory." The old man picked up the handkerchief and touched a corner to his left nostril. "Morgan, are you thinking of bringing Sebastian to the service?"

"What?"

"He was so much a part of her last year, of her life, that I thought—"

"No." Morgan got to his feet and stepped away from the desk. "I have to go, William."

"Of course." It took longer for the older man to stand and walk around the desk, and it was all Morgan could do to wait and return the quick hug. "And you're right. Sebastian shouldn't come."

Morgan had hoped for a quick and easy escape, but William followed him out of his office and through the reception area where Ahern's assistant/secretary met Morgan's eyes and smiled, sadly, but didn't offer any verbal condolences.

William opened the office door and held it for Morgan. "I know how hard a time this is for you and your family, Morgan, so if there's anything else I can do, please don't hesitate to call."

"I will, promise."

"I'm so very sorry for your loss, Morgan."

"You, too, William."

Morgan could hear the old man begin to cry again as the door closed between them.

⋆ ⋆ ⋆

"Damn, Morg, I'm so sorry."

Morgan accepted the condolence and scotch and soda with a nod. It was just after ten in the morning, but who was going to deny a man the comfort of friendship and twelve-year-old single malt in his moment of grief?

No one in the cozy office off the casket display room, that was for sure.

"Thanks, Chet."

Morgan took a sip and almost forgot how to swallow. A long intake of air helped but only marginally. He'd called his friend after going into work for just long enough to let his manager know what happened and ask for the morning off to deal with funeral arrangements. He got the full day off with pay and managed to escape with only a few heartfelt condolences before the majority of the staff arrived.

Chet had been waiting for him in the main lobby with the bottle.

"Smooth, huh?"

Morgan nodded. He'd asked Chet to go light on the pour, and if that was light, he'd hate to find out what heavy was. "Very."

Chet finished off his glass and lifted the bottle. "Again?"

Morgan covered his glass with his hand. "I still have things to do and don't want to find out at the funeral that I picked a neon-pink casket."

"Not to worry. I already sold that one." Chet sighed and put both the bottle and his glass back on the small bar behind his desk. "You're right, you have things to do. But not as many as you think, so hold on to your glass." He opened the laptop on his desk and hit a few keys, then turned the screen to face Morgan. "We had this on file since your dad's funeral, but your mom called me about six months ago and updated it."

Beneath the Munn Family Funeral Home and Mortuary masthead were the words PRE-PLANNING WORKSHEET and his mother's full name: Christine Anne Morgan Riley. Below that was a stylized rose and below that a list of eight topics:

Type of service: Traditional
~~Related events:~~
Reception: TBA
Attendees: TBA
~~Officiants and Eulogizers:~~
~~Prayers and Readings:~~
Songs and Music: TBA
Pallbearers: Morgan Riley
Chet Munn
Robert Lowell-Walsh
Charles Lowell-Walsh
John McIlveen
Steven (Shen) Wan, M.D.
William James Ahern (alternate)
Charitable Donations: The Ground Floor Loft (Chestnut Hill, PA)
Casket/Liner: Londonderry Gray/Marshmallow Cream

He didn't even get to pick out the casket.

Morgan took a drink and barely noticed the burn.

"Scroll down if you want to see the memorial announcement."

Oh boy, something to do.

It was a standard white card with a gray border and black lettering – ***Celebrating the Life of Christine Morgan Riley*** – beneath a photograph of Sebastian standing next to a grave. Her life and death in black and white and shades of gray. With model.

"All you have to do is pick the date…any ideas?"

"What's the usual time frame?"

"Well, unless there are religious reasons that require a near immediate burial…a week more or less." When Morgan didn't say anything, his friend nonchalantly nodded to the Munn Family Funeral Home & Mortuary wall calendar. Naturally the photograph was one of his mother's. "How about ten days from now? That will make it Friday the 8th…oh, just before Mother's D— Oh, shit, Morg, I'm sorry."

"It's okay, Chet. Yeah, let's go for the 8th. Time…uh…late afternoon? I know that's rush hour but you know how my mom loved shadows."

Morgan was very proud of himself; he'd managed to say that without taking a drink.

So he took one as a reward.

Chet added that to the checklist on his mother's worksheet. "Good. We can start the visitation hour at 5:30 to give people time to get here and then the gravesite service to follow?"

"Okay."

The sound of key taps was almost soothing.

"What about the reception?"

"Um…."

"We have a reception room that can accommodate about one hundred attendees, but I have a feeling there might be more than that?"

Morgan took another swallow. "Probably. Can I get back to you on that, Chet?"

"Sure, but you really don't have a whole lot of time. I can get the announcements out as soon as you give me the names of the people you want to invite."

"You don't have to do that, Chet."

His friend patted the laptop. "Already in the contract. Your mom didn't want to burden you or Holly in any way. So…any ideas?"

Um. "Let me call William…mom's agent…maybe he'll have an idea."

"Good, you do that and I'll go hit the vending machine in the break room. Some of it is even real food."

"Nothing for me, thanks, I'm not hungry."

"I don't care if you're hungry or not, you're going to eat something to soak up that booze you just finished. Be right back."

Morgan looked at the empty glass in his hand and carefully set it on the desk. And just as carefully dialed the agent's number.

William picked up on the second electronic ring. "Morgan. What can I do for you?"

"William, do you have any idea where we can hold the…the memorial after…everything? Chet can't do it here because there's not enough room and I also need a list of names. Do you know who mom's friends were? I know some of them, but not all of them, and did you know that she pre-planned her own funeral? I didn't know that…." Morgan stopped when he finally heard himself. Maybe food wasn't such a bad idea. "Sorry, William."

"No apologies necessary, Morgan. I didn't know about the pre-plan, though that does sound like your mother. As for the announcements…I've just brought up your mother's mailing list and I'm afraid it's rather extensive. Your mother had a great number of professional friends and admirers, as well as business acquaintances, but I can cull the list, if you like."

Morgan didn't have to think about it. "No, just send the whole thing to Chet."

There was a moment's silence. "Done. As for anyone else, I'd suggest you look in her address book or, what I did when my own mother died was to look at her Christmas card list. Any overlap of names won't be a problem, I'm sure. Now, all we need is a place for the reception. What date did you decide for the funeral?"

"May 8th."

"I have an idea for a venue, but might have to do a bit of professional cajolery first." He sounded like his mother's agent again and not the broken man Morgan had left only an hour before. "Tell Chet I'll cc him the information when I send it to you. If it works out. Fingers crossed."

Morgan leaned back in his chair. "Fingers crossed. Thanks, William."

"No, thank *you*, Morgan. Thank you for allowing me to do this for her."

Morgan ended the call as the door opened behind him.

"William has an idea for the reception. He has to find out first but he'll let us know as soon as he can."

"Good old William," Chet said and handed him a paper-towel-wrapped sesame-seed bagel smeared with cream cheese and strawberry jam.

"You got this out of a vending machine?"

"No, one of my embalmers brought them in this morning. Her dad runs a deli." He reached behind him and opened a dorm-sized refrigerator, pulling out two bottles of water. "Unless you'd rather have processed cheese-flavored cardboard snacks."

Morgan shook his head and took a bite. "Mmmm."

"So we may have a venue. Great."

"And William sent you a list of names. It should be in your inbox and I'll send you one when I find my mother's address book."

"Or you could just drop it off."

Morgan took another bite.

"With her outfit."

And almost choked. "Outfit?"

"Go down the wrong pipe? Drink some water. Yeah, the outfit your mother's going to be…for the funeral. It doesn't have to be fancy or new…you'd be surprised at some of the ensembles we get. A few still have price tags on them. But you knew your mom better than anyone, so just pick something you think she'd be happy with…and if you think she'd like a party dress…then bring a party dress. And don't worry about getting it cleaned, we'll do that here."

"Full service, huh?"

"You know it. Hey, look, I know it's hard and if I could do this for you…."

"I appreciate it, but—" *It's one of the few things that's left for me to do.* "—I still have to find the address book…if I can find it."

"You might want to check her computer for a Christmas card list. What's so funny?"

"Nothing, just…nothing. Sorry."

"Don't be. I don't get to hear a lot of laughter in here. The receptions, yes, but not here. This isn't the fun part. And since we're on the subject…how many death certificates do you think you'll need? I can give you twenty to start but can order more if you need them."

That seemed like a lot. "Let's see…the hospital already has one and you'll need one…that's two, and I'll need one to close out her bank accounts so I can transfer the funds…that will make five, no six, and another for her financial planner…and I'll probably need to send copies to her utilities and refuse company, but I'm not sure about that, although I will need one for the IRS when I file her final tax return and her life insurance and…I know I'm missing some things. Can you think of anything I haven't covered and why are you looking at me like that?"

His friend had been watching him like a pay-per-view sporting event.

"It's just nice being in the presence of someone who already has some idea of the more mundane aspect of death."

"Just part of being a banker."

"I thought you were an accountant."

CHAPTER SEVENTEEN

It felt wrong going back into that house, her house, and I'm not just saying because it was empty. I'd been in there alone plenty of times before. I'm not saying I was a latchkey kid but sometimes I'd come home from school and find a note taped to the newel post from my mother telling me where she was – with her camera, naturally – and when she might be back and that I'd either find dinner in the refrigerator or money to order whatever I liked.

Unless it was the second Monday of the month and then she'd put the money on one of the takeout menus she never threw out with her selections circled in red pen.

No, I wasn't afraid, it wasn't that. I know that house as well as I know my own face. I grew up there. I lived my childhood in those rooms. Even after I grew up and moved out, it was still my house…part mine…mine and hers. But it still felt like mine.

Before that it was my father's and hers and mine.

Before that it belonged to them, my father and her.

Now it's just mine.

Except it's not.

Somewhere I'd become a visitor…still her son, still on the deed, thank God, but not a part of it. It's still her house and probably always will be.

And that's what made it feel so wrong about walking in like nothing had happened, like I belonged there.

But I don't.

You know why they say you can never go home again – because the home you had is gone. The house might still be there but the home, the place where you lived, doesn't exist anymore. It can't.

I remember when I was little, I liked to stand at the landing at the top of the staircase and look over the railing and think how far away the floor looked. It was like standing on the top of a mountain. Now it's not that high.

Perceptions change as you grow up. Staircases aren't that tall and rooms you used to race around aren't as big as you thought they were. You can't go home again because the home you remember is only a memory that doesn't quite match the real world. It might look the same and smell the same and have the same wallpaper or paint or bathroom fixtures but it won't be the same house you grew up in. Too much time and life has passed between then and now.

★ ★ ★

Morgan closed the door as quietly as he could, but the snap of the latch bolt sliding into the strike plate echoed up the stairs and down the hall into the kitchen, momentarily filling the empty rooms but passing too quickly.

He'd been in the house alone before, but there was always something of her still there…even if it was just the knowledge that she'd be back.

Morgan closed his eyes.

The house wasn't supposed to be quiet. There'd always been some kind of background noise – music, thuds and clinks of the water pipes, creaks and groans of floor joists, the rasp of windblown curtains, the sound of wind chimes from the backyard, her voice – always some sound.

Most of them where still there – the clunks and rattles and wind chimes – he could hear them but the house was still quiet, and that quiet had nothing to do with sound.

It had everything to do with loss.

Stop it.

Morgan took a deep breath and felt his nose wrinkle. He should have opened a window before he left. In the three days since the paramedics took his mother away – *God, only three days* – the urine stench had had time to marinate. And mutate. There was a sharp chemical reek that made Morgan's eyes water.

Jesus, the developing chemicals in the basement.

What was he going to do about all those chemicals? There had to be a procedure for getting rid of them; he couldn't just dump them down the drain.

Could he?

Morgan took out his cellphone and opened the notepad app, added *EPA disposal/developing chemicals* to the growing list that included *carpet (rip out and replace?), paint/clean/pro, lawn service, storage unit, find address book/Xmas list, funeral clothes.*

He deleted the last two entries and put the phone away. With any luck he'd find what he needed without having to tear the house apart or look into too many drawers, drive back to Bala Cynwyd and....

And what?

He'd been given the day off to 'take care of things', so the *last* thing he wanted to do was to walk into the branch and be bombarded with sympathy and sad looks and condolences and have to tell them his mother had died before she got a chance to see the basket or balloon, and that he'd left the balloon floating in an ICU room and the basket in the surgical waiting room.

And he'd even forgotten the get-well card.

Dammit.

Of course he could always check Zillow again.

Morgan hadn't even thought about selling the house until his wife asked what he planned to do with it. Up until that moment he still thought of it as his mother's house. Did he *want* to sell it? That wasn't a legitimate question. Obviously, he had to sell it; there was no way they could afford the upkeep or taxes.

Could they? His mother's estate alone could probably handle that and there'd be money coming in from the sales of her photographs and calendars for some time to come.

They could afford the house if he wanted to keep it and it would save him God knows how much on capital gains tax. Morgan didn't know how much his father had originally paid, although he could find out, and the last time his mother had it appraised in 2017, it was skirting the million-dollar mark.

Last night's Zillow estimate was $1,195,431.00.

But not selling the house would mean – *being closer to work, having a real backyard, putting Hannah in a top-notch school system* – he'd have to live there.

Besides, his mother had always joked about turning it into The Christine Morgan Riley Museum of Photographic Art.

I talked to the neighbors and they think it's a wonderful idea.

Which would give him a great tax break.

"What do you think, Mom?" Morgan whispered as he walked to the gallery.

"What the hell?"

There were more photographs hanging on the walls and lining the shelves and they were all of Sebastian.

And just like that the decision was made.

He'd give the photographs to William to sell, bring in an appraiser for the antiques and an estate agent for everything else, then toss or keep or give away whatever was left, clean what needed to be cleaned, repair what needed to be repaired and put the house on the market as quickly as was humanly and legally possible.

But first he had to find his mother's address book and pick out an outfit.

The urine and chemical smells were stronger in the living room, but Morgan ignored them the same way he ignored the manikin, half-hidden behind the arm of the chair where the police officer had put it as if it was playing a game of hide-and-seek.

Déjà vu all over again.

Morgan was checking the drawer on the reading table when his mother walked in from the dining room, the hem of her oversized white pintuck blouse billowing out behind her.

"Morgan! I thought that was you."

He almost knocked the reading lamp off the table. He did knock his mother's cellphone to the floor.

"I'm sorry. I didn't mean to startle you."

The woman was older than his mother, somewhere hovering near the late-eighties mark, although she'd seemed that age for as long as Morgan could remember, and wore sunglasses around her neck instead of a camera. She didn't look anything like his mother. Except for the blouse.

Morgan picked up the phone and put it back on the table. "That's okay, Mrs. McIlveen. I didn't hear you."

"I was out back watering. If it's already this hot I can't imagine what summer will be like. I saw you drive up but...." She took a deep breath. "I've been coming over to water the plants and turn the lights on at night. Your mother and I made house keys for each other. I'd come over to water when she flew out to an opening or spent the weekend somewhere taking photographs and she'd do the same for me when I visited my grandchildren in.... Oh, Morgan."

Morgan nodded and helped her to his mother's chair, avoiding the spot directly in front of it where she'd fallen and prepared himself for another bout of weeping that could easily eclipse William's. But Mrs. McIlveen surprised him.

"I'm so sorry, Morgan." Her voice was thick but steady and even though her eyes glistened the tears didn't fall. "Was it...?"

Morgan squatted in front of the chair, still holding her hands while the manikin looked on.

"It was very peaceful."

"Good." He must have looked surprised. "When you get to a certain age, like your mother and me, it's not death you're afraid of, that's the easy part, you only worry about the path that brings you there. I am glad it was easy for her."

Since the doctor didn't say otherwise, there was no reason to believe it wasn't. "Amen."

"It will be hard to look at this house and not see her or Sebastian. They were always together since she brought him home."

Morgan glanced at the manikin.

"Was there anyone else? That you saw my mother with?"

She shook her head. "No, just Sebastian. Would you like me to tell the neighbors or would you rather do that?"

"I should, but...thank you. The funeral's on the 8th at Graybryer Memorial Gardens and you can tell everyone they'll be getting a mailed announcement for the service and reception. In fact, that's why I'm here. You wouldn't happen to know where my mother's address book...." The tears finally came, but they fell softly and without fanfare. "Oh, God, Mrs. McIlveen, I'm sorry, I shouldn't have gone on like that."

"No, it's fine. Just...I'm fine." The old woman took a deep breath and used a corner of the blouse to wipe her eyes. "She gave me this, you know? I saw her wearing one just like this when she and Sebastian were outside and told her how much I liked it and a few days later she brought me this. It didn't happen often but sometimes we'd both be wearing it and it always made her laugh...and say we could be twins." She cleared her throat. "Sorry."

"There's nothing for you to be sorry about, Mrs. McIlveen. In fact, if you'd like any of my mother's clothes, I think...I *know* she'd love you to have them."

"Oh, Morgan, I couldn't."

"Please."

"It wouldn't be right to just...take them."

"Well, how about this...." Morgan took the old woman's hands the same way he'd taken his mother's in the hospital. "I could use your help and that would be a fair exchange, wouldn't it?"

"I suppose. What do you need?"

"This might be asking too much and please feel free to say no, but I have to pick something for my mother to wear...."

The old woman's smile folded across her cheeks. "I would be honored, Morgan. Do you know what colors we're working with?"

It was a very nice way of asking the color of the casket and liner without actually saying it. He'd have to remember that.

"Gray and white."

"She'd love that. And I think I know the perfect going-away outfit. You don't think she'd want to wear a dress, do you?"

"Whatever you chose will be fine." Morgan stood up and helped her to her feet. "And please, if there are any clothes you'd like...as a remembrance, just put them on the bed and I'll have them cleaned and bring them over to you."

"Nonsense. If I do find something I'll show it to you and clean it myself." Morgan took her arm and helped her, slowly and carefully, up the stairs to his mother's room. "Did you say something about your mother's address book?"

"Yes."

"If it's anywhere it's probably in the desk in her office, or the computer. I use the tablet my son gave me as a coaster, but your mother loved computers." Morgan let go of her arm when they reached the upstairs landing. "I'll check her nightstand if you like."

"That would be great," Morgan said, but the hallway was empty and he could hear the scrape of plastic clothes hangers being pushed across a metal rod as the old woman ruffled through his mother's closet.

Going-away outfit…check.

That just left finding the address book and/or Christmas list to get and he could leave.

The door of his mother's office, a converted guest room at the front of the house, was open, as were all the doors on the second floor with the exception of the door to Hannah's bedroom. Maybe Hannah had asked his mother to keep her door closed whenever she wasn't there. Because she was growing up and needed her privacy.

And since that was something else he didn't need or want to think about, the gods took pity on him.

Morgan found both his mother's address book – which was one they'd given her two Christmases ago – and a flash drive labeled CHRISTMAS CARD LIST/2021update.

He felt almost giddy when he walked down the hall to his mother's room and to make sure the feeling didn't go away, Morgan stopped at the threshold.

"Found them." He held up the address book and flash drive as he leaned against the doorframe.

"Yay!" Mrs. McIlveen tossed his mother's long black sweater-coat next to a pale gray sweater on the black-and-white floral bedspread. Black-and-white-and-gray-and…. "What do you think about this?"

She disappeared into the walk-in closet and came out holding a shimmering silver and blue dress Morgan had never seen before.

"Isn't it lovely? Oh, I know, it's completely inappropriate for the occasion but I just love it."

"Keep it."

She didn't even attempt to put up a fight. The dress joined its more sedate companions on the bed. "If you insist, but I have no idea where I'd wear it. Maybe to dust when I'm feeling blue…that would cheer me up…unless my son is there and then you'll have to tell him I haven't lost my mind." She disappeared back into the closet. "I thought I had the perfect outfit in mind, but your mother bought so many beautiful new clothes, it's really hard to decide."

Morgan straightened but didn't leave. "She did?"

There was more rattling of hangers. "Oh my, yes. Loads of them! And in so many colors. Do you know the first time I saw your mother in something other than black or white I almost didn't recognize her? Can you imagine?"

He could.

"But, it's that certain age thing again…one day you look at yourself and say 'why not?' Oh, I think these…." She handed Morgan a pale blue silk scarf-tie blouse and white linen slacks and hurried back to the closet. He recognized the slacks. "And *this*."

The vest was long and made of a sheer material the color of mist and morning and rain and water and floated behind the old woman like a cloud. "Isn't this beautiful? I saw her wearing this the other day when she was walking with Sebastian. She looked so happy." Morgan saw the wrinkles around her mouth deepen as she handed him the vest. "I think these will do."

Morgan hooked the three hangers over his fingers. "I think so, too. Thank you, Mrs. McIlveen."

"Shoes!" Mrs. McIlveen hurried to the closet and came back with a pair of low-heel white leather pumps with peek-a-boo toes. What his wife would have called *Septuagenarian Date-Night Shoes*. "These will go perfectly with the outfit. Do you think pantyhose or knee-highs?

Knee-highs...they're much easier to get on." That seemed to be the right answer because the old woman nodded as she crossed the room to his mother's dresser.

"Top right," he said. "She was always getting runs and sending me up to get her a new pair."

"You're a good son."

Present tense, not past. Morgan liked that and felt a smile starting, which immediately changed direction when Mrs. McIlveen opened the top left drawer and pulled out a pair of his mother's panties and bra.

They were both at a loss of words. Chet hadn't mentioned those two particular items and Morgan really didn't feel like calling to find out.

Mrs. McIlveen folded the panties and nylons into the bra and closed both drawers. "I'll just put these in a plastic shopping bag. I know where your mother kept them in the kitchen. I'll come back and finish this later."

"Thanks." Morgan slung the clothes over one shoulder and stepped back into the hall, taking Mrs. McIlveen's arm again when they reached the top of the stairs.

Morgan let go of her arm when they reached the bottom of the stairs and draped the clothes over the newel post while she headed for the kitchen. Morgan caught the manikin still watching from behind his mother's chair – *peek-a-boo* – when he turned to follow.

"Looks like Mom went on a spending spree," he said when he walked into the kitchen. It was still early enough that the kitchen was mostly in shadow, the air was cool and still, the smell of coffee and cooking and lemon dish soap missing.

There was something though....

"Here you go." Mrs. McIlveen handed him an ACME shopping bag, handles tied together. There was a large black trash bag over her arm.

"I don't think I'll need that for the clothes."

She looked down at the bag as if she'd forgotten it was there. "This? Oh, no, tomorrow's trash day so I thought I'd clean out the refrigerator. I was going to check anyway, but now I guess we should toss everything?"

"I can do that. You've already done a lot."

"And you have much more to do. Let me do this. My son always comes over to take out my trash so he'll do the heavy lifting. Please."

Morgan guessed it came from having been raised by a strong-willed, independent and determined woman, but he couldn't say no.

"Okay, but same deal as with the clothes, if you find anything, especially in the freezer, just take it. Mom didn't like to waste food."

"Don't I know it." Laughing, Mrs. McIlveen opened the trash bag as she walked to the double-wide refrigerator/freezer. "Your mother brought me enough Thanksgiving leftovers that sometimes I didn't have to cook for a week! But I'm not a big fan of Chinese food."

She opened the refrigerator door and Morgan immediately recognized the smell.

"Chinese food."

"Oh yes, your mother loved her Chinese food, but it's a bit salty for me." The top half of the old woman disappeared behind the open door as she began dropping takeout containers into the trash bag. A *lot* of takeout containers. "And I know what you said about wasting food, but there's just so much of it."

"There is?" Morgan headed for the refrigerator. "We…I mean she only had it once a month. The second Monday."

"That's right, I remember when you used to do that," Mrs. McIlveen said, still filling the bag, "but not for a while."

"No."

"Well, I guess that's why she started having it delivered. Oh, dear, most of these are almost full."

Morgan came around to the front of the refrigerator. Except for a gallon of chocolate milk and a carton of eggs, the shelves were lined with takeout cardboard and plastic containers.

"She wasn't supposed to…. Do you know how often she—"

"A few times a week," Mrs. McIlveen said and gave Morgan a guilty, I've-been-caught look. "I'm a snoop, what can I say?"

"Mrs. McIlveen, was my mother seeing someone?"

The guilty look changed to shock. "Someone as in a gentleman friend?"

Morgan nodded.

"No." She shook her head. "No one came over that I saw and, like I said, I'm a snoop. There wasn't anyone. Except Sebastian, of course, but I don't think he counts. No, your mother was alone."

Your mother was alone. "Yeah, okay. Thanks, Mrs. McIlveen…I really should get those things over to…. But I can stay…."

"No, I'll call my son. You do what you need to do. And Morgan—" She held onto the bag as she turned toward him. "I'm so very sorry."

Morgan leaned down and kissed her cheek. "Thank you, Mrs. McIlveen."

Her cheeks reddened. "Remember, call if you need me to do anything else."

"I will. Shall I lock the door, or will you?"

"Lock it. I'll go out the back. Bless you, Morgan."

Morgan looked straight ahead as he left the house, which, as it turned out, gave him a clear view of the single daffodil in the middle of the front lawn.

Where the snowman had been.

* * *

Chet was with a client when Morgan came back, so he handed the clothes and shoes and baggie to the receptionist and left after accepting another professional condolence and thanks for having chosen the Munn Family Funeral Home and Mortuary in his time of sorrow.

When he got back to the car, Morgan thought about texting his friend and suggesting he cut the appreciation tagline since it sounded uncomfortably similar to what every flight attendant says when their airline touches the ground, but decided it wasn't worth the effort.

For all he knew it was a standard practice in the funeral biz.

Chet called when he was pulling around the funeral home's circular front drive.

"Morg, sorry I missed you. Ari gave your mom's things to the mortician and I'm about to head out to pick up your mom.... Oh, is that you?"

Morgan glanced in the rearview mirror and saw his friend wave through the black transit van's windshield. He pulled into the curb, stopped and rolled down the window.

The van, a cargo model, pulled up alongside. The passenger-side window was already down. Chet waved his cellphone and turned it off. Morgan did the same.

"How are you doing?"

"Not bad."

"Truth, Morg."

"Okay...how about I wish this was over. Is that a feeling?"

Chet nodded. "Better. Oh, and your mom's agent called. Wow, what a venue, huh?"

Morgan waited. "Are you going to tell me?"

"You mean he didn't call you?"

Morgan looked at his phone. He'd turned off the sound, but his voicemail indicator was flashing. He thumbed the sound back on.

"Yeah...but why don't you just tell me."

"Okay...are you sitting down?" Morgan lifted a finger. "Okay. The Philadelphia Art Museum's Ruth and Raymond G. Perelman Building. Is that unbelievable or what? If there's a heaven, your mom is doing the cha-cha."

Morgan couldn't help but smile at that mental picture. "That really is amazing."

"He gave me all the details, so I'll start work on the announcement card when I get back." He stopped smiling. "We'll do her proud, Morg, I promise."

Morgan gave Chet a thumbs up as the van pulled away and was about to follow when his phone rang.

And almost let it roll over when he saw the Caller ID.

"Hi, William."

"Morgan, wonderful news! I've contacted the Philadelphia Art

Museum and, with your approval, we can hold your mother's memorial reception at the Ruth and Raymond G. Perelman Building."

"That's great." Morgan tried to force enthusiasm and failed. "Really, great. Thanks."

"It is. Have to run, but I'll call later to discuss the details. Your mother would be..." His voice broke. "I'll talk to you later, Morgan."

"Okay."

Neither of them said goodbye and Morgan was about to put his phone away when he saw there was still a voicemail from William J. Ahern waiting for him from the night his mother died.

Morgan turned off the car's ignition.

—You have one new voicemail from...William. J. Ahern.—

Except it wasn't from William.

"Morr-an, ing suhbaa-znn."

—Message saved.—

CHAPTER EIGHTEEN

You know those times when you simply want to go into a dark room and lock the door behind you and just sit there…maybe with a drink, hell, maybe with a whole bottle, until the world forgets where you are?

No?

Lucky you.

Well, that's what I wanted to do, but I went into the office instead because it was still early enough that I knew if I went home there was a really good chance I would lock myself away with a bottle and I didn't want my wife or daughter to see me like that.

So I went to work and everyone treated me like I was made of glass and that was fine.

It's very awkward, you know, to be around someone who's just suffered a loss…there's only so many times you can tell them you're sorry or my prayers are with you, or, my personal favorite, at least she's at peace.

My mother would have.… I don't know what she would have done.

But for the most part my coworkers pretty much left me alone and that gave me the opportunity to pretend to be working while I actually read articles on how to talk to your children about death.

But it's not as simple and easy and straightforward as they would like you to believe.

Not by a long shot.

But I was confident I'd be able to do it…the hard part was deciding what to make for dinner.

I'll explain.

Hannah had cheer squad practice after school and Holly's one of the coaching assistants, so it was my turn to make dinner and I knew that whatever I made, it would always remind her of the night she found out her Grammy died.

See the problem? Pizza? Wawa? Daddy's Famous Canned Spaghetti and Scrambled Hamburger? Fish sticks? Chicken tenders? They're all Hannah's favorites and one of them was going to be sacrificed.

No, I was definitely not going to order Chinese food.

★ ★ ★

Morgan turned off the oven when he heard the patio door open and shut, and met them in the hallway. His daughter did a quick cheer routine that included a kick and spin and ended in a hug around his waist.

"Hi, Daddy!"

"Hi, back at'cha, Hannah-Banana. That was really cool."

"Yeah, she's really coming along. You'd be proud of her."

"I am proud of her," he said and met his wife's eyes. She shook her head and shrugged. "Hannah, go wash up. Dinner's almost ready. Fish sticks and sweet potato fries."

That was their daughter's favorite-*favorite* dinner and one Morgan had originally rejected from his list early, but if there was a chance she'd eat anything that night, her favorite-favorite might do the trick.

Hannah did another routine – pirouette, crouched and then a jump, arms raised in a V. "Yay, Daddy!"

Morgan watched Hannah high-kick into the downstairs powder room and put an arm around Holly's shoulders. "Yay, Daddy."

"How are you doing?"

"Okay."

"When should we tell her?"

That had been an even bigger question than what to make for dinner. Before dinner and she might not want to eat, after dinner and she could toss it back up.

The night his father died, Morgan and his mother had had dinner and watched TV and gone to bed as if it was just another night, then he waited until he was sure she was asleep before going downstairs and vomiting in the hall bathroom.

He hadn't eaten a sausage and green pepper pizza since.

"I don't know."

Hannah came out of the bathroom. There were water spots on the front of her *WEE-YELL Cheer Squad* t-shirt and her face was still wet.

"Daddy, Coach Denise asked me to ask you to ask Grammy if she can take our cheer team picture again like last year? We have county competition in two weeks and need a new team picture."

His mother had been the squad's official photographer since Hannah joined cheer.

"I'm sorry, Morg, I didn't get a chance to speak to Denise alone."

"It's okay, Mommy, I told Coach Denise that Grammy is sick but you said she'd be better so can she? If she's better?"

Morgan looked at Holly. "You know, I forgot to make a salad, would you mind, hon?"

"I can do it later."

"It's okay, do it now. And while you do that," Morgan held out his hand, "Hannah-Banana and I will have a little sit-down in the living room."

His daughter beat him to the couch. "Are you gonna call her now, Daddy? It's not late."

All the articles he'd read on explaining death to a child – without causing irreparable harm or immediate trauma – might have differed on the how, but more or less agreed that the child should be told as soon as possible after a loved one died and emphasized using plain and simple terms that are appropriate to the age of the child.

His mother had done that. *"Your father's dead, Morgan. Be strong."*

"Come here, baby." Morgan patted his lap and an instant later she filled it. "You know Grammy was in the hospital."

His daughter nodded. "Because she's sick. Is she better?"

"No, Hannah, she's not." Morgan looked up when Holly came into the room and sat down next to them. "Grammy was very sick."

Morgan felt his daughter tense in his arms. *She already knows.*

"But she's in the hospital, like before, and the doctors made her better."

"Yes, they did, but Grammy wasn't as sick as she was this time and sometimes a person is so sick even doctors can't make them better." Morgan turned his daughter's face toward his. "Hannah, Grammy was too sick to get better. She died. I'm so sorry, Hannah."

Her body went rigid then collapsed against him, sobs rolling through her body in waves. All Morgan could do was hold her and let her cry while his wife stroked her back and whispered it was okay, everything was going to be okay and the fish sticks dried out and the fries turned into cardboard and the salad got warm.

When the deep sobs tapered off into snivels, Morgan handed her off to Holly so he could grab a couple tissues from the box on the coffee table.

"Oh Hannah, I'm so sorry, baby." Holly was rocking her slowly back and forth, the way she did when Hannah was a baby. "I'm so sorry."

Morgan held the tissues until the sniffles faded into an occasional hiccup and he was able to wipe her face.

"I know how you feel, baby, and it's okay to be sad. I'm sad, too. We all loved your Grammy very much and we will miss her for a long, long time. Right now it hurts so much it makes you feel empty inside, but it will get better. We won't ever forget Grammy, but the empty will go away, I promise. Here, blow your nose."

Morgan held the tissue while she blew, then folded the sopping wad into a ball in the palm of his hand.

"Daddy?"

"Yes, baby."

"I didn't say goodbye."

Morgan leaned forward and put his forehead against her so she wouldn't see the tears in his eyes. Daddies could do a lot of things, they could hold snotty tissues and rescue spiders from bathtubs and push you on swings and tell you your grandmother died, but they couldn't cry in front of you because that was too scary. Daddies had to be strong and brave and resilient even if it was only pretending.

"I didn't either, but you know Grammy loved you very much, right?"

She nodded.

"And love doesn't go away. So we can still love Grammy inside." Morgan touched a finger to the middle of his daughter's chest. "In here, can't we?"

Hannah nodded again. "I miss her."

"So do I. Your Grammy was a big part of our lives and we're always going to miss her, but I don't think she'd want us to be sad for too long, do you?"

Hannah shrugged. "Daddy?"

Morgan rubbed his eyes as he sat up. None of the articles he'd read mentioned a question-and-answer period and he hoped he was up to it. His wife nodded at him with tears in her eyes.

"Yes, baby."

"Do you think Grammy's taking pictures in heaven?"

Morgan looked at Holly and smiled. "I think there's a good chance she is."

"Yeah," Hannah said, "Grammy was all about the work."

His wife laughed and kissed the top of their daughter's head, and for a moment the world almost felt normal again.

"Daddy?"

"Yes, baby?"

She looked up at him, her eyes glistening and wide. "You need to go get Sebastian from the babysitter and bring him home. Here."

Morr-an, ing suhbaa-znn.

"Hannah, I don't think—"

"You *have* to, Daddy! He's all alone now. He *needs* us."

"Oh, Hannah." Holly shook her head. "Honey, Sebastian doesn't need us."

"Yes, he does, Mommy! He's just little and he's alone. He's probably really scared." She began crying again. "Please, Daddy, he's scared!"

Holly began rocking again, which made it hard for Morgan to cup Hannah's chin. "Hannah, baby, Sebastian isn't scared, he isn't anything. Sebastian isn't real, you know that."

"But he *is*!"

"Okay, okay, Hannah, shh." Holly began rocking faster. "Calm down."

"Grammy said Sebastian was like my baby brother. Grammy said…." The snivels returned. "He is real, Daddy. He is!"

Morgan took a deep breath. *Thanks, Mom.*

"She was just pretending, like you do when you play with your dolls. Sebastian isn't real, baby, it's just a prop…something Grammy used for her photographs."

"N'uh uh. Sebastian *is* real and he's *alone* and he's *scared*!" She wiggled out of her mother's arms and stood in front of him, her whole body shaking. "He's *real*!"

"*Enough!*"

He'd never yelled at her before and he'd never spanked her…and of the two at that moment, yelling was the better alternative and had the same effect. She stopped shaking and ran out of the room.

"Hannah…come back."

They found her curled up behind the sofa-recliner in the family room.

"Hannah, please." She peeked over the armrest…peek-a-boo…like the manikin. "I'm sorry I yelled. I won't do it again. Will you come sit down with me?"

She got up slowly and tucked herself into the corner farthest away from him. Holly remained standing just in case she took another runner.

"Hannah…."

"Please, Daddy. He's all alone."

"No, he's not." Morgan felt his wife's eyes on the back of his neck. "He's…with Mrs. McIlveen." *Jesus, Mom, look what you're making me do.* "You remember Mrs. McIlveen, she's Grammy's neighbor."

His daughter nodded. "With the little white dog."

Morgan nodded even though the little white dog had gone over the Rainbow Bridge when Hannah was still a toddler. She remembered it only from the photographs his mother had taken of her and the dog for the *First Encounter/First Friend* series.

"Yes, with the little white dog. Mrs. McIlveen has been taking care of Sebastian and she was your Grammy's best friend so…I think it will make Mrs. McIlveen feel better if Sebastian stays with her…for a little bit."

"But you'll bring Sebastian home after Mrs. McIlveen is all better."

Morr-an, ing suhbaa-znn.

"Of course he will," Holly said and saved him from being a total liar to his only child. "Sebastian's fine. So…do you feel up for fish sticks and fries?"

Hannah shook her head.

Goodbye forever, fish sticks. "How about a peanut butter and jelly sandwich?" Morgan asked.

"With strawberry jelly?"

"Is there any other kind? Okay?" She nodded and Morgan heard Holly give a sigh of relief. "I'll go make them right now."

"And while Daddy does that," Holly said, "we'll go clean up."

Morgan went into the kitchen and dumped the near-blackened fish sticks and fries into the trash. And because he already felt like the worst father in the history of the world, and that included the elder god Cronus, who ate his own children, Morgan ignored the loaf of organic twelve-grain and made the sandwiches with honey wheat.

It wasn't much in the way of dinner, but it was so ordinary that Hannah might not connect it with her grandmother's death the next time she had it for lunch.

Morgan smiled at his wife and daughter as they walked into the kitchen.

"Perfect timing," he said. "Dinner is served."

CHAPTER NINETEEN

And I guess that brings us up to the funeral.

Oh, and just to let you know, Hannah doesn't like strawberry jelly anymore.

★ ★ ★

It was perfect.

The dark clothes, the visible but controlled sorrow, the long, sinuous shadows cast by the late afternoon sun that crept ever so slowly toward the burial site, the carefully placed floral arrangements, the open grave and just the hint of the casket it held.

All that was missing was her, his mother, with her camera, telling him where to stand and what to do with his hands so he looked natural.

Morgan improvised by standing next to the grave, hands clasped in front of his dark gray suit, with his eyes downcast in the perfect pose of solemn and/or pensive grief, and his back to the sun so his shadow fell on her casket.

She would have crouched low to take the photograph, giving the impression that the viewer was looking up from the grave.

It would have been a quintessential Christine Morgan Riley photograph.

A Man's Grief – Mother and Son.

She would have loved that almost as much as what would have certainly been the final photograph in the series taken from above and shooting down at the Londonderry Mist with Marshmallow Cream satin casket – gray and white like he told Mrs. McIlveen – that rested snug and firm at the bottom of the grave, covered in shadows and the long-stemmed white roses Chet had given each mourner as they arrived.

It would have made a beautiful photograph – black shadows, white roses, gray casket.

Morgan shifted his weight and felt a rock move beneath the synthetic grass carpet the groundskeepers had laid out around the grave. His job was essentially done – he'd read Mary Elizabeth Frye's poem 'Do Not Stand at My Grave and Weep' while the casket was being lowered – but he still needed to stand and accept condolences as the mourners left. His wife stood next to him and held his arm.

They'd asked Hannah if she wanted to come or if she'd rather spend the day with Coach Denise and her daughter. Coach Denise had suggested the playdate herself when they told her the news and it was the option Hannah picked.

When Morgan dropped her off on the way to the cemetery, she'd told him she wanted to remember Grammy alive and happy, and it'd been one more sign his baby wouldn't be a baby much longer.

Morgan had been glad he was wearing sunglasses.

Then she'd asked him again to bring Sebastian home and his eyes stopped burning.

"How you holding up?" Holly asked.

Morgan took her hand and gave it a squeeze. "Okay. How about you?"

"My feet hurt. I shouldn't have worn new shoes."

"No one should."

"What?"

"Nothing. Why don't you go wait in the limo for me. I shouldn't be much longer."

"You sure?"

Morgan looked at the dozen or so mourners filing past the grave. There'd been almost two hundred people attending the funeral, but a good number of them – gallery owners, reviewers and clients mostly – had left after the memorial, either thinking the gravesite service was more for the immediate family and friends or in the vain hope that they could avoid some of downtown Philadelphia's traffic by getting to the reception venue early.

"Yeah, go on. Chet looks lonely."

They both turned toward the stretch limousine parked along the curb a few rows back from the gravesite. His friend had declined their invitation to sit in the back with them, opting instead to sit with the driver so he wouldn't intrude in their time of sorrow.

Morgan wished he had.

If they had walked from the mortuary parking lot to the gravesite, it might have taken four or five minutes, but driving along those same roads behind Chet's fully restored 1970s black Cadillac Hearse, nearly identical to the one he and his mother had followed at his father's funeral, took almost ten.

All of it passed in silence inside the limo's massive backseat while Morgan and Holly held hands. Chet being there would have been a diversion from the last few weeks.

"Okay, I think I will," she said and touched his arm before following a group of mourners down the gentle rise to the road.

Morgan watched Chet step away from the limo to take Holly's hand as she approached, and tossed the rose he was still holding into the grave. It landed on top of the others, not special, not unique, just one among the others...like him, not like her. His mother had been unique and special and one of a kind and now she was gone.

"Goodbye, Mom, rest in peace. I love you."

The tree shadows had covered the road by the time he got to the limousine. Holly was already in the backseat, shoes off, left leg over the right, rubbing her toes. Chet was standing by the open door, his coat – dark navy, not black – tossed over one shoulder.

"I had an idea and your wife thinks it's a good one."

Morgan ducked down when he reached the curb so he could see her face. "Oh?"

Holly smiled and continued to rub her foot.

"Yep," Chet said. "I was just telling Holly about a funeral tradition called the libation for the dead and got to thinking that it might be a nice thing to do for your mom. I've got a bottle of *Esperanto Añejo* tequila from a previous libation ceremony and it's really good tequila...eighty dollars a bottle."

Morgan stood and looked back over his shoulder. The shadows had deepened on the hill, diluting the colors from the floral arrangements and giving them a gray tone among the paler headstones and the black hollow of his mother's grave.

Black. And white. And gray.

In the morning the grave would be filled in and the flowers set around it until they withered and were tossed in the industrial-sized dumpster next to the mortuary's loading bay.

Chet was looking at him expectantly when Morgan turned around. "We really need to get to the reception…."

"I don't mean now. I thought the three of us could come back after."

"That sounds lovely," Holly said, "but just for the two of you."

"Are you feeling okay, hon?"

Holly nodded as she refolded her legs, right over left, and resumed rubbing. "Fine, I'm just tired and this way Hannah can come home early if she wants to. I already asked Jim and Tessa and they'll give me a ride back. Is that okay?"

Okay? It was as close to divine intervention as Morgan could have wished for – his daughter was at friends, his wife, in wanting a few hours of peace and quiet after a week…no, ten days of death and all that it entailed, had given him permission to do the one thing he'd been longing to do since the night his mother died.

Get drunk.

Morgan tried not to look as excited as he felt. "Well, Mom did like her margaritas, but eighty dollars is a bit expensive…."

He pantomimed pouring a bottle and Chet smiled. The sky was still bright, but on the ground it was almost getting too dark to see.

"As much as I loved your mom, and I did, she gets one drink. As for the rest of the bottle…well, let me just say I can attest that the sofas in the lobby are perfect for catching a few Zs, if it comes to that."

Tempting. "Okay."

"Okay." While his wife scooted across the backseat to give him room, his friend grabbed his coat and held the door until Morgan was inside. He tried not to, but couldn't stop himself from looking at the grave as the limo pulled away.

"It's been a long day."

Morgan leaned back against the seat and nodded. "Sure has."

"But it's going to get better."

"I know."

"And Hannah will be okay."

"I know."

"I've been thinking that maybe we should go back to the house tomorrow and get Sebastian. I think it will help."

By *the house* she meant *his mother's.*

By *we* she meant *him.*

By *I think it will help* she meant *so she'll stop whining about it.*

"I'll think about it," he said.

And by that I mean No way in hell!

★ ★ ★

Morgan could look at the trays of champagne weaving in and out of the crowd and sip his ginger ale without regret. He'd had a glass, raised just after he and his wife arrived, in memory of his mother. It was good champagne and he'd relished the sweet/sharp apple-peel tang as the bubbles burst against his tongue and palate, but he had a bottle of golden tranquility waiting for him.

All he had to do was get through the rest of the evening.

A woman walked up and raised her flute. Morgan returned the gesture with his deceptive highball glass.

"Your mother was a phenomenal talent," the woman said. "There'll never be another Christine Morgan Riley."

"No, there won't."

"Are you a photographer?"

"No."

"Pity."

That wasn't the first time Morgan had heard that sentiment.

But he stopped taking it personally shortly before Holly left.

Morgan didn't know what favors or coercion or magic William Ahern had used to obtain a private function room in the Ruth and Raymond G. Perelman Building of the Philadelphia Museum of Art, but the end result was much more than a private memorial. The museum wanted to move the reception photographs into a public gallery as a retrospective exhibition of his mother's work.

Christine Morgan Riley (1949-2022)

A Life in Black and White/The Sebastian Series.

If there were such things as ghosts, he could easily picture his mother standing at the front of the cavernous room filled with the photographs she'd taken of the manikin, hands on her hips, head cocked to one side and maybe tapping her ethereal peek-a-boo white pump against the floor and muttering, "Of course they give me this, now that I'm dead!"

Morgan lifted his glass to the photograph directly in front of him. It was one of the first she'd taken of them at Graybryer, with the manikin standing naked at one end of a child's grave while he stood at the other. He'd thought it was morbid while he was posing, but now he saw what his mother had done. The photograph, *Always with You*, showed that love doesn't die.

"You were a phenomenal talent." Morgan raised the glass higher. "Top of the world, Ma."

"*White Heat*," a voice to his right said. "That's one of my favorite movies."

Morgan turned and nodded. "Mine, too. Hers too, I guess. I remember we always watched it together when it came on. 'Top of the world, Ma,' my dad used to say when she got a new show. She'd tell us about a new gallery opening or something and he'd say 'top of the world, Ma'. This is amazing, William. It really is."

"So, you think she would have approved?"

Morgan kept his ghostly fantasy to himself. "Oh, my God, yes. This would have made her very proud."

William nodded. "I think so, too. I just wish I could have done this for her when she was still here. To you, Christine." He lifted his flute to the ceiling then downed the contents. Morgan tensed, ready to grab the old man's arm if he suddenly lost his balance. "Top of the world, Ma, top of the world. I've been talking to the museum and they'd like to buy Sebastian."

"What?"

"Morgan…sorry, I don't mean to interrupt—" It was the company's CEO and after nodding apologetically, he continued to interrupt. "—but my wife and I are leaving and I just wanted to give you my condolences again. And to tell you how wonderful I think your mother's work was."

"Is," William corrected him. Morgan bit the inside of his cheek to keep from smiling. "Christine's work still *is*."

"Of course," the CEO said. "I didn't mean to imply—"

"And we always buy her calendars," the CEO's wife said, obviously feeling left out of the interruptions. "In fact, our son just gave us the Sebastian calendar for Christmas. I tell all my friends Christine Morgan Riley's son works for my husband's company. Will there be any more?"

It took a moment for Morgan to figure out what Mrs. Head Office/Owner was asking. "I believe so. Oh, I'm sorry, this is William Ahern, my mother's agent."

William nodded. "How do you do. And to answer your question, that's up to Morgan to decide. There are more than enough photographs that have not been made public, so if Morgan wishes to continue marketing his mother's work, then yes, I can assure you that there will be more calendars to come."

Both the CEO and his wife looked at Morgan with something verging on awe.

"Well, we certainly hope there will be. Your mother's work was… *is* remarkable." He shook both Morgan's and William's hands. "I'm so sorry for your loss, Morgan."

"Thank you."

"Interesting people," William said.

"Yeah…what did you say about the museum wanting to buy the manikin?"

"They want to buy him first for the exhibit of your mother's work and then possibly as a permanent installation piece. They're offering twenty thousand."

Morgan almost dropped his glass. "For a manikin."

"No, for Sebastian. It's a fair price but they hinted they'd be willing to go as high as twenty-seven thousand five hundred."

"Jesus." Morgan finished the ginger ale and replaced it with a flute of champagne. Which he also finished. "You're joking."

"No, why would I?"

"Because it's just a store dummy, William. My mother got it in a going out of business sale."

"And Vincent Van Gogh only sold one of his paintings while he was alive, *The Red Vineyard*, for 440 Francs in 1888…that was about seventy-six in US currency."

"I understand, William, but I can go online and buy another manikin just like it for probably less than seventy-six US currency."

William shook his head. "No, you can't, Morgan. I looked. I had thought about buying one for my office reception area but…. Well, your mother was not only against it – 'There could only be one Sebastian' she told me – but threatened to find another agent if I pursued the idea. Of course, I knew she didn't mean that, but I understood.

"Sebastian may only be a manikin that your mother bought on sale, just like any other manikin, but it was your mother's talent that transformed him into something else. Sebastian has become a cultural icon, Morgan, and that's what the museum is buying.

"Although I'm sure there are probably private collectors who would pay even more for him."

"That's nuts."

"No, Morgan, that's art." William exchanged his empty flute for a fresh one without missing a beat as a tray went by. "And may it continue."

Morgan did the same, with a bit less grace.

"What would Mom say to that?"

"To the Perelman buying Sebastian…she'd say no. She wanted you to have him. Well, Hannah, actually. Your mother knew how much your daughter loved him, almost as much as she did herself." Morgan watched the cut glass catch the light as the old man lifted to drink. "We talked about it once, after her accident in December...she worried what would happen to Sebastian when she...after she was gone. You get to a certain age and you start thinking about things like that. I said I'd take him, you know, to ease her worry, and she reminded me that I'm older than she is...was. A card your mother was. So she said she wanted Hannah to have Sebastian as a little brother. Did she never mention it to you?"

"No," Morgan said...but she sure as hell mentioned it to Hannah. "Tell the museum they can have it for free."

"What? No, I certainly will not. Your mother wanted Sebastian to be a part of your family, Morgan. For Hannah."

Morgan finished the champagne and felt the room tilt ever so gently. He should have eaten more before the funeral.

"Hannah doesn't need it, William. She has enough toys. The museum can have it."

"Fine." The old man's shoulders and back straightened almost imperceptibly. "But considering the amount of revenue his presence will garner, I feel it is in your best interest to neither sell nor give him... excuse me, the manikin in question—" He lifted the flute when Morgan began to argue. "—but to let the museum display him on an extended loan. This way you still have the option, should you decide to honor your mother's last wish and take him home."

It took the rest of the champagne before Morgan was able to swallow most of the anger.

"Did guilt work with Mother?"

William met Morgan's stare and held it, for a second, before exhaling back into a more natural slouch.

"No. Your mother knew her own mind and once she made it up no amount of logic or guilt would dissuade her. Obviously you inherited that trait...more's the pity...but what's the harm if I...or your lawyer draws up a six-month loan agreement with the museum? Just six months where Hannah can come by and see him...*it* and know it's still hers. At the end of that period you can either give another six-month option or put him on permanent loan…or sell him. Six months is a long time for a little girl and you know how quickly children grow up. Who knows what she'll be interested in in six months' time?"

"Yeah, who knows. You really should have been a lawyer, William. Very persuasive."

"Contract law became a hobby of mine when your mother became my client. Just think about it, will you do that?"

"Sure."

"Thank you."

They toasted each other, and while Morgan could still feel the tension between them, he wasn't going to take responsibility for it. William had stepped over the line. Whatever collateral relationship Morgan had established with the old man because of his mother was beginning to fray. Although he'd still have to deal with him regarding his mother's photographs, once the reception was over Morgan would be able to treat him like any other professional acquaintance: with practiced detachment.

And there was no better time to start practicing than at that moment.

"I don't think I got the chance to thank you for this," Morgan said, nodding toward the room. "It's a wonderful tribute."

"Thank you."

Two words and nothing more. The old man had more years of practice.

Morgan cleared his throat. "Can I ask you one more thing, William?"

"Of course."

"My mother changed in the last few months…I'm sure you noticed… and I'm not just talking about her buying new clothes or cutting her hair. She had someone in her life, didn't she, William? Don't deny it because you think it'd be disloyal to her…I *know* she had someone. So, all I'm asking is if he's here."

William didn't so much as glance toward the crowd of mourners. "No."

"I don't understand. Wasn't he invited?"

"In a way."

Morgan tightened his grip on the empty champagne flute and felt the stem snap.

"Stop playing games, William, why isn't he here?"

The old man smiled. "Because you wouldn't bring him."

"Bring.... Are you talking about the manikin? Jesus Christ. I told you to stop playing games. Look, if you're not going to tell me, fine."

"I don't care if you believe me or not, Morgan, but the truth is that there *was* no one in your mother's life besides Sebastian, because her life was about her work and he was part of that life. I'm surprised you never saw that. Your mother was an incredible artist and I will treasure the time I was allowed to stand in her shadow, but all things must pass. I'll be handing over your mother's contract to my associate. She'll be contacting you in a few days, at which time you can convey any changes you may wish to make to her.

"It was a privilege, Morgan. Now, if you don't mind, I'll be leaving." The old man held out his hand and waited until Morgan had transferred the broken flute to his left hand and wiped his right on his coat. "My deepest condolences on your loss."

It would have been the perfect last line if William had just continued walking away, but he stopped after just a few steps and turned around.

"Your mother loved you, Morgan, and was very proud of you."

Morgan watched him walk away, then looked down at the palm of his hand. It wasn't champagne. He watched the blood fill the narrow slice that cut his life line in half.

Fitting.

"Jesus, Morg, what did you do?"

Morgan looked up as Chet popped a marinated stuffed mushroom into his mouth and pressed the used cocktail napkin against the wound on Morgan's palm. The vinegar marinade stung.

"It's just a cut." Morgan held up the broken flute. "They don't make these like they used to."

"Guess not. Excuse me." Chet grabbed one of the circling waitstaff and carefully deposited the broken flute onto the tray. "Do you think you could find a Band-Aid?"

The woman's eyes widened when she saw the blood seeping through the napkin. "Yes, sir. I'll check."

"There but for the fear of a lawsuit go I.... Lemme see." Morgan lifted the napkin and sucked air in through his teeth when it stuck. "Not too bad and nothing a little medicinal tequila won't cure."

Right, the tequila. Morgan folded the napkin in half and made a fist. "Thank you, doctor. Hey, Chet, do you think we could postpone the libation thing?"

"Oh, sure, no problem. I shouldn't have suggested it in the first place. I know what you're going through and I just thought.... We'll do it some other time. The one thing about tequila, it doesn't go bad."

"Thanks, Chet, and I will take you up on it. Soon. That's a promise."

"Any time," Chet said, "and anywhere. Have bottle, will travel. Oops, cheese it, the cops!"

Morgan turned to see the museum's security guard walking toward them carrying a mini first-aid kit. Before his errand of mercy, the guard had stood at the room's entrance to ensure that the mourners limited their museum visit solely to the reception.

"I was told you might need this, Mr. Riley?"

"Yes, thanks."

"Here, let me." Before Morgan could react, Chet had taken the kit from the guard and opened it, then proceeded to tear open a sanitizing towelette. "Open your hand, Morg. This might sting a bit."

It stung more than the vinegar marinade, but only until his friend had covered Morgan's palm with a thick waterproof bandage.

"Couldn't find anything bigger?"

Chet made a face and handed the kit back to the security guard. "Try to help, right?"

The guard nodded. "Yes, sir. Mr. Riley, the museum will be closing soon. Would you like me to make the announcement?"

"I'll do it. And thanks." Morgan held up his palm. The guard nodded and walked away.

"Okay, Cinderella, party's over." Chet caught him with a surprise one-armed hug. "Take care of yourself, Morg. Talk to you soon."

"Thanks, Chet."

His friend gave him a backhanded wave and disappeared behind the easel-mounted photograph of the manikin standing next to the snowman on his mother's lawn.

Morgan wished he hadn't broken his flute.

"Excuse me!" He used the same tone and volume he'd used at all of his mother's gallery shows – loud enough to be heard over the overlapping conversations and other background noises, but without shouting – until he had everyone's attention. There was still quite a crowd.

His mother would have been pleased.

"On behalf of my mother, Christine Morgan Riley, my family and myself, I want to thank you for the kind words and for coming here tonight to honor both my mother's memory and her work. Because as a friend of hers reminded me this evening, my mother's life was her work...which means, these photographs...*all* her photographs are pieces of her life frozen in time. It's like the poem I read...don't stand at her grave and weep, she's not there...she's here..." Morgan waved his bandaged hand at the photographs. "...and here. My mother is immortal...matted and framed and hanging in galleries and homes around the world. Just her and her friend...."

He had everyone's attention now and all of them, including Chet and the security guard, looked confused.

What did I just say? "So...thank you all again for coming."

To fortify himself for the last ordeal of the evening, which would be to stand at the door and thank each mourner personally, again, Morgan helped himself to another flute of champagne and downed it in one long swallow.

It wasn't as if there was a bottle of tequila waiting for him, after all.

He handed the empty flute to one of the waiters.

"Top of the world, Ma."

CHAPTER TWENTY

You know the rest.

★ ★ ★

Morgan didn't know how he got there.

The last thing he remembered was hearing thunder crack overhead while he was walking to the parking garage to get his car and looking up into a face full of rain.

He didn't remember how long a walk it was – although it had obviously been long enough to soak through his coat and pants and dress shirt – or how he'd navigated downtown Philly Friday night traffic or missed the turnpike entrance…or how he ended up parked in his mother's driveway at…

Morgan looked at the heads-up display on the dash.

…at 12:43 in the morning.

When he left the museum, it was 10:00 pm.

Where had the time gone?

Morgan was reaching for the Bluetooth app on the display when his hand changed its mind and turned off the car instead. Which was probably a good idea. He remembered his wife thought he'd be spending most, if not all, of the night with his friend Chet drinking tequila – *yes, remember that* – so if he called now to tell her he was sitting in his mother's driveway without knowing how he got there, she would just worry.

Or ask him how much he had to drink since he was obviously having trouble with his memory.

Morgan also remembered Holly was a bit of a worrier and could get extremely vocal.

That he remembered.

He also remembered he still had clothes at his mother's house...and dry clothes plus coffee and maybe a catnap on Hannah's bed and he might remember how he got there.

If not, he'd be warm and more awake and better able to drive home.

"Good plan," he told the car as he left it and repeated it to the house when he used his key to unlock the front door. "Good plan."

And added: "God bless you, Mrs. McIlveen—" for keeping the living room and hall lights on so opportunistic burglars wouldn't know the house was empty.

Or that it wasn't, momentarily, empty.

Morgan toed off his shoes at the door and left damp footprints through his socks across to the stairs. He left the socks on the floor next to the bottom step, his suitcoat over the newel post and, after unbuttoning it on the way up, his dress shirt over the second-floor railing.

He didn't worry about trying to remain incognito. Any of the neighbors who were still awake would see his car in the driveway and come to their own conclusions as to why he'd come back to his mother's house.

Morgan hit the upstairs light switch and squinted as he walked barefoot down the hall to his daughter's room. One thing he needed to remember was to bring back some boxes so he could pack up her things and bring them back h—

He stopped when he reached the door to what had been his room, then his daughter's, but now had a blue teddy bear-shaped name plaque hanging from a silver picture hook.

SEBASTIAN'S ROOM

The bear rattled against the door as Morgan opened it and reached in to turn on the overhead light.

The pink-and-white girl's room, Hannah's room, had become a boy's room again, but not his.

The hand-me-down twin bed that had been his and then his daughter's had been replaced by a small bed in the shape of a racing car with built-in guard rails. It sat on the floor in the middle of a rug designed to look like a racecourse. The sheets were bright blue. The spread, tossed back, was covered with racing flags. The pillow had the indentation of a small head.

"Jesus Christ."

His mother's copy of *The Wind in the Willows*, the one Hannah had wanted to take home, sat on the bedside table beneath a race car lamp.

There were three toy cars on the rug, two lined up on the painted course, the third on its side next to a pair of little boy slippers. A child's bathrobe lay puddled on the floor next to the bed.

Morgan recognized them.

—help Mama she won't get up please, Morgan, help Mama—

The only things in the room that didn't match the racing car theme were the pictures on the wall. The largest was over the bed. It was similar to the photograph she'd had at the Christmas party. It was another self-portrait of his mother and the manikin. His mother was facing the manikin; the manikin's blank head was facing her.

His mother was smiling at it.

And it was in full color – a picture, not a photograph.

There wasn't a single photograph in the room. They were *all* pictures, all framed, all matted, all of his mother and the manikin.

Childish crayon scribbles on white paper, the kind Hannah used to make when she was little, decorated the closet door and lay scattered across the child-sized desk in the corner. Morgan had to admit it was a nice touch.

If this was the background setup for a photo shoot.

He might have been too drunk to remember how he got to his mother's house, but he wasn't drunk enough to believe that. What had William said – that there was no one in his mother's life besides Sebastian?

"No."

Morgan walked over to the desk and picked up one of the scribbled pieces of paper. In the lower right-hand corner, almost indistinguishable from the scrawls and jots and squiggles that covered the page, was a name. A child's careful, block-lettered name.

S E B A S T I A N

The color picture above the desk showed the manikin standing next to the desk, one arm extended, a bright yellow crayon taped to its hand.

Sebastian Goes to School?

Yeah, it was a studio. She'd set it up and had just been... experimenting with the digital camera – taking pictures – until she got a new camera. And once she did, she would have taken more black-and-white photographs and then found something else and the manikin would go down in the basement and only be brought out at Halloween.

If she'd lived, her obsession with the manikin would have died.

"She wasn't crazy."

Morgan exhaled and reached for the closet door – hopefully she hadn't gotten rid of all his old—

"*Jesus!*"

The manikin was still wearing the pajamas it had on when Morgan last saw it, standing behind the chair where the officer put it – *Mama fell down! Help her, Morgan. Help her!* It'd been pushed into a back corner of the closet, half-hidden behind a row of little boy's clothes (size 2T) that hadn't come from the boxes of his hand-me-downs in the attic. These were new clothes, some still with the labels – high-end, kid's boutique labels – on them, everything from play clothes to formal wear.

A row of tiny shoes marched across the closet floor in front of a tower of cardboard boxes marked *Hannah's things*. A much smaller box marked with an *M* sat on the otherwise empty sweater shelf. Morgan took it down and found a pair of work socks, his cross-trainers, jeans and his Eagles sweatshirt.

Morgan slammed the door shut and made sure to turn off the light before carrying the box into the bathroom to change.

He'd have to thank Mrs. McIlveen, or her son, for packing up his things and putting the manikin in the closet – if he remembered.

★ ★ ★

Yawning, Morgan turned off the hall light and used the porch light seeping in around the gallery's curtains to find his way to the chair.

His plan was to rest just long enough to let his body synthesize the champagne sufficiently for him to wake up and remember driving home. That was the plan. All he needed was a quick nap.

Just for a few minutes.

He wasn't going to fall asleep.

But when he did, he dreamed he heard a child crying and even though Morgan knew he was asleep and that the sound was only part of the dream, he was a father and he couldn't stand to hear any child cry even in a dream. So when he opened his eyes and saw Sebastian standing in front of him in his little boy pajamas with racing cars on them, with his arms reaching out for comfort and the sound of crying coming from him, Morgan knew it was just a dream.

But it was a sad dream. Sebastian was crying because he was alone and scared, a child whose mother had gone away and was never going to come back.

Daddy, you have to get Sebastian. He's all alone. He needs us.

Morr-an, ing suh-baa-znn.

Morgan, bring Sebastian.

Leaning forward, Morgan lifted Sebastian onto his lap and for a moment the little body remained stiff and cold, but then, in the way of dreams, the hard plastic softened and grew warm and curled against Morgan's chest.

"It's all right," he whispered. "I know you're scared, but it's going to be okay. You're not alone. I'm here now. I'm here."

In the dream Morgan closed his eyes and slowly began rocking Sebastian back and forth until the sobs faded and the breathing deepened into sleep. It was like rocking Hannah when she was a baby.

"Good boy, that's right, just sleep. Everything's going to be okay. I promise."

He didn't dream after that and woke up to the sound of birds and a pale golden light filling the room. Still half asleep, he tried to lean forward and felt something hard and cold and stiff against his chest.

Morgan opened his eyes.

The manikin was lying across the arms of the chair, its head resting on one armrest, the legs, minus their stand, across the other, the stiff body hovering above Morgan's lap. The metal stand was on the floor in front of the chair, exactly where it had been standing in Morgan's dream.

"It was just a dream."

Because it wasn't a child, it was a store dummy, a manikin his mother bought on sale and turned into a cultural icon. Not real, not alive, nothing but a molded piece of plastic that was stiff and cold and faceless and had a folded piece of paper wedged into the narrow space between the thumb and index finger of its right hand.

Morgan pulled the paper from the stiff fingers and unfolded it. The printing was childlike, scribbled in blue crayon and matched the signature on the scribbled drawing upstairs.

please don't leave me morgan take me home

Morr-an, ing suhbaa-znn.

Bring Sebastian home, Daddy. He's all alone. He needs us.

Sebastian.

Morgan folded the paper and pressed it against the bandage on his palm.

It hurt.

He wasn't dreaming.

CHAPTER TWENTY-ONE

My mother wasn't crazy.

And neither am I.

I'm not.

★ ★ ★

"Isn't that right, Sebastian?"

Morgan looked in the rearview mirror and smiled.

And Sebastian smiled back.

FLAME TREE PRESS
FICTION WITHOUT FRONTIERS
Award-Winning Authors & Original Voices

Flame Tree Press is the trade fiction imprint of Flame Tree Publishing, focusing on excellent writing in horror and the supernatural, crime and mystery, science fiction and fantasy. Our aim is to explore beyond the boundaries of the everyday, with tales from both award-winning authors and original voices.

•

Other titles available by P.D. Cacek:
Second Lives
Second Chances

Other titles available include:
American Dreams by Kenneth Bromberg
The Haunting of Henderson Close by Catherine Cavendish
The Garden of Bewitchment by Catherine Cavendish
The House by the Cemetery by John Everson
The Devil's Equinox by John Everson
Hellrider by JG Faherty
The Toy Thief by D.W. Gillespie
One By One by D.W. Gillespie
Black Wings by Megan Hart
The Playing Card Killer by Russell James
The Sorrows by Jonathan Janz
Will Haunt You by Brian Kirk
We Are Monsters by Brian Kirk
Hearthstone Cottage by Frazer Lee
Those Who Came Before by J.H. Moncrieff
The Sky Woman by J.D. Moyer
The Guardian by J.D. Moyer
The Last Crucible by J.D. Moyer
The Goblets Immortal by Beth Overmyer
The Apocalypse Strain by Jason Parent
Stoker's Wilde by Steven Hopstaken & Melissa Prusi
Until Summer Comes Around by Glenn Rolfe
A Killing Fire by Faye Snowden
Fearless by Allen Stroud
Resilient by Allen Stroud
Screams from the Void by Anne Tibbets

•

Join our mailing list for free short stories, new release details, news about our authors and special promotions:

flametreepress.com